HERO TOWN

Also by Bryan MacMahon

Autobiography
The Master
The Storyman

Novels
Children of the Rainbow
The Honey Spike

Short Story Collections
The End of the World
A Final Fling
The Lion Tamer
The Red Petticoat
The Sound of Hooves
The Tallystick

Plays
The Bugle in the Blood
The Honey Spike
The Master
The Song of the Anvil

One-Act Plays
The Cobweb's Glory
The Death of Biddy Early
Fledged and Flown
The Gap of Life
Jack Furey
The Time of the Whitethorn

Translation
Peig: The Autobiography of Peig Sayers of the Great Blasket Island

Travel
Here's Ireland

Children's
Brendan of Ireland
Jack O'Moora and the King of Ireland's Son
Patsy-O series

BRYAN MacMAHON

HERO TOWN

A NOVEL

BRANDON

First published in 2004 by Brandon
an imprint of Mount Eagle Publications
Dingle, Co. Kerry, Ireland, and
Unit 3, Olympia Trading Estate, Coburg Road, London N22 6TZ, England

ISBN 0 86322 322 2

2 4 6 8 10 9 7 5 3 1

Mount Eagle Publications receives support from
the Arts Council/An Chomhairle Ealaíon.

Jacket painting: *Listowel Square* by Liam O'Neill
Author portrait by Liam O'Neill
Jacket design: Anú Design (www.anu-design.ie)
Typesetting by Red Barn Publishing, Skeagh, Skibbereen
Printed and bound in the United Kingdom

To the Heroes and Heroines

Author's Note to the Editor

I hope to leave you with a draft copy of *Hero Town*, my *magnum opus/magna opera*.

It is an attempt on my part to pull the threaded beads of incident, the doings of a small community, in through my senses, to distil the raw material in my brain and let it issue through my fingertips through the ballpoint of a pen on to paper where it can be reconstructed by the reader.

I have chosen what I call familiars to see me through. These are words or phrases incongruous or outlandish or prosaic or mesmeric or whimsical or reverberating but which of their nature defy definition. I see them as offering some sort of coherency and continuity and as providing something of an exotic coupling so often referred to by Koestler in *The Act of Creation* and *Janus*.

Perhaps this is too highfalutin an explanation. Perhaps I am giving way to the impishness of an imaginative child or the wickedness of a witch stroking a mangy tabby or even the antics of a gaudy clown. Honestly, I'm not sure. But what I am sure of is, I can tame and slash and pound and sew and condense and stick together what I've got in a montage that will provide its own instinctive entity.

Of course, I'm being ambitious. Even foolhardy. But whatever the verdict, I'm hell bent on seeing this effort through to some kind of finality. It's with me too long for me to abandon it now. I have read widely in the genre, and I find reading about any community, no matter how isolated, truly rewarding if, of course, it is apprehended in a believable, interesting, artistic and human fashion.

May the dedicated ghost of Maxwell Parkinson hover above us both.

Bryan

Editor's Note

"A work is never finished – it's abandoned."

I can now fully understand this statement uttered by my father, Bryan, some years ago in reference to writing. I have found this to be true also in the area of editing.

The request in my father's will that I edit the manuscript of *Hero Town* did not lie easily on my shoulders. The novel, written in the 1980s, had rested in my Dublin home for some twenty years in safe keeping while his autobiographies *The Master* and *The Storyman*, together with short stories, competed for his energy and inspiration.

As an "unruly son", I recall saying to him when he retired from teaching in 1975 that I would give him ten years maximum to empty what he had in his head and not to be carrying it all to the grave with him. The horizon beckons for all. As a history teacher, throughout my career I valued the contribution of his generation and recorded him extensively on tape and video on topics of which he would not talk in public. Creativity and inspiration were his gifts.

I had cut my teeth in editing for my father in *The Master* and *The Storyman*. Admittedly, for me this was a labour of love. Little did I think that six years after his death I would still be editing his work. "Scissors and paste," he called it. A patient wife, computers, family and close friends at home and abroad advised, directed and encouraged me to continue when the text and task overwhelmed me. For their support I am indebted.

At all times I had a "reader over my shoulder". It was easy to hear Bryan's voice reading the text, a voice from childhood reading aloud in the room above the family kitchen table. The jigsaw pieces were all set out. I am confident that the pruning and the editing of this text retains the real voice of Peter as he walks the Square (Diamond) of his beloved Hero Town.

Something done.

Maurice McMahon

Editor

JANUARY

Here, in the middle of nowhere, the centre of everywhere, lives the pedagogue Peter. A right dry old book, Mulrooney. Yes, ancient before his time. Peter, otherwise Ped, Peddah, Peadar, even Master, unhitched, an En-Tee. Forty years young; forty years old. Teetering on the edge in his school on the corner of one of the fifteen streets in the town. Speaking to, or for himself, by a gear shift of the personal pronoun, first person, second person, third person, the pedagogue reminisces, addresses, narrates, constantly suppressing a tendency to flibbertygibbety, to indulge the idealistic daftness tincturing his blood.

A man with semantic familiars, the familiars are important— demons which attend him at times obediently, at times willfully the reverse. This pedagogue has the secret ambition, has the secret obsession to void the bowels of his imagination. His food, the town and its inhabitants. Cut them up, suck them in through the apertures and tentacles of his senses, digest the buggers, belch on occasion, then finally crouch and void them in the form of literature.

The town runs on milk—milk in its several manifestations, condensations, coagulations and reincarnations. A constituent of billiard balls even! Casein. When the wind is from the south-west. Phew! It must be a whey day! Town a nipple: countryside a swelling breast. Suck, child, suck. Milk the first food and the last.

The Town an opaque nipple. By straining his eyes Peter the Pedagogue can see vaguely through cavity walls, brick walls, flimsy partitions and the handful of mudwall cabins that somehow have lingered.

To the west lies the sea. The hills look down on the town. There are almost four thousand citizens; from citizen to citizen there extends a mesh of interwoven ticker tape. Criss-cross— Christ's cross. The ticker tape manifests itself in a thousand colours, tints and hues, that extend to points far beyond the little burg, to exotic places.

The streets are narrow and intimate. As a concession to a mythical sunshine or an act of hope offered to the Sun God, there is one white out-of-doors plastic pub table in which a red and yellow parasol is inserted when, on a July day, the mercury soars to seventy-four Fahrenheit. Not the case now in goose-pimpled January. The citizens have their house fronts and shop fronts decorated by painters, sign writers and door grainers. Men not afraid of colour. With curlicues and horses' heads depicted wherever a flat surface offers space, blood brothers to the tinkers of the outlands who slam violent colours on the shafts and tailboards of caravans and flat carts. Horror vacui—the monks had the same disease. Everything comes right. There is a wild inbuilt sense of rectitude. Something like a bubble in a spirit level.

Here also the citizens sniffle, suffer from cystitis, pick their noses, utter yells on festive midnights, grow lusty in season, file their fingernails on unpointed, unplastered walls, bounce ivy berries on tarmac, swap stories, strum tambourines, spit on the floor and call the cat a bastard. The theory to be proven is that they are human. Even heroic. Hero Town, Peter calls it.

*

What the hell is heroic about it? Are all its citizens brave and admirable? *Good God—no.* Of what then does their heroism consist? *They're truly human. They understand human relationships. They preserve social equipoise. If a man raises his head in pride they lower it: if he lowers it they raise it. It's an unarticulated law. It's handed down. Without courts. The people have familiars, totems and taboos. They preserve the life of the imagination. They communicate in the shorthand of the nerves. They adore stories. What Peter-I propose doing is as follows. But there, tiresomely I tend to repeat myself. I propose to treat the town much as I treat the children in the school beyond. For the school is a micro of my micro. Fingersnap— silence! Fingersnap—spring to attention! Fingersnap—talk volubly! Fingersnap—sing "The Crazy Billygoat" in Compulsory Erse!* Simili modo, when Peter-you fingersnap in the reminiscent literary sense. Your fellow citizens will talk, quarrel, grovel, intrigue, succeed or fail in lovemaking, backbite or strain as a consequence of a constipated stool. Let them cavort, dance naked and be condemned from altar steps or sing in traditional fashion, be demure or devious, and all this by means of the cut out, the fold in, the montage or collage of words and phrases achieving perhaps haphazard beauty by the recognition of a politeness in the conjoined disparate.

For Peter the familiars are his witches' cats reincarnated in various forms. His effort is largely one of threading the bright beads (the minor epiphanies of the passing day) on the catgut of the passing year. And his prayer is as follows: *May Christ direct my trembling pen.*

Watch the pedagogue stroll abroad on this early January day down a main street, its mouth opened to the south-west.

"Happy New Year to you, Sir."

"Many happy returns."

The town clock under the steeple in the square stands at a perpetual quarter after twelve. Peter-he is now mentally admiring his own *History of the Barony of Clanconnor* in the window of the town bookshop. Published in the county town by the same firm which published the county newspaper. It's a bad stepmother would blame the publisher for using the columns of their paper to blow up the book to the proportions of a classic. Peter-he dreads the day when a real scholar will come along and destroy his reputation. He never articulates this terror. Still he was brave in publishing the story of Black Davy's "Child of the Ferns". Bracken evokes erotic images. It rustles and is dry and secretive in summer on a sunny hillside.

*

"Fierce heat, that bulb," said the old tinker, as light-blinded and itchy-skinned she entered the first ever bedroom she could call her own. Outside the wind was a querulous woman whingeing as she blackmailed the male countryside.

In the harness maker's shop, Buddy Daw, strategically positioned to observe the comings and goings, talked about a blind man being dragged across the road by his guide dog whose seeing eye had become a sniffing nose with the passing of a bitch in heat. "Missing death by inches, the blinder."

"It's not right to make jokes about a personal affliction," the harness maker's son says with a barely perceptible wink and a smile of triumph to the silent listeners. All agree by murmuring— Buddy Daw is a great rise. And obscenities leap off his tongue as he flounces out the door. "We're one up already."

The others release their laughter and yell. In Hero Town what else is there to do?

Hero Town now turns into a mid-winter Cape Horn. The weather is malignant. "Not many out last night welcoming in the New Year," Peter comments. The harness maker, under a naked bulb, continues to dig deep with the awl.

*

About women, Peter mused. *Hold everything! What jobs or errands did Margo give me to do? Sisters are as bad as wives: the same sense of bossery without any of the creature comforts. Jesus! Euclid had the same problem. Women are, were and will be perambulating mysteries to men, and to themselves. Peter-I would like to peep through a blindless bedroom window from the heart of shrubbery to see a woman seated at a dressing table. Comb, brush, neck torsion, head tilting, nostril flaring, finger tipping points on the goose-extended neck, the touching of the eyebrows, the kiss pouting lips to receive the tippy-tip-tip of the red, red, red lipstick. SShhh? What's that? A slate, mock innocently fluttering from its lofty perch over and over and down on its edge shattering on striking the roadway edge on.* Lucky man Peddah, you. That could have trepanned you.

*

The year opens before the striding schoolmaster. It is New Year's Day! "Spuds will be ferociously dear," a man comments. "What with all the bad weather we're having." A pair of men sit chatting on adjoining pub stools. "The curse o' God on dole-drawing big farmers who've done shag all for the economy of this country except supervise the mechanical sucking of a white liquid out of a cow's tits once or twice in the day." Then he adds, "They do feck all else. Wan of these days spuds'll be dearer than bananas." Spuds are blackening in the pits—I hear the plaint again. Same every January. Same ring of men, townies. Spud-setters trying to manipulate the market according to the pair.

*

Peter . . . you like middle-aged widows, don't you? *Now that you ask—I do.* And why do you like them? *Hold up your head, Peter-you . . . this is Peter-I talking to you. I like them because it appears to me that constantly having to recall the handiness of their dead mates, they tend to tolerate all kinds of wild male behaviour.* Go on! *There's nothing to go on about.* Could it be that you look upon them as teachers? *Of what?* Of what do you think, you ape.

Progress is being recorded in the market in the town. The bronze turkey, an imported sonovohoor himself who displaced the good old goose in the green field grazing as Yuletide provender, now gets the toe cap in favour of the white turkey. The electric carver has displaced the knife blade scraping across the flagstone at the back door. True, true, true the good many coloured chrysanthemums still blossomly adore the host on the High Altar. *Peter-I wonder if I will die wondering. How beautiful (for others) are the shoes of the biblical beloved. Middle-aged widows as instructors of the ignorant among whom pedagogues may certainly be numbered.*

Outside the streets are an absolute puddle: the final Christmas trees still glow in their several colours, and in upstairs windows the electric candles too are here and there in evidence. Knock— knock at the front door. Margo, a widow herself, having only her son Andrew in Dublin, answers the knocking.

"We're doing a school project on local superstitions and curses and the nun said Master Mulrooney might help us." Three nubiles, Peter verifies from outside the bathroom door. "Peter!" Margo's tone of voice indicates instant antagonism directed at the girls.

How can Peter-I keep a semblance of dignity with this instant antagonism established in the hallway? In the living room with its copper and mahogany addressing the three . . . it's pishogues with eggs, Robin-Run-the Hedge, forgewater, broom tea, and finally the whole contraption of pishoguery resting on a boy's sunken chest cupped and up-drawn in a tumbler. We're only one step from Voodoo brother. It's out there on the hills yet. Alive and kicking. No woman yet, Peter. *None.* Good God, you're sub-human.

*

Word moves quickly through the town that Shivers is dead. What comfort can familiars or servants offer now in the face of communal loss? His own worst enemy. Shivers. The poor devil, suave and harmless. Part of us has vanished. The likes of Shivers don't appear in the *The History of Clanconnor.* Oh no! Our

Shivers was O'Caseyesque who glittered as a broken mirror—one piece erratically reflecting errant, the rebellious part of Peter-me.

Our refined conman who without raising his voice wormed his way into the affections of everyone in town. We are diminished. How to talk a priest out of his second overcoat ("It doesn't look the thing, Father, at a graveside—it lowers the offerings"), how to lead in the winner of the Gold Cup at Cheltenham, oh how to flatter a barmaid. Oh, Ssssh, the sibilance of sorrow succeeding the surcease of Shivers Sullivan is suggestible in sudden solemn silences.

Where? SsssShivers. Dead! No?

Yeh. The harmless hoor. Begod he was witty. Got a cerebral haemorrhage yesterday evening. Shifted back to the Bons. Into a coma—out like a light. His aged father is in a daze. The old man cackled with ancient pride and glee whenever Shivers returned to tell of an adventure.

The mirror in me catches his splintered face. No more will he wash his gleeful hands in air. (If you like, Father, I'll take the choir—I'm not at all bad at that kind of thing). No more will he help to make beds in the Hospice of the Infirmary of the Convent of the Holy Sepulcher in wherever it is and where he wintered in the role of gardener, if you please, holding the spreading bed clothes on the other side of the bed from a middle-aged nun (according to himself) a consecrated virgin in the convolutions of the menopause who goes into semi-convulsions perilously close to the threshold of epilepsy every time Shivers, appraising the woman with deadly accuracy as regards timing, utters a fornicatory, defecatory or micturatory adjective at the crest of a recital when he thought his dedicated virgin with the dint of uncontrollable laughter would surely get a seizure. The nun loved it, he said afterwards. They're starved for that kind of thing. Shivers dead. I hope to Christ they'll put Shivers on his obituary notice in the paper. At St Elton's hospital Patrick (Shivers) de Lacy, greyhound trainer, man about town and wit—beloved son of his town and his time. Shining Tesserae of the mosaic of outback existence. Deeply mourned by his aged father, his fellow townspeople and discerning exiles from Denver to Basra. Requiescant in pace. The mirror. Shivers in the mirror. Just a glint.

*

Stand here, Peter, ould son. Right here at Dick Haley's corner on this first sunny day of the opening year. Place your back against the benevolent white painted oil painted wall. Cock up your face. Close the eyes. Be blissful. First a happy New Year to Margo and yourself. Now open your eyes; isn't that the happiest prospect in the whole of creation. They can keep Sunset Boulevard, Champs Elysees, and Ganders Market in Hamburg but leave me this. Inhale comrade. Again. Note the sun glinting on the bountiful breasts of Granuaile herself up there on the wall. Watch the barber at his upstairs window watching us. Watch the Little Flower trundling her bicycle across the Square, a load of messages on its carrier as she faces for the church to pay a visit to the Blessed Sacrament. Take the visit from her and she's no more. Isn't this heaven? The opening year. And poor old Shivers—box open, box shut—that's the story of life. One box the womb, the other the coffin. Peter, in the last twelve months you and I have seen the end of wakes. Paddy Mary's Funeral Home scooptewsled the wakes in one bare year. People wouldn't know now how to behave at wakes. The protocol will be lost. Like the "caoin" or the fairs. The lovely cow dung after the fairs. It's wet and oozy. Inhale comrade. Stock take. Will we see the end of marriages? Eh? And of the Catholic church? Eh, comrade? Calvary versus electronics. Stop that talking to yourself, Peter. I hear you muttering about Shivers. Make a New Year resolution. Be blissful. Get a dame. Ah. Paradise. Inhale. Any day you can pull up my trousers, eat six or seven Kerr's Pinks and consider myself slightly solvent I feel well.

Up there in my perch on the hill I look down and read the town by its smoke signals. *Who's at home? Who's away? Who's in bed? Who's up? Who has changed from turf to coal? Et cetera.*

What have I now in the way of familiars? I've got Black David's by-blow in the bracken, the Crazy Billygoat, a blind man seeking canine bookends and Shivers. Cumulative and traditional. The "run" in the folk story. A literary device.

Again the Pedagogue ponders, at times being jarred, cossetted, enthused or depressed by the imagination, on the life he seeks to project in hieroglyphics. No woman yet, Pedagogue*! None, not a skirt on the horizon.* I can't fathom it—every second person one passes is, on average, female. You're not the other thing? *No!* Is it the Holy Ghost? *Yeh, sort of.* Let me tell you it can hit a man in one of two ways—the Pilly Willy or the Holy Ghost. The Holy is the worst of the two. You'd want to watch out, Peter Mulrooney.

*

"We'd badly need a couple of factories, Tom."

"Shut up that bloody talk about factories."

"Why, Tom?"

"What they call stagnation I call happiness and peace."

"Not so! Not so."

"Progress as they see it, to me is poison. O well, I say it as I see it. What I mean is, my prayer is May God in His infinite mercy and long distance telescopic understanding vouchsafe . . . whatever the feckin' hell vouchsafe signifies but it's a damn nice word just the same . . . Vouchsafe . . . the word derails me . . . that we never ever get a factory in this kip of a town. For me getting a factory is the same as asking me to ram gob and nostril against the exhaust pipe of an oil burning old tractor. Still and all, Vouchsafe is a dinger of a word."

"It is indeed."

For Peter, vouchsafe didn't quite ring. But it sparked off the effusion. Standing at the sunny corner appraising Paradise, he realises that subliminally his eye is that of a hare. He can see in the spread of 180 degrees.

This while the dead bell bongs above as the people wait for the bright coffin to emerge from the church.

*

"Sheila Cronin phoned," Margo said.

"Oh!!" from Peter.

"She wants you out to luncheon at two o'clock tomorrow. Little Christmas Day." Peter pondered ponderously.

"Herself and her three daughters. They're all at home. I said that you'd be there."

What the hell are these women up to? Peter asked himself. Does Margo want me to get buckled, so that she'll then be free on the side of the street to take a second mate. Or is she just cocking me up and chuckling to herself? Enmeshed in a conspiracy of women, he will drive out after last Mass.

There was no pretence. At the door buxom Sheila said, "We're out to trap you, Peter!" (For herself or one of the daughters?) The hall was warm. A Christmas tree festooned and glinting but no children to enjoy it. (Peter thought of the house of Bernardo Alba.) The young women were beautifully dressed. They had obviously been talking at length about the invitation. They sat down around him on low seats. The bird had just been taken out of the oven. Inhale. Red-faced Sheila bustling and saying sternly to the two, "Pour out the sherry!" and as Peter demurred she chortled, "All in now, say grace, Peter." He did so—sonorously scholastic. The fumes of the wine and turkey filled the room, as the colours of the clothes, yellow, green and virgin blue, danced around the cherries—red berets on the heads of gondoliers in the prows of melon gondolas.

Sweet God, the eldest girl has filled up my wine glass. Again, I'll be befuddled. Nice kettle of fish if the Guards make me breathe into the bag on the way home. Talk on, dear women. Talk on. Even if you seek to delude me or entertain me or are sentimental because of the memory of your dead Ma and grandma, it doesn't matter a damn.

You are natural and gracious and womanly. And it is your feast day—the Christmas of the Women.

The mantelpiece is a brilliant card shop. And in the corner is the crib, its figurines anticipatorily touched with the blood light of Calvary the while it celebrates labour pains, afterbirth, donkey apples, awkward Joseph, and of course the One and Only.

Eating, the Pedagogue drifts out into bliss. And because of his bliss the women became blissful too. Intrigues forgotten, they became their utter, and to Peter their different authentic silver. *"I could do worse,"* Peter told himself echoing a saying of Margos. He then added, *"To hell with the familiars."*

Catching sight of his own flushed face in a mirror as the meal ended. *"I am now a mixture of Black David, the Crazy Billygoat and rubicund,"* Peter told himself. Standing in the doorway, the moorland declining to a ravine clothed with the blackthorn, he inhaled deeply before socially kissing each of the women goodbye. As he left the gateway his arms uplifted, his subconscious noted something that surfaced later. The wee flowers of the winter jasmine pegged against a wall. Like yellow ornaments set in errant hair. It occurred to him that the little blooms were also feminine and were watching him demurely. "We spy," they seemed to say.

Although Christmastide was at an end, it was still lingering in the air of the classless town. Ever since the so-called ascendancy had been burned out or shot out in the early twenties, tuppence ha'penny ceased to look down on tuppence. He was revered who could entertain. The people, frustrated with political struggles, sought leaders who could provide fellowship and the laughter of fellowship. There was an awareness of nature as a large wheel turning whether one watched it or not, an inward examination of the mystery of everyday material.

*

"Gentle Child was here looking for you," Margo said later in the kitchen.

"What did she want?" Peter asked.

"I didn't ask her."

"Was she upset?"

"Gentle Child is always upset. Your tea is almost ready. Don't delay."

Outside there was a clinging mist of rain. The evening Angelus was ringing on the television in the houses that he passed. The amber street lights carried aureoles of rainbow tints.

"Gentle Child was rapping at your door, Mr Mulrooney."

"Did she go up or down?"

"I couldn't say. Likely down."

Where are you, Gentle Child? All of twelve years of age. Are you up this laneway hiding in the dark? Are you under the jeweller's canopy? On the little road of dusk that goes down to the roaring river? Where are you, Gentle Child? Ah, there you are, standing in the recess of the dank doorway.

"Hello, Denise."

"Hello, Mr Mulrooney."

"You were looking for me."

"I was . . . Can I hold your hand?"

"Yes, of course. What is it?"

"I have a tumour on the brain. I'll die soon."

"Nonsense, Denise."

"It's true, Sir. I heard the doctor whispering it to my father."

"Is that what you wanted to tell me?"

"No."

"What is it so?"

"I'm not sure whether I wheeled out the baby or not."

"In the go-car?"

"Yes. One minute I think I wheeled him out and the next minute I'm not sure."

"There's no go-car on the street."

"Are you sure?"

"Of course I'm sure."

"Will you walk with me, Mr Mulrooney?"

"I will indeed."

"I'll let go of your hand if anyone comes."

"Fair enough. Come along. Did you have your little operation?"

"They were afraid to go deep, Sir. For fear I'd go blind and lose my wits. So they closed up my head again."

"You'll be fine now. Here we are. In you go."

"Mr Mulrooney?"

"What is it now?"

"Would you ever go round by the back and peep in the kitchen window. Come back then and tell me if the baby is there."

"Sure. Don't stir."

"Is he there?"

"Yes, of course. Sitting up in his baby chair with a spoon. And laughing."

"Thanks, Mr Mulrooney. Goodbye now."

"Goodbye, Denise."

*

Know what I think? There will be no winter! The climate has changed. I'd say that the island of Ireland has floated out into the Atlantic so that now it serves as an agent of bifurcation of the Gulf Stream which now laps and circles all its coastline. *Would you now?*

"Take Tosselli's Serenade," the old fellow whispered out of his mouth corner. The Pedagogue took it. It's a Jim Dandy, 100 per cent foolproof method of seducing females—all other conditions being equal, of course. Peter hangs on for dear life to the coat-tails of the conductor, wondering when the pay hatch of comprehension will open. Then, "Like a golden dream in my heart ever smiling," old Jonathan utters through a gas mask of halitosis. "Golden dream heart ever smiling" each word a ringer a dinger and a spell binder, "What care I for life without you by my side," spoken or sung in the proper tone of voice is mesmeric, hypnotic or whatever you'd require it to be to suit the amorous circumstances. She wouldn't be bloody well human if she resisted. Eh? Are you with me, Peter?

What? What? Oh. Sorry, wha' did you say? I was thinking of something else.

Of what were you thinking if it isn't amiss to ask?

Winter jasmine. That kind of stuff.

Is it long since you got your head examined, Peter?

I never got my head examined. Why do you ask?

Ah nothing. Nothing at all. I'm in a hurry home. A call of nature, he said, turning on his heel and walking away like a cut cat.

"Dotage, I daresay," with a thin lipped smile. Peter-he then added, *"Nothing for these boring buggers but to give 'em the Gandhi treatment."*

*

It was bound to come on the roller coaster of the rhythm of life in the small place. Peter noticed that invariably after the celebrations of the Year's End and indeed Beginning, depression was to be expected. Let 'em call it what they like, but what Christ suffered in the Garden of Gethsemane, wasn't that depression?

"You can't fight the troubles of the mind, Peter, but you can dodge them. Get busy! Get involved. Get tormented. Enlist! Get involved in a war. Anything is better than this. And what's more, you have the wrong idea totally of Josephine," Peter is told as he stands listening. You could tell Josephine the killing of a man. She lets on to be demure and sedate. But break the wall of the sandcastle reserve and as your waves come lashing in she'll crumble before you in laughter. She's liable to say anything then, this saint of a dame. If I had my day all over again, she'll maybe say, I'd flog it around the Burlington—the highest bidder to be declared the purchaser. Nuns are the very same—their fertile imaginations oscillating from the sanctuary to the boudoir and back again. Josephine, Peter, is the woman that would educate you, my bucko. Do you know, Peter, of the ungovernable power of the mind? And fingertips have in their own right a mind and a well padded body possessing the total range of the five senses, all fusing, willy nilly to the obedience of touch in the ultimate of frenetic human love. Do you realise that 90 per cent of all diseases are psychosomatic in origin? What starts originally in the mind, ends eventually in the body. Parts of the body already have achieved autonomy. Peter, your body is a host of republics.

Schoolmaster, she is the lassie whose company you should cultivate. Watch her eyes narrowing the next time you come in contact with her. Without uttering a syllable her eyes will say, "I could teach you a great deal." And so she could—Josephine. A woman in a million! Behold the undiscovered volcanoes that lie inside there in the unseen space between the fingertips. Examine them before you go to bed. Talk to them. They're good listeners. Promise 'em goodies. They'll repay your kindness a thousand fold. But Josephine—she's an express from trap to line. An empress, and an educator too.

Basra! Tosselli's Serenade melts in the heart. Slogans.

*

The pedagogue wasn't quite sure how to handle domestic freedom. Margo, his widowed sister, acting on intuition or hunch or god-knows-what-class of vagairy decided to go South to the foothills to visit their older sister who was married to a roguish auctioneer. Peter had to "drum up for himself". He was unused to the silence of the house; it seemed out of kilter without the constant "Wipe your shoes," "Give the backyard a rub of the brush," "No turf up yet?" "That tie is a holy show on you," "Do something about that downdraft," and "Wash a handful of spuds for me." Orders, injunctions, admonitions, cautions. He ended up cooking a rack chop, an onion, some mushrooms and dumped the lot into a buttered Pyrex dish. He persuaded himself that it was appetizing. True. A creative comfort spiced with male freedom.

*

Excuse me, Mr Mulrooney. Peter-I you. Small town pedagogue. Gabhaim pardun agat. Excusez-moi, monsieur. It's all cat's shit, Toselli and Josephine, all this in the environs of an obscure hamlet at the world's end. Heroic? Sweet you Eternal and Preternatural Deity—what is the man talking about?

Human relationships, Sir.

Shivers, winter jasmine.

All food for the imagination, Sir.

And this is heroic?

Yes, in the context of sitting on a three legged stool of spirit, mind and body.

Do you think anyone will heed?

It might head off what corresponds to myxomatosis in rabbits. You see, mankind, like water, in an enclosed U-tube, tends to find its own level. An achievement. Even heroic.

If you're still in charge of the local primary school, Mr Mulrooney, God help the children entrusted to your care and tuition.

*

Then came the first daffodils. Imported but nevertheless harbingers. Imagination or its elder sister intuition could be said to be a female attribute, and whenever its kinetic qualities appear in a man they couch for the female side of his nature. At times male imagination appears to correspond to his dry teats, ornamental, there for symmetry, a stirring question mark, a cause of spontaneous laughter to women, twin microcosms contrasting with twin female macrocosms which buttress their claim to utility.

Stretched out in bed in the early afternoon the pedagogue ruminates. He experiences the beauty of silence despite the grinding revolutions of a concrete mixer in the back road. He imagines the sediment in the well of his agitated mind as settling gradually on the bottom of his consciousness. Women and the war with women are paramount in his thoughts. Now the voices can come through.

Peter boy, I know that your sister Margo and yourself are the very best of friends but by nature a woman is apt to be overbearing, bossy and in certain cases tyrannical. You'll never get the better of her by force—it's about as sensible as smashing up an oyster with a hammer instead of flicking it open with a knife blade. Nobody can understand women—not even themselves. Force—no! Guile—yes! Listen now.

Take Margo. She gives you the works. For why, she doesn't know but perhaps she could know if she tried to isolate causes. Recently she's on the razzle-dazzle. A mixture of Nero and Idi Amin. What you do to counter Peter-this, Peter-that, Peter-the other, is to pretend to be getting odd. Begin with trivialities. Mutter. Look vacant. Gradually work up to a climax. Do you smoke—no? Well buy a packet of fags unknownst, take three out of it and put it in the last place a person would leave such an article. Still retaining the vacant stare, walk down to the end of the yard and gaze up at the sky. Be sure that she's watching! If it's dark or duskish even you might consider letting down your trousers and relieving yourself beside her beloved chrysanthemums.

These are opening gambits. Next think up queer sounds. Pretend to stagger, while letting on you don't know that she's on the watch. She'll then begin to pet you. I'm for your good. The Pope of Rome has to carry on like this to keep the nuns who housekeep for him in order. Otherwise they'd issue papal bulls. Schoolmaster, this is neither Algebra nor Trigonometry. This is the chessboard of life. Move, pedagogue, move! Else the women will checkmate you. Move forward, brave pedagogue!

*

Hear the rain hammer off the galvanised roofs of the outhouses at the rear of the streets. Watch the hail dance on the iron. Note the wind—swirl creating all sorts of diverse patterns of rain and hail, feel the cold blade of frost winter placed flat against the morning cheek. Hear the doors and windows rattle. Sense the people of the town huddling down against the harsh weather. Intuit what they have to say. Ready, Peddah?

"As long as you're in this town, Mr Manager, don't ever again call me out of a counter-queue of the bank to chat in your sweat-box. It looks as if I owe you money which I don't!"

Watch the terrier in Donegan's door sniffing the upstreet wind: watch the way the wind moves the fur around his shivering nostrils.

*

"Be careful, Maney, the wind is high."

As a young woman in her twenties, the labourer's daughter looked after the big farmer's infant son. He was from what you'd call wild Catholic gentry. Now even when she was in her late eighties and he in his mid-sixties, there was a powerful bond between them. Footless drunk in town late at night or in the early morning hours, the publican would get a hackney driver to drive the farmer home. "Maney's or the house?" the driver would enquire of the drunken man as they approached the arch of trees in the foothills. "Maney's" with a drunken snore. "You can pay me next Thursday," the driver'd say as the farmer dug deep for a roll of notes. Right! Where's my brandy? Crouched outside the window of the cottage and clutching the almost full bottle "Maney," the farmer would growl thickly. After a stir in the room and a muttered word, first the door, then the half-door would open to reveal the shadowed outline of the old woman. Her lower nightclothes show white and her shoulders covered with a black woollen shawl. Her feet are bare. There is a growl from the farmer as he staggers in. The driver turns the car and grinds off but not before he sounds his horn in signal to the great house in the trees where a moment or two later a light flicks off.

Inside the cottage, "That you, James?"

"That's me, Maney."

Placing the fat bottle on the table the farmer staggers to a low sugan chair on one side of the hearth. The old woman closes the bedroom door behind which her husband is sleeping. She takes a low seat opposite the farmer and rakes the embers of the dying fire under the black cavern of the chimney. For a time none of the pair speak. They resemble mother and son or grave-faced lovers. Their heads now close together he begins to mutter then to talk. She listens. Their eyes on the ripening fire they continue to drink and talk gutturally and at times in syllables with long intervals between them. This until dawn whitens the window. A tinge of red to the new day finds the farmer's head sunk on to the woman's knees. At last the farmer drags his body upright and prepares to go. "Good luck, Maney," he says. Having closed the door behind him the old woman pads back to bed.

*

On Saturday when there is no school Peter Mulrooney rises late and saunters down the already aired town! He does so with a certain sense of adventure—the postman could well bring him a letter from far-off Indiana, he could meet Tully Daw armed with a new mildly bawdy story. Behind the plate glass the old harness maker drove the blade of his awl through a harness strap. He's an important tessera in the mosaic of Here and Now. But wait, the man must be given time. Squeezing a drop from the point of his nose he looked out at the hail dancing on the pavement and cackled, "There'll be dust on the roads yet!"

"Peter," he says, "I've seen one revolution: you're seeing another."

"What revolution have you seen?"

"Didn't I see the English in the full sway of their glory and the Irish like pigs in puddles. In this very town too."

"Carry on."

"I saw the Protestant church surrounded by black coaches with grey horses snortin' oats. Coachmen dressed up to the veins o' nicety—with the three banks controlled by the other crowd. Out there at Rahaneenagh at ould Mrs Croker's big house a tenant couldn't get married without the dame's permission. You daren't wet a salmon line in the river nor course a hare along their turbary. They made the trains halt close to their demesne even where there was no railway station. What are you talking about, man, with those Ghosts of yours. They could bring you from the gallows with a word or plank you right up on it with another. I've seen all that tumbled and humbled in my eighty years and six. So I have, Scholar—witnessed a revolution."

Granted. No familiar there, Peter concluded. It's like this, he deduces. What are we but Alices compelled to pass through the looking glass of the imagination so as to find reality. To every man his particular series of revenants. Still Peter has Black David, Gentle Child, Vouchsafe not to mention Winter Jasmine. Each man must find his own series of phantoms like a mantra, such as latterly crept in here among us from distant eastern beliefs and philosophies.

*

True for the man. Peter-I live here at a moment which can squarely be called a hinge of time. Change! All around me here there is nothing but change. When have I seen a wake, that tribal ceremony which was in its full health and strength a few short years ago? Now it's "Hello! Yellow! Is that the Funeral Parlour! My father is after dying. Will you pull up the van to our back gate about six o'clock when the news is on the Teevee." Rights of way are being growled over, beaches are being fenced off, streams have notices on trees telling anglers to clear off, fields are ultra fenced so that the town loners cannot hunt a rabbit. Even the High Altar is reduced to a slab and the browbeater of a pulpit bulldozed to be replaced by a lectern. Sniff the air—the acrid smell of coal where once turf reigned. Traditional concepts of God, Christ and the Virgin are subject to revision and the word myth is used as a term of contempt.

Peter-I am a medieval person. I see changes in womanhood too. Traditional woman is a lure, an anodyne, an instigator—the salmon fly of love. Love is no longer indicated through the medium of chocolate, wine or two pigs. None of that! The women's programmes on the radio exemplify it. All their talk is of emissions and penetrations. They're burstin' to gossip biologically before all Ireland. Is it any wonder that we'd have pisheogues as an antidote to such claustrophobic activities? Or that I would treasure in my heart of hearts the beloved constancy of such as Gentle Child or liquorice allsorts that have weathered the years? A nor'easter skinned and scoured the long street. It hardened the cement tits of Mother Erin who insisted on presiding over the door of a pub. Meanwhile as the home-grown daffodils make their appearance the day lengthens by a cockstep into light.

*

And then, Peter—we buried the Gentle Giant. The sound of the deadbell is still in our ears. Deserted from the Free State army in 1942. Not enough jacking action. Enlisted again in France. *I always know when people are going to die, Peter-he told himself. They come telling me anecdotes about their lives. Don't want their individual histories, the only ones they truly know and have lived, to be erased. That's why Gentle Giant stopped me lately. Must watch out for that in future; it's a sign that they feel death approaching. Prone white, cold under the timber cover—the Gentle Giant counterpart to Gentle Child. Other places have no monopoly on gentility.* In front of the altar whereon are placed two flowerpots of life ageless the plain coffin lies. The Dean chants but above the chant is heard the roar of explosions on Dunkirk beach.

*

Talking each day for six hours on end leaves Peter exhausted. But, ould son, you know the way out. Down street as if walking on eggs. Speech reduced to a minimum. Look neither to left nor to right; you bear the brimming vessel of your mind. Another drop and it will spill over. It's a balancing act like the old lady at the fountain with the pail of water on the circular pad on her head. Not far to walk. Salute people superficially. Sit at the table in the warm kitchen, this without opening your mouth to Margo— must let the sediment of the mind settle, murmur acceptance of the farmhouse vegetable soup, sniff the boiled mutton and the parsley sauce, accept ceremoniously the three waistcoat-bursting Golden Wonder spuds. Then the slow climbing to the room high above the street, the half stripping of one's self, the easing into bed, the sigh that indicates tension dropped, the gentle taking up of narcotic bedside book, the seeping sense of ease, of shrugging off harness. Then down, down sediment settling ah into ssssssssssssslee-ee-eep . . .

*

"Let me put my hand in the full-o-silver pocket of your apron, Anastatia Beggarwoman." How warm everything close to her body, even the coins.
"You've done well, Anastatia."
"Not bad, Sir: if you're ever short let me know."
"The town is good to you."
"Begged properly this town is worth £6,000 a year," this with grave sincerity.

She too has a life to live and a part to play. Even now the familiars seem devoid of comfort. Then unexpectedly, a strike by the electricity workers plunged the town into darkness, and all laughed. Exhilarating at first but then depression set in. Calling this place Hero Town is utterly self-deceive. Cowardorf, Jackalburg, Scabbyville, Ballybollocks, Buggerboro, Lousythorp—names likes these would have suited the place better. You know well, Peter-you, that womanless heirless as you are, stuck here for the balance of your puff and you're determined to persuade yourself that it is a homely kind of place. No use for you to reject these thoughts as tribal treason. Only for the familiars— a hilarious semi insane type of occupational therapeutic club, acceptable only to its deluded creator you'd go utterly scatty.

*

"By the way, Peter, are you interested in that lassie over at Madigans?"

"Who said that?"

"No one. Just that ould Tomas saw you looking after her in a certain class of way."

"Are you trying to cause mischief, Jim? Along with the footin and the firewater he's dotin'. If I know ould Tomas his brain box is capable of concocting anything."

*

"The tank on the roof is leaking," Margo said. "I didn't sleep a wink with the dripping. Since Andrew died I haven't one to do a hand's turn."

Steady, Peter counselled himself. Let it pass. Don't let Margo or old Tomas here rupture your precious inner life.

Anastatia Beggarwoman, Gentle Giant, Finger Pickers of Ireland stand by me now. Be ye my consolation in my hour of trial. The bloody frost and snow will pass and its aftermath will leave us in better humour. Hold the footing for a day or two. Endure the claustrophobic sense of living in this small place. It can be liberating in times of anguish when the citizens all gather in and protect the wounded one. They have the psychology of crows cawing at a wounded crow and of cawing angry defiance at a hawk! What I am, Peter told himself, is a son of the old woman who lived in a shoe. I have crawled into the ultimate recess of the toecap and there with scholarly pretentions I scribble with a goose quill, setting forth my reactions to my mother and my vociferous siblings and to the existentialist resentment I hold and treasure against my unknown father. A preordained task, to indicate the reactions of a huddle of humans in a particular time and place. It's an anthropological study. "Be all things to all men," and in the asylum of the toecap with the miniature figures of the familiars flitting in and out, you Peter possess a fortified tower house complete with barn in which to take refuge from the constant bombardment of the personal and the emotional, from the pig slurry of the passing day.

"'Twill burst in the middle of the night!" Margo said, "and flood ourselves and our neighbours." The snow continued to polka dot downwards outside the patterned glass of the window.

Funny how Jim noticed that I had noticed the chemist's assistant at Madigans. I didn't realise it consciously but I must have looked at her in a novel way—intuitively or some such. Did I look at her in the manner of a lazy salmon watching a lure out of the corner of his eye but too indolent to pursue it—some part of his fishy brain idling with the thought of chase and capture. Eh?

That's it! Woman the lure, the salmon fly, the minnow, the spoonfast twirling in ale brown water. In her role as fly she has the tinsel of the body, the skirt of the hackle, the flare of the wing as well as the hidden point and barb of steel! She knows intuitively and instinctively the whole gamut of the love-angler's trade or craft; she can measure moment of wind and rain, of water temperature, of pause and on rush of spate filling or receding and she revels in the struggle of the fish in play. Capture or surrender her goal, the only moment when she appears to be touched with pathos is when the fly is removed from the gasping mouth of the caught fish and all her finery is momentarily daubed or tarnished with blood, mud and slime. But dipped in the running water and her wing finger— caressed she resumes her role as if nothing had occurred. Or so it appeared to the pensive pedagogue.

Ah well. Hold on, Peter-you. All this talk about females. And the only female you vouchsafe to enter the holy of holies of your inner chamber of mental ruminations is Gentle Child. You did mention Anastatia the beggarwoman and flirted with the idea of allowing a certain Sheila to enter, but you seem to have thought better of it. So much for practice and preaching, carrissime pedagogue.

*

And still through the many incongruities and disparities inherent in the opening year, the wind of steel blew, the leak in the tank arched and arced like a boy pissing, the electric wires joining the next house to his sparked and fused and stank and smoked as bared wires were joined by the falling raindrops, and snow was seen as slush and not as an adventure. Binds of disparate feather of memory flitted in and out of Peter's brain, and were momentarily examined as by a sudden switching on of the pocket torch of the brain, and as speedily rejected when the light was snicked off. But the rejection was later seen only as a setting aside, for back came the phrase of incident, the snippets of conversation, the waves of brain, the insights, the fugitive if disparate bricks of which the house of day was built.

January ebbed. The black smoke of the great Christmas candle was a memory only—the very last candle Old Joe moulded with its smoke swirling against the white ceiling, with Margo farting fire for fear her firmament would be fouled. *"It's only for a minute," Peter whined.* Purely symbolic. From a man who lives on symbols and not on reality. Ah there's the cock of the opening year, his comb a morning flame strutting from under the shabby elder trees of winter and into the widening day. Up goes the sky. Out into the midden heap goes Peter's childhood memory of the old storyteller, the last of his histrionic line as he mimicked the instructions of Bellman Christ from the pebbly shore. "Cast on the other side"—and with the yells of piscatorial triumph, the slur of sandals on shingle, the smell of charcoal and frying fish, the Son of God, a smell of death yet clinging to his single garment, plays the new role of chef and most deftly turns the fish on the impromptu frying pan.

As the wild marmalade cat leaps down via the branches of the bare lilac in the back garden and miaows his hunger, Peter's mind leaps forward to hiker-time. It won't be long now he tells himself before they tramp past the window down the street. Adventurous but absolutely untutored as regards the human resources of Hero Town, dull of its familiars both living and dead. Peter too longed to have the courage to go forth with a young woman into the Pyrenees. *As far as Peter-my experience goes in these matters it is likely to remain theoretical. Keep your ears open and learn something every day.*

Today you wouldn't have out a coarse brush.

Cold bloody weather. Peter—the phlegm in his windpipe, his head clogged, his bones aching, his feet blocks of igloo ice—lies stretched in a high room hung above the traffic-hissing street sipping a mixture of hot cloves and Vitamin C.

When he had drained the tumbler Margo started nagging about the ballcock of the lavatory cistern. "A child could fix a ballcock," she said as Peter's snooze was gone for good and glory. What the bitch forgets, Peter told himself, is that a ballcock has a cunning brain. A ballcock can refuse to bow its head, can fail to let the flange or whatever it is fall into place, can leak or corrode the nail that holds it in place, can snap off and float fair and free in its circumscribed swimming pool and manifest its intransigence in a score of devilish ways. A child could fix a ballcock indeed.

*

Zorba the Greek, creature of Kazantzakis—he was your bottler. No mercy on women! "The poor things were weak," he said, "and one has to help them." Or words to that effect. All round him in the street corners and in the hotel he saw clowns and clots of youngsters, many of them he had taught in school, and in the matter of dealing with feminine psychology they seemed to be light years ahead of him. Crackerjacks! The cinema poster in the window gave some flickering awareness of the necessity to save the whale. The world would wake up one of these days and find that Stripey and Moby and Salar were extinct. Save the Whale, Save the Salmon.

Then a thin reedy voice whispered, "Save the Schoolmaster!"

*

Peter could hear the shrill cries of the kids in the street below as they rent the silence. He could hear their shouts, even recognise individual cries. Yahoo!

Sleet on the streets. The drumming of hail on the windows. The hot water bottle gone stone cold. Margo down at Hallissey's gossiping like mad. *I have no encumbrances. I could go to a hot climate. Ah well, everyone has a black mood. Piles, cystitis and pruritis dormant. Haven't got migraine for years. Sinus not as bad as it was. The year is opening up. Soon be back to form again. Will have jizz, capernocity and function. Tosselli's Serenade. What strange birds of light and darkness flit in and out of my brainbox. Go, man, go!*

In the yard below the buds of the lilac tree are pregnant women. *Which of the five rooms of consciousness do Peter-I the Pedagogue now inhabit?*

Winter is gone. Tomorrow is St Brigid's Day. Gather round me, familiars. Comfort me. Tosselli. Kazantzakis, and dear dead Shivers. Place your hand in mine, O Gentle Child, my small surrogate daughter. Let us go forward, comforting each other into the greenery of spring. Let us not forget Miss Delamere and her paper lovers pressed to her breast. Come along, dear—fellow soldiers fighting side by side with me at the front of loneliness.

FEBRUARY

Steadfastly the borough, creaking a little in its timbers, moves ahead with a forward thrust into spring, battling the while against rain and wind and most acutely in a personal sense, a quiet silent fight is waged against the evils of loneliness, of nervous stress arising from real or imaginary sources, dread of the cardboard 4 a.m. giants towering above sleep in the dark. Environmental change is seen as an ominous crack appearing in the pillars that uphold the certainty of life: a landmark obliterated is a tragedy that strikes deep into the emotional mechanism of the old. Juvenile delinquency, alcoholism, drugs, contraception, abortion, divorce are the dark underwater clouds appearing on the horizon. Unfulfilment and jealousy continue to lurk in shady corners of the conscious or unconscious. Yet despite all odds the parish moves ahead on the turning carousel of the year. Peter-he sees himself and his fellow townspeople as luggage, shuddering, shaking, falling sidelong, moving round and round in the terminal building of an airport, each item waiting to be snatched and taken from the circular moving contraption called life—and borne elsewhere for new adventures.

*

On a bright morning Peter was endowed with the privilege of seeing snowdrops raising their heads above a few inches of snow.

The biddy boys were now a lingering memory. Somewhere, far away in the mysterious world outside, a space-shuttle rose from bulging smoke bearing its burden of astronauts and a cage containing three arthritic rats. Three of the crew had surnames beginning with Mac and the teacher rejoiced. He was addicted to Celts. It was a standing joke behind his back. The Court Clerk sniggered at his preoccupation with Celtic mythology. His companion Steevy Harrisson, back from the UK, cursed "The Shagging Celts", saying they invented sweet bugger all beyond the safety pin, like that on the back of the Tara brooch.

"I had to go native over there or else stick out like a sore thumb Paddy in the sight of everyone and even of my children," back from England after thirty years complete with an upper crust English accent. "It was a difficult choice to make, but thanks be to God who gave me a good musical ear, I achieved my goal. I went to bed one night, a thooleramawn caterpillar of a Paddy: the following morning I woke up, butterfly of a Saxon. Magic! I bagged up all about the Royal Family, and the teams in the Soccer Divisions. Honest, I contemplated turnin' Protestant, but since they never went to Service I just took my foot off the Roman Catholic accelerator and it worked. Called the IRA all sorts of sods—protective coloration this is called in case you don't know. But it's bloody hard to keep it up I can tell you. I came back to Ireland every couple of years to relax, to return to type, to correct my perspective, to lay aside the mask and breathe deeply and naturally into all the remote fibres of my lungs and my being!

"Ah, A . . . a . . . ah. The English are different. Sweet God, for one thing among the English you must never mention death. I went to the house of a neighbour who had died: I even turned up at the cremation of the corpse; they never spoke to me after, no more than if I had walked upstairs in their house without leave or license. Guilty of obscenity. We were barbarians, intruders. Different? Chalk and cheese, I tell you.

"Easy for you to talk that way from home, Peter. Are you listening to me? I had to take all this into account when I decided to become a cultural, social, political, and superficially religious transvestite! I'm tellin' you I earned my citizenship papers over there across the water! There is a gulf, sonny boy! As wide as the Atlantic Ocean between the English and the Hanamandeels! And I crossed it, by God.

"Another thing, Peter, it's hard to have patience with this kip of a town. How's that? There he's up, my perished bacach with oodles dumped below in the bank, brandy and Cordon Bluh and summer in the Bahamas. And now he's off to get a shilling dinner at the Charity place above. The meal subsidised by me and you with our church gate donations and our rates. Life is topsy turvy.

"Did you see Madam on Sunday, Schoolmaster? She was two in from you in your seat. Hair superbly groomed, With her haute couture and her haute coiffure! Well, let me put you wise.

"This day ten years back that girl was togged out as a biddy with the Clash crowd, her face daubed with polish and soot, a biddy doll cradled in her arms, and she's going from door to door collecting money for the Clashers to have a booze. ('Disgraceful effigies of St Brigid our beloved patroness'—Fr Irwin called this custom.) A good warrant to belt the tambourine she was. Let me tell you how the change came about.

"She's living with a man—somewhere in the North east coast of England. A quiet countryish area. This man is making a fortune out of what? Out of worms and maggots for anglers. The pair of them hang meat in an outhouse. At a certain point in time out come the maggots by the million. Scoop them into boxes. Post 'em off. Cash the cheques! I'm not mocking her—I'm praising her. She's minting money. No wonder she's dressed like a princess, come a long way that one.

"A transvestite—that's myself. Like herself one of the very few who crossed the cultural divide—your humble and obedient servant, Steven Harrisson, Esquire."

Cordon Bluh, Peter told himself, the Cultural Transvestite and the Trio of Arthritic Rats mucking about in space.

*

Is there a world outside the town? Does it impinge on the activities of Hero Town? Most certainly. And at times it casts a tragic shadow.

Margo in an old full-length green knitted garment wanders about the house at all hours. Looks into space. Is tempted by the alcohol in the sideboard. Creaks back to bed. Peter listens. He decides at last to give advice.

"Listen, only for the school, I'd go up with you in the bus to Dublin. Well, you have Monica Dee with you anyway. When the witnesses get into the bus keep your mouth well shut. In the hotel, trust no one—not even waiters. Do you know what you're going to say? You do. Let's hear it."

When I went down in the morning to see if he wanted anything the door was ajar. I pushed at it and went into the kitchen. Old Moss was lying on his side with his head on the flag of the hearth. Under his grey hair there was a pool of blood. Cups were smashed around the floor. The drawers of the dresser were pulled out and odds and ends, papers mostly, were scattered around the floor. The goldfinch was going mad in the cage. I went out into the street and sent word up to the Barracks.

"Good. That's fine. That's clear. Don't add or subtract. Go to bed now. And forget it. 'Tis easy sleep on another man's wound.

"Above all don't blab to strangers. Ten chances to one they're from the newspapers feeding off the Court. You hear me?"

I hear you. I've a better head for these things than yourself.

*

Hello, Father Joe!
    Hello, Tully.
    That was a great sermon you gave on Sunday.

Thanks, Tully.

I was just saying to Peter here that I'd ask you to do something for me.

Sure, if I can at all I will.

You haven't the Blessed Sacrament on you? No! Okay. You see this bit of an ash crop. Hold it. Right. Peter the pedagogue here and myself are going down on our knees here—no not to pray—hold on, Father.

On your knees? Here in a corner of Main Street on Market Day?

You have it, Holy Man! Go on. We'll stretch out our hands like this. See.

Yes!

Now when we're down on our hands and knees, Peter Teacher and myself that is, I want you, Holy Man, holding the ash butt firmly in your priestly paw to get up on our backs. Every second turn that is.

What's this in aid of, Tully?

And to give each of us, again in turn, a good skelping across the rump with the ash butt.

What's the meaning of this, Tully? Why should I do what you say?

Well, it's like this. If anyone asks me, especially one of the Metropolitan Know-Alls, and the Libber crowd we see on the Tee Vee panels, if one of them asks me a straight question that is, I want to be in a position to answer with perfect truth, that yes yes, the Irish, especially the inhabitants of the rural and small town areas, are priest ridden.

The other way around, Tully!

What? Give you the crop?

I'll get down on my hands and knees, and let you get up on my back where you rascal the laity, you repressed, have been for the past three years since I was transferred here from a godfearing parish at the foot of Carintwohill.

I'll say this for you, Father. Wherever you came from, you were educated in a bright school. You never kept a cat until he killed a mouse.

I'll leave the last word to the man of the Cloth. Collar from Rome: manners from home.

Good day to you, Father Joe.

Good day to you indeed, Turlough O'Daly! For brevity addressed as Tully Daw. Oh, and here's your ash crop.

Hold on to it, Father. You never know the day you'll be hoisted into the saddle and become a PeePee!

Too much o' you in me for that to come to pass. Good luck whatever.

(Peter-he would like if this dialogue really took place because together with being a local historian, he's also a craftsman in making imaginary dialogue.)

*

From the nearby shop a customer's call from within beckons Peter. Hey Peddah—you! The voice hangs in the air. Shiverer in breeches! Cowardly cat! What about Eoghan Roe? I hear you're saying a few words about him at the Commemoration.

Yes, I am. What about him! I know his story better than you!

Eoghan Roe—Sugar Mouth Eugene. A class of a schoolmaster too. Like you. Didn't get half your chances. Born and died in the middle of a mountain bog forty miles from here. And now they are commemorating his bi-centenary.

Tell me more.

This awkward galoot of a hedge schoolmaster—cum—labourer—cum—Jack Tar—cum infantryman—cum—poet . . . cum womaniser packed more into his short thirty-six years! "One hundred and twenty women whom I deprived of their reputation," as he said himself. Unlike you Peter! God Almighty. A waste of good life giving it to you! Afraid of your shadow. Afraid of the parents. The inspector. The Parish Priest. Wimmin!

But the bould Eoghan Roe of the O'Sullivans, scholar . . . If you had half his guts!!

Guts! Named off every altar in Munster, husbands on his trail. Had to skidaddle and join the British navy. Drank in St Johns of Newfoundland. Faking scurvy in Britain. Discharged begod. Returns to Kerry. "Father, I'm opening a school." I know the school you're opening. Would you ever announce it off the altar, Father. No women this time—as God is my judge—no wimmin this time!

What a hope, Peter! Rambling labourer one day, schoolmaster the next, but always a poet with waterfalls of words tumbling, tossing, cascading in beauty out of his mouth. Munster his El Dorado—everywhere women that were like gold. But only for a belt in the head of a tongs in Killarney he'd have lived to be an old man only the girl they set minding him was good looking. Got out of the bed to chase her up the mountain. They hoisted him back. My poor ould hoormaster. Game to the tail! Give me my pen till I write my farewell? A crowd around the bed gaping at the wonder of Munster. Pen and paper put before him. Propped up, poor ould Honeymouth Eugene. The pen falls out of his fingers. His eyes glaze. Down run the sands when out of his hands, the pen . . . the pen . . . the pen . . . all over then!

So?

So! You poltroon of a pusillanimous panty-waisted pedagogue, you have a lot to learn. Go forth à la Eugene into the many lands. Explore exteriorly. Introspection taken to excess is fatal. I've seen you talking to yourself a good deal lately. I believe that even a nervous breakdown can be halted by travelling ten miles in a bus or train. Clean the crowded blackboard of your mind, Peter. Come Easter, come Summer, sally forth east, west, north or south. And come back with courage to purview your pitiful putrefying problems. Madigan is the word and Madigan is the man! No—the woman I mean.

Peter. About yourself and that local history you wrote let me give you a word of advice. You'll never be considered a writer in the truest sense of the word until such time as you go around deliberately insulting people. That's a basic law in scabby suppurating Ireland. If you are courteous and genial and thoughtful and sensitive to the susceptibilities of other people, observing the ordinary norms of behaviour, you'll be mentally pigeonholed by the community, well, if not as a moron, certainly as one who by any stretch of the imagination cannot be called a poet or a literary person. The cure for this deficiency is to learn a few picturesque soldier words and phrases of slang—even if occasionally blue—the language of dockside, pub, mess deck and barrack and the irrepressible wit of errand boys and costermonger.

Cant and lewd slang—they're beauties. Pick out the ones that sound pungent, picturesque and peculiar and boy, before you know where you are you're elected President of the Irish Academy of Letters. The Latin ones should give you a touch of classical swish. Any eedjit can say "Eff off!" But how about pudenda and fecundo and fellatio. Eh. You won't do it of course. Once I've advised you my duty is done.

I know!

You reckon me a parasite. Well, the mistletoe praises the apple tree from its crevice of growth in the branch and the sea lice of the nether fin praises the freshly run salmon. So the parasite is important. Nor should the parent ever begrudge the presence of the parasite nor the tithe of food—sap or oil or blood or literary fame—it needs for sustenance. It should always be a patient, generous, courteous bountiful host.

Yet tell me, how is it that all the bloody cranks, contraries and verbal monomaniacs of the barony pitch on me to utter their outlandish perorations?

*

"Oh. The doorbell isn't working. Were you knocking for long? What can I do for you?"

"I want to speak to you in private, Mrs O'Hannigan."

"Can you say it here?"

"I could but I wont. I said . . . in private."

"Very well. Step in. You're Mrs Kinleen from the place above?"

"That I am!"

"I have an appointment to play bridge so I can't delay."

"This appointment might be more important than the one you have."

"That remains to be seen. Sit there."

"You know why I'm here?"

"I have no idea!"

"You have an idea. And more than an idea. It was told to you this morning when Guard Hallissey called to see your son. And failed to find him."

"Oh!"

"Don't mind your Oh! I came about the attempted rape of my daughter Babe Mary last night. I'll make it plainer for you. Your son Denis and young Ahern from over the hill stopped her in McGonigle's arch at a quarter to eleven last night when she was coming back the short cut with a bag of chips. Ahern pulled down her knickers and your son attempted to rape her."

"My son Dan was in bed at ten o'clock last night."

"He was not and you know it."

"Are you calling me a liar?"

"I'm calling both you and your son two potent liars. And if that's your attitude I'll be off and let the law take its course. And I wouldn't be surprised if there was five years following it. So good night to you, Mrs O'Hannigan."

"Wait now! Don't be hasty. Young people are always playing. Hot blooded too."

"Only for Jim Linnane was passing at the time and they ran when he shouted at them they'd be up on a more serious charge. But it's bad enough as it is. I don't seem to be making any headway with you so if he's not at home I'll call to the shop tomorrow and see your husband."

"This can be fixed between you and me. Has your daughter made a statement?"

"Statement? She was shivering and moaning all last night and all today. She'll make it smart and lively when the Guard calls at ten o'clock tomorrow morning. Mrs Ahern is to see me later tonight—phone her if you like and verify it. The pair of you had better be lively. My husband Martin isn't in his right mind this minute."

"What are they but children. Wait. We could come to some agreement."

"Are you trying to buy me off?"

"Not at all. Only if the little girl got frightened in . . . the rough play . . ."

"Rough play! You'll tell me next the elastic broke on her knickers."

"She's entitled to a little comfort say . . . a hundred pounds."

"I've no business here. Take your hand off the knob of the door."

"From each of the boys that is . . ."

"No, nor a thousand pounds from each of the boys as you call them. Let me out of that door or I won't be responsible for what I'll do."

"Look. We were always friends. Wasn't your Martin working for my father-in-law? He was never done praising him as a lad. My last word . . . say £250 each and we'll forget it ever happened."

"Make it £400 each and I'll try to pacify Martin."

"There's no meaning to that. My last offer—£350 each. I'll speak to Monica Ahern. Don't break my word. And don't get the girl's name up in court. 'Twill follow the child all her life. You've more to lose than we have! Say £350 each."

"I'll talk it over with Martin."

"No. Agree now! I won't let you out the door unless you agree."

"But Martin. ."

"You're the boss. Everyone knows that. Don't break my word. We are a long-tailed family with influence in this locality. We might be in a position to do one of ye a turn yet. Say you will. Go on, say you will."

"All right so. £350 each. In cash!"

"And no statement."

"No."

"That's that so. Thanks be to God the weather is soft. I'll let you out quietly. Good night now."

"Good night."

*

Peter woke at the unearthly hour of 3.45 a.m. He couldn't go back to sleep. The damn time of eerie morn when the pushed down, the semi-digested trouble of the day invariably surfaces. A tintin tabulation in his cloosheens. His legs shivering. *Sweet God, am I going to have a nervous breakdown? I will be an oil rag in school tomorrow.* The belly too was banjaxed, nervous dyspepsia a young doctor said it was when Peter having described his symptoms confessed he had adequate bowel movements only on weekends and during school holidays. Plip, plop, hurrah. It's a constriction of the muscles of the bum gut, the doctor said. No problem. Go to sleep after school. As easy as that? No nervous breakdown. *Well what-do-you-know! Plip plop hurrah!* He avoided the creaking board in the floor, and tiptoed down the thirty-two steps to the kitchen. Careful, that step creaks outside Margo's bedroom door. Coast clear. In the darkness, Peter sat on a chair facing the window on to the dimly lit street. The street was quiet. Cars travelling to the Hydro Electric station wouldn't begin to pass for another hour.

Peter took stock. *I have lived in a small town all my life. And I dare say I shall teach on adventureless to the bitter end. Meanwhile, let me try to define my environment. To itemise its characteristics, to verbalise the utterly familiar but mistily imaged.*

Item: A small town is a place where the walls are made of glass. If you are liked in a country town, the inhabitants will by unspoken consent conspire to conceal your sins; the converse is also true: if you are not liked, God help your reputation.

Item: In a country town the barber looks at your hair, the cobbler at your boots, and the confectioner and butcher at your flimsy white wrapping bag. Brown paper parcels by their shape alone become transparent—all tell their individual tale.

Item: In a country town the character is prized and the storyteller is King. Sickness is drama and death is a curtain falling on a play.

Was it due to the initial repercussion of spring that the schoolmaster now found himself bombarded by familiars?

He had escaped from their clutches for some weeks but now he could not help comparing himself to a vessel at sea being attacked from many points of the sky by the tracer bullets of familiars. Bang! Maggot Girl kept calling from a shed in the English midlands as she most artistically scooped maggots from a hanging haunch of rotting meat into a large blue plastic basin.

She exercised a powerful recurrent fascination for him. The pedagogue drained his glass of water. He felt good now that he had isolated certain characteristics of his surroundings. Outside, the wind blew harshly. It rattled the window frame. Peter stole up to bed.

*

In the lee of corner shops the storytelling went on. The tellers of tales, the anecdote merchants, were crouched a little against the skinning breeze, while others huddled indoors. "Is that you, Mother?"

"'Tis! That you, Maimie?"

"Did you get the pains since?"

"What pains? Oh, they're eased up all right. Buttercup calved!"

"Did she? 'Tisn't calves are troubling me, Mother. But the Stock Exchange."

"The live stock exchange I'm interested in, girl. Your father is delighted with the way the Friesian heifers are turning out in spite of having lost a Friesian bullock St Brigid's Day. But the other springers are calving great, Thank God. They'll market well."

"The stock market was bullish, Mother. Ernest was worried. Everyone fine out here, but below in the bank non-stop buying and selling. Pure panic stations—he hardly slept a wink. Walking the floor into the small hours. Being a Bank Manager is no fun, Mother. The rooms of the Bank House here are huge and hard to heat."

"I'll tell you a good one, Maimie. You remember Angel Gabriel, the Jersey heifer calved on 25th March? Well she was in calf to the best bull from the insemination centre. And when the calf was born—didn't Angel reject her own calf. We were in a right predicament. Right or wrong she refused to let the calf suckle her. What harm but we washed her carefully after she was dropped. Bond washing it was called."

"You might have seen it in the papers, Mother, investors selling Government bonds at inflated prices before dividend day. Making a pile of money and paying no tax on it. It drove the Exchange crazy entirely when the Government came down on it. The Government brokers too held the reins on transactions."

"So I said to your father, 'What you'll do now is this. Go into the Mart. Explain your position. Sell your calf and get a good price. Then buy the best Jersey calf you can find. Bring her home. Angel had taken a dislike to the smell of her own calf. I'll bet you anything you like she'll let the new calf suckle her. The pounds will walk up on her then.' "

"The Irish punt struck a new low, Mother. Ernest was in a pucker as to what he'd do with the money he had salted away in Maidenhead and the Channel. You know what? He lost a great chance of buying a field in the west that'd give five prime sites. No use crying over spilt milk."

"Milk! Very minute the fresh calf was put under her, Gabriel let her suckle away. After a few days her coat shone as if it was polished with oil."

"Oil? Ernest had over a Big Ten in Atlantic Viscid. At first it soared. All last week the value of the shares was up and down like a yo-yo. A pure nightmare."

" 'Matthew,' I said to your father, 'stop up the first night so as to make sure Gabriel doesn't turn against the new calf.' Give him his due, he did."

"Talking of dues, Mother. Ernest had to foreclose on a farmer last week. He tried every way to avoid . . . you know."

"Foreclose on a WHAT?"

"On a farmer. He had 583 statute acres and he refused even to service the debt. Wouldn't even answer a letter. What harm but if he sold 183 acres he could have cleared it no bother and would have enough left to stock his land. There was a bit of a fuss by the farmers when he was taken off to Mountjoy, but it blew over! Know where we're going for our holidays this summer, Mother, taking Cynthia and Ronnie with us—the Seychelles in the Indian Ocean."

"Hold on there, girl, now! Was it your Ernest clapped that poor unfortunate farmer from the South-east in jail? The case that was in all the papers?"

"He had no option, Mother!"

"Well bad luck may melt you. And him as well as you. How quickly you forget that you were reared on a farmer's bread. Wasn't I short-taken to send you to a laddie-daw of a boarding school where they put high notions into your empty head. The long years your poor father spent scouring drains and drawing stones to make land of this place. Aye and standing cattle at fairs and his old frieze overcoat a ton weight with the dint of rain."

"Mother!"

"Ah shit for Mother! Ernest with his golf and his rugger at Whiterock and every time you come on the phone your only tune is how hard it is to get domestic servants, babysitters and charwomen. The Seashells Islands in the Indian Ocean. Bridge, golf and tennis! That's all your cock . . ."

"Mother, listen!"

"Your poor father and myself were bloody lucky if we got a week at Lahinch in late September when the work was finished and the iodine was in the sea water".

"You're being most unreasonable . . ."

"Don't ever forget, my lassie, that both your father and myself gave every second turn up nights watching the sow farrowing in the back kitchen in case she'd eat or smother the bonhams. With only the light of a tin lantern, and we perished with the cold. Far from boarding schools we were reared. But you . . . Ernest . . . and Cynthia and Ronnie."

"Listen for a moment, Mother."

"Don't bother ringing me again until that poor man is back in the bosom of his family. Mountjoy Jail! Fine for yourself and your Ernest talk with your bellies staunched in the Big Bank House and your arses to a coal fire and your money in the Channel Islands. And don't darken my door but as little. You hear me!"

"Mother! Mother! Dear God she's gone. Impossible to time her. Getting worse as she grows older. I'd better keep this to myself. I'll try her again when she cools off. Maybe Ernest can do something about the fellow in jail. Life is hard, very hard at times! My nerves are in tatters"

*

Now now, Peter-you—Stinoff! Peadar, Pete, Pedagogue, how now? You have decided to find a centre of silence wherein you might think things out. Sunday afternoon. Damp and cold. The town silent.

The question is the familiars. The mind coalescing creatively on globules of words, on nouns proper and common, images of all sorts that are units, lego pieces, bricks—that kind of thing. Familiars? They adhere like the newly laid eggs of the apple snail.

They comfort like Angora wool. Trouble is one is forced to resort to words to convey these images. Words that interpose between the mind and the sensory target are a confounded nuisance. Gesture, as on the stage, the shorthand of the nerves, is far more powerful. Words should be outlawed.

Yet, still the search for the mantra, the Open Sesame, the assembling of a jigsaw puzzle, the coalescence of the disparate with its random beauty goes on. Words and images reacting almost chemically to each other. As man to woman, as woman to man, reacting at once and knowing, knowing, knowing.

Cut ups, fold ins, montage and collage of incident, and dialogue seek intuitive but inexplicable harmony. And you hope to achieve this goal in the context of a bum country town on the western edge of the known world. In the context of a girl bone-feathering maggots from a chunk of rotting beef, of imported daffodils, and Bonds.

That's correct. Selecting comrades and mates. Old shoes finding old stockings. Mating and giving birth to minor indelibilities. Haphazardly they will come upon me or through the medium of coincidence or as single spies. Eoghan Roe shaking hands with Toselli.

You'll be locked up, Pedagogue.

Maybe so. I'll have a lot of fun before that.

Why do you call them up, the familiars?

So that eventually they may feel at home trying out the philosophical furniture of my mind.

*

It wasn't everyone could make porridge, Peter muttered, with the first tentative stir with the old gold coloured spoon. Porridge, bran and honey ensured the perfection in conformation, texture and colour of the postprandial stool! Watch it, brother. Since days historically prehistoric porridge has a habit of bubbling and boiling up rather surly and gluttonously pouring over the lip of the cooking utensil and down to hiss on the electric ring. Burnt porridge in the air would bring Margo out in her dressing gown and downstairs like a fury. There is no timing of her lately. Ah . . . just right. Too early to take the cream of the porridge up to Margo and get off to a good start in domestic affairs. Pour. The porridge jells on touching the cold dish. Lovely!

Sweeten with honey, raise, break the umbilical cord of dropped sweetness, hold over, allow to drip. There it goes, a pattern of concentric circles liquefying like the blood of St Janarius as it touches the hot surface of the porridge.

"Porridge," as the old prosthetics doctor said, "puts a poultice to your inside first thing in the morning. Allied to bran-nuts it is good for the bowels."

*

Down in the town the parish clerk was bothered. No fun being a parish clerk. Money and the excitement of ceremony—okay that's granted. But at the break of day entering the sacristy and checking that the picture covering the knob of the secret wall safe was not askew after the night. A sigh of relief. Burglars had not yet discovered what lay beneath the pictorial camouflage. Then entering the Sanctuary itself, as Keeper of the King of Kings, the sanctuary lamps seems to wink as if to say, "About bloody time, you holy loafer. Come on, lad, do your stuff!" The protocol of genuflection must be observed even in the context of an empty church. He looks over his shoulder at the great empty nave. The arena of my triumphs, he tells himself. Where I stood wreathed in the smoke of incense against the backdrop of an altar dressed and ablaze for benediction. I looked down over great congregations. I saw myself as others see me in this moment before handing the thurible to the priest.

Now for sounds in the empty church. The echoing footsteps, the clang of the single sanctuary side gate; they took away the other gates in the New Reformation. The rattling keys, the back swing of bars and bolts on doors, the admission of the last dark of first day. The first worshipper. Biddy the Bike, a dame obsessed with the godhead—she whom the intellectual barbarians of the metropolis heterogeneously lump together as "Country craw thumpers".

And what is Biddy doing except seeking to participate in the offering of dawn/sacrifice to God, in a type of ritual as old as the human race. Ha ha brother, what the half-baked buckoes of humanism choose to overlook is this—that they themselves offer sacrifice to lesser gods.

The parish clerk, an expert on ceremony, has twin foes whose ferocity increases according as age advances and he begins to revolt against the burden of traditional duties. "Brass and bells will drive me crazy!" he complains, swinging on the bell rope. The priest agrees: "Must make enquiries about dipping," he murmurs. "Dipping?" the parish clerk asks. "What's that?"

"The article said the candlestick is dipped in a solution of liquid brass and it needs no polishing thereafter."

"That buttery yellow," the clerk explodes. "It'll be done over my dead body!" He pauses as the priest continues. "Have the bell automated and programmed. You won't have to ring the Angelus or the Mass bells then."

"You mean it will ring by itself? Holy God!" the clerk says as he slams the door behind him. "Automated! Daniel O'Connell makes children by steam." The priest has heard the historical reference. He smiles to himself. Ah, times change! But the heterosexual business remains basically the same. But not for long as test tube babies and uterine something or other are mentioned.

*

By 10.30 a.m., the women of Hero Town sieve through the streets in search of food for the body and stimulants for the mind. Gossip at this hour proceeds at its traditional pace and with its traditional rhythm.

Face to face, gravely absorbed. "What happened her except what happened us all—a belt of the old nerves."

"Poor Jack is putting his Purgatory across him in this life with those wild children of his."

"May Gold help me to bear the cross of my poor brother's death. Big lovely lovable Mick, a steamroller of a man. If I live to be as old as an eagle I will never forget the kindness of the people of this town."

High above two gulls planed across the raw spring sky. Except for the schoolmaster no one looked up from the streets of the town. Peter, secretly and imaginatively extended his arms to either side, mimed the birds' flight towards the breaking waves of the broad Atlantic which again set Peter thinking about the Funeral Home idea that had crossed the same waves and opened recently in Hero Town. Grandpaw's cadaver could now be collected at the back door in a canvas sack, shuttled discreetly in an unmarked dark blue van to the Home or Parlour or House of Rest or Some such, where the poor overripe banana would be stripped, hosed, washed, shaved, then robed according to the choice or pence of relatives and laid out in a coffin. Perfect example of the depersonalised and deodorised mortal remains of a Loved One. Whiskey in the wings. All amusements and occasions of sin, especially at wakes, strictly forbidden by the First Commandment. That's death. Now where's life. Looking through the sitting room window.

*

And you, Bomber Harris—how about your sins? Peacefully dying in your bed at ninety-one. How about the times as a young man when you shat down bombs on Dresden killing thousands in a short space of time? You who sowed the quick red harvest of annihilation returned to base to sleep the sleep of the unjust and to grow pucely apoplectical at the thought of a few Irish "subversives" placing a tiny pyrotechnic device in a West End boutique so as to call attention to the woes of Old Ireland.

Dresden. Glow, firecracker in the boutique, glow!

The second crop of the daffodils is now on the altar. Margo will show a spark of civilised dependability once the daffs arrive to be followed later by the primroses. *Winter is past. Welcome, O flaunting bugler of spring, failte romhat.*

After the recent burial of her husband Old Angela Trueblue, white hyacinth in hand, walked up the hill and looked down on the sullen mystery of the town. "I lost my comrade and there is a great vacuum beside me. But my loss is as nothing compared with the loss I am about to come in contact with, at first hand."

In a dark room of the north-facing thatched cottage a young mother is dying of cancer of the womb. She has four children, the eldest eleven, the youngest crawling about on the floor. She had refused to go to hospital. "I'll die where I've made my home," she kept saying, "with my children around me and my man darkening the bedroom door."

Angela, product of a mixed marriage, pushed open the half-door and entered. "Here, Hazel," she said addressing the worn face in the bed, "look, it's spring." Scarce knowing whether to laugh or to cry the patient compromises with a slow spreading smile: "Yes indeed, Miss Angela, it is spring!" The fox cub eyes of the daughter who had been holding her mother's hand shifted suddenly from one to the other of the two faces above her, but betrayed nothing definite as regards her reactions. A watcher if present would have reached a variety of conflicting conclusions.

*

With the ringing of the Angelus Bell at noon, Peter found himself considering again the case of the Parish Clerk. Something that was common to both the Parish Clerk and the Pedagogue was the fight against superstition. Peter however through his interest in folklore secretly confessed himself the less committed of the two custodians of the Faith, capital F. The clerk was hell-bent against rural cures; he took the note from a succession of denunciatory pastors determined to stamp out the last embers of paganism and superstition in a credulous community that at times lacked faith in antibiotics and Christianity as they should. Forge water, broom tea, and graveyard herbs, a never-ending list!

But though the old remedies were dying, their practitioners conveyed that their death would not be hastened. In the fullness of time, resources relied upon in crisis for thousands of years would vanish naturally. Meanwhile the three eggs in the confession box of the missioner gave him food for thought as he raised the roof roaring about pisheogs. Peter wouldn't be surprised if one of the first spacemen was found to have smuggled a rabbit's paw into the capsule before blasting off for the moon. To protect him. Yahoo.

Peter decided to stick to honey and porridge. Those are for the body. For the imagination there were the primroses, Angela Trueblue, superstitions—not to mention Bomber Harris. Quite a good bag of mixed birds there. Hang 'em by the feathers till they fall to the ground. Before cooking.

*

"Hello, Mrs Mac."

"Hello, Johnny."

"I'm sorry about Brendan failing the exam again."

"What's that you're saying, you brat? He did no such thing. Who told you that? For your information my Brendan got Second Class Honours in his Second Arts, with the option, mark you, of resuming University Studies any time he wanted."

"I didn't mean anything by what I said. Honest, Mrs. I was just going to the delicatessen."

"Come in here to my hall off the public street. Stand there on the mat till I read your pedigree. You're the son of a bitter father and a poisonous mother. Both your grandmothers could piss arsenic. So where would you be got? If you want terriers, breed 'em. Stand there, you feckin' little serpent, till I show you the result of my Brendan's exam. Read it there in black and white.

The cheek of you! No one belonging to me carried the bag around the countryside gathering small green praties from the farmers and playing the bones not knowing a crotchet from a crubeen. Stand your ground and hear the truth. Yourself and your feckin' delicatessen! Far from delicatessens you and yours were reared. I'm a quiet woman. Graduation! Your sort has graduated from the periwinkle to the prawn cocktail, from the fist of grass to the Baby Soft, beggars on horseback! Go on with you now! And if I hear another peep out of you about my Brendan in Sligo I won't be responsible for my actions. Scoot!

*

Hey, Schoolmaster, are you still going on messages for that sister of yours? Well stop it! You're succumbing. To women. For your own sake, not mine, stop it. Look at me! A galley slave to a Community of consecrated virgins in that convent over forty eight years. What's that in your hand? Ground cinnamon. You've succumbed. Your sister's apple cake. Traitor! You're a pure mutt, even from the nipple. Biddy with the hiccough and your sister Margo, all tyrants spreading their infernal empire. So for God's sake, Peter, stop. Don't succumb. You hear? *I hear you. Don't succumb.*

*

From the centre of the silver slant hiss of the morning shower the silver ferule of an umbrella raised aloft shines like a far chalice exalted. "Who dat man?"

"That am de doting bishop back in retirement in his native town on his way to de Sisters' chapel to celebrate a quiet mid-morning Mass." The ex-bishop, mock mild now, spent twenty-five years as chairman of an ecclesiastical court of matrimony in Chicago and heard the seamy side of wedlock. No two ways about it. Spent a score of years and more discussing academic points regarding menstruation, fornication, blood and bras. Poor chap. Lost one-third of his diocesan clergy in a gush and rush for the exits and mock free air of post-conciliar liberty. Played on his nerves. Grew senile in a month. Some of his priests married nuns. The only females with whom they had come in close contact. God love the poor old man! What goes on in his head?

Peter, pondering, perceives the prelate pass. On the old graveyard wall ivy berries begin to grow fat and sleek. Dark olive green good at bouncing on footpaths—the berries. Their means of getting away from the parent bush! Unlike the thistle they possess no parachutes. Just a bounce. The Lord God must have said to the ivy bush: "To thy berries I shall bequeath a bounce. Go forth, increase and multiply."

With a bounce?

Massa, dat am a bouncer.

A dancehall bouncer?

No, Massa, de Lawd's own green berry ivy bouncer.

I see.

*

But now at the Corner Shop, John-John the grocer is bouncing and putting on a show from behind the counter for five women customers, as his wife is busy making up the parcels. John-John is not idle.

Holding the change from the fiver (the customer might think of buying something else) John-John surveys the shop-full of women. Then he speaks.

"In the next reincarnation, I'll come as a woman. I'll have two titties here in front, both firm as half melons, yet shaking like jelly, with a protruding backside that's begging to be pinched. A man is only a glorified jackass. And when I am reincarnated I hope to God and His Blessed Mother that I get a husband as good as that woman there got," points to his wife.

Handy Annie, his wife, tutts as he goes outside the counter crouching at the bag of potatoes. "Look at that for ankles!" John-

John proclaims, his face vermilion as a result of crouching, catching a woman by the ankle. "Look at that for a calf. Look at that for a knee! If I have thighs half as good as that in my reincarnation I'm past the post."

"Get up, you scamp," his haughty wife cries. He gets up, his face flushed again not from shame, but from crouching. "Next time round I'll be wearing tights and a cross-the-heart bra Men are simpletons, with their cowdunged corduroys. I'm looking forward to the next life and the part I'll play. High heels, Italian shoes. But skillets of possibilities! There are drawbacks, big drawbacks. I'll lower my voice, Sally—you're an understanding woman.

"Some of women's moon troubles will prove a bit of a chore, but so is shaving. One balances the other. As a woman, I said. The next life. Holy Mary Mother of God, pray for John-Johnny who's gone to the bad. Oh! Look out that door and see the retarded children coming out of the coach—back from Lourdes. Loving God watch the little fellah working his arms. Incontinent day and night. They're great girls that went out in charge of them. That's Christianity with a capital C. I'll have no more joking for the balance of my day. That finishes me with fun. A man doesn't realise how happy and lucky he is. Nor woman either. God love 'em. I'll take out your box, ma'am, and load it into the boot of the car. They're little primroses so they are. Primroses of Christ, that's what I call them, an endangered species. Soon they'll be all put to sleep after birth. As abortion postscripts. Man's inhumanity to man. Is it any wonder I'd look forward to reincarnation."

*

In the late evening, the pedagogue pauses and looks upwards from the corner of the square. Overhead in a scattered but elongated file the rooks are flying eastward heading for the populous rookery of Kilveeney Wood. Since dawn they have been scavenging all over the barony and almost at the same time every late afternoon they converge herringbone fashion towards the main backbone of the homeward file eventually to hover and circle clamorously over the branches of the trees beneath which the walls of the ruined mansion crumble away.

Caw! Caw! Nervous creatures the crows: they have reason to be so. Sixty-five years before their great great grand-parents were, in the grey light of dawn, startled by a volley of shots, and as they rose in a clamour of protesting caws an old brave bird must have looked down and seen a titled member of the ascendancy vivid in a red dressing-gown lying barefooted on the crisp grass adjacent to his monkey puzzle tree. The shots had hardly died away before scandal rose clamorous as the cawing of thousands of crows, cawing the Crown Jewels filched from Dublin Castle some years before, a pride of pederasts entrenched in power and suicides. Caw-caw-caw for an enquiry that touched the Royal hem of an overseas emperor thoughtful at breakfast. Caw-caw say the rooks on their way home above the streets of the town as they return to Kilveeney Wood.

*

"Peter, you're the very man!" *Sweet God it's Flossie Donnelly.* "What I want you for is this, and this for yourself alone. I'm writing a history of this town and the country round."

Divine God!

"No I won't intrude (laughs) on your territory at all. And I'll be asking you to have a look at my history book. As regards what they call a foreword, two or three thousand words from yourself will be fine."

"Flossie, before you go any farther I'm blind as a bat with eyestrain. This comes over me all of a sudden, so I'm out of action. I'm not refusing you, Flossie. 'Twould be a bad act for me to do that."

"Jealousy is at you! There's friendship for you. Say no more, Peter Mulrooney. If you said you'd do it now I'd refuse you. I hate something given with a perished heart. You bring that from your mother. Good day to you. And that you may have the luck you deserve. Whatever that is."

Where are you, Gentle Child! Why do you not come gently to my aid? Jeez that was a narrow escape. Is it any wonder I'd have migraine.

You lied, Peter. *Of course I did.* You have no eyestrain. *None whatsoever.* Any excuse? *Yes, my sanctified patron Peter of the Brazier was a liar. Standing in the courtyard, when accused of being in the gang of Jesus, he blustered, I know not the Man! Are there any cocks left in this town? Or is it altogether incarcerated hens laying paper eggs? If there is one cock left now is his time to crow. Let me offer him a cockcrow in case he has forgotten how it sounds. Ready? Cock-a-doodle-doo! That should pacify Flossie Donnelly, if she is equipped to interpret. Which indeed I doubt.*

*

Every morning of the week in which the moon cycle of her daughter-in-law ended, as the old mother-in-law came slowly downstairs, the first thing she looked at was the young woman's waist. The old lady never varied her routine. Her movements were uneasy until such time as her son had finished his breakfast and gone off to work on the farm outside the town. The young wife often teased her mother-in-law, inventing excuses to go here and there so as to avoid the question which never varied at this time of the month.

At last the young woman allowed herself to be cornered. Then came the whisper from the old lips, "Did you get our friend?" The younger woman could sense the old woman's disappointment the moment she answered, "I did, ma'am!" Then the old lady would sigh and say, "Next month, please God, he won't arrive at all."

"That's what she said to me long ago. 'Our friend,' she called it, the bride now a mother-in-law herself whispered to the red-faced Peter. "Now I find myself asking my own daughter-in-law the very same question. 'Well Doreen,' I say, 'any trace of our friend?' And disappointment is in my heart when she says, 'Yes, ma'am.' And simpleton that I am, I say without realising what I'm saying, 'Next month, please God, he won't knock at the door at all.'"

All this kind of chat drives me up the bloody walls, Peter-he told himself. It vexes me, puzzles me and upsets me. In her essence it appears to me that every woman, young or old, vicariously or actually is a she-cat purring over a litter of kittens, licking them and nosing them up to the teats. I give up. One seldom finds a breach in the wall of women's whispered confidences to each other, as I have just experienced. She must have a reason for being so open with me. Is she pointing me in the direction of her daughter Junie—now twenty-seven or so. I'll be on my guard. The tender trap and all that mumbo jumbo. Still Junie isn't a bad looker. We'll see who'll outfox whom. If she takes me for a randy passer domesticus she'll have another think coming. What am I but a simpleton and an outsider at the door that is slammed in male faces. Here and there a chink of light as has been granted to me today. Friend or foe, curse or blessing—you pays your money and you takes your chance. Ponder on, Peter-you, an innocent gom of a deluded schoolmaster in the context of an arsehole of an Irish country town.

*

And still the complaint about the stray dogs lingered on. "This town," the neighbour complained, "is full of Bingo dogs! It's only a question of time till we have rabies." Bingo Dogs that the elderly rustics bring into town in hordes on a Sunday night to play the curse-o'-God game called Bingo in aid of parochial funds in the Fiesta Hall, realising to a man, and woman, that dog licence time has arrived, bring their curse-o'-God mongrels with them from a ten-mile radius into this town where they tuft out the tykes on to the road or alley. They're too squeamish to shoot, drown or hang the buggers, so they foist them on us in the town with the result that . . . will you look at instep of my shoe!"

"'Tis no laughing matter."

*

The humour of a small town being firmly based on the faecal and its ancillary functions was a left-handed tribute to the sense of intimacy obtaining among the citizenry. It wasn't everybody one would discuss these activities with. They were never indulged in the presence of outsiders. It was a counter-poise of sorts to the grim reality of such imperial gents as Bomber Harris whose energies were directed toward a form of genocide.

Yet again, mostly the other familiars which abode with him were positive as opposed to negative; Sambo and Co. were wholesome people all saying yes to life.

From the higher ground outside the town the pedagogue allowed himself the Lenten luxury of a modest smile. Ah, what a vista lay below him when Peter viewed the leafless woods below, the distant mountain tops white with the sky-guano of snow, and the surface of the river a steel blue pane of thin ice. Brrr! But it was cold! Brrr! The single eye of the little bridge on the edge of the southern world like that of a blind old boatman. Peep! Brrr! This wonderful panorama should banish all negative forces. Somehow it doesn't. Imagination is in revolt and occupying key positions in the Pedagogue's brain box.

*

The voice of an old man snarling at the Market Arch, "Go away, you bastardin' tinker lover," still rang in Peter's ears!

Five beautiful girls. Young women now—gathered in the semi darkened recess of the arch of the Flour and Meal Store in the Diamond, obviously waiting for the bus to take them to a disco. Hair glossy as they emerge into the light of the street lamp. Limbs beautifully fluid in Levis. Peter-he on his way to evening Mass suddenly realised that they were tinker girls whom, when they were in their very early teens, he had been called upon (the old nun who had nothing else to do) to act as an audience for their prowess in reading and recitation. What a change since he had first noticed them. He had tried his best to see them housed, to school them in some fashion. Clamour! Savage opposition from Christian people! "If you build a tinker's house near me, Teacher, I'll cut my throat on your doorstep!" The threat was enough to upset Peter.

Five beautiful young women. Ready for the sexual road. In time, their parents had got houses. Nubility now expressed in terms of giggling and pushing. They had Peter under observation and were putting on an act.

"Well, well. Which of you read the lesson about Michelangelo for me?"

"'Twas me read about the Pope's painter. And he upside down in the chapel ceiling painting people without any clothes!"

Loud roars.

Five beautiful young women, off into life, their parents never knew the widening of horizons; the first generation able to read. All their forebears knew was beggary, wood smoke, dampness and tuberculosis. "We're off to the disco at Eastcastle. The lads from Traveller's Hill will be there, we know them all!" So they're keeping to their own. "Here's the bus. We're off. Good luck, Sir."

"Good luck."

"You're not married yet, Peter?" (Giggles)

"No!"

Who dat now?

That am de tinker girls ready for life, Massa.

The submerged irritations of the day resurface in the mind on awakening at 4 a.m. Hero Town was asleep. Peter stood at the window looking down on a street rain-scoured and rain-drenched.

It was a struggle keeping February at bay. 'February, I dread you!'—the old people said—the internal apparatus of Hibernian skulls as sensitive to atmospheric pressure as the mercury in a barometer, reached an all-year low during dreary February. There were other brain pressures just ahead, for spring in its initial stages sent novel vibrations through the brain.

Within me there's an urban guerrilla—a dour enemy to defeat. What will send me back to sleep? "You married yet, Master?" Women harbour these guerrillas too—terror of vasectomies and cystitis and herpes zoster. Voices! Voices!

Shoo! Scat! Beat it! Some of you are not familiars but intruders and imposters. I'll have no truck with you. Standing here in the morning dark I call upon the daffodils to blow their bugles. Come heralds and trumpeters, signal the perennial resurrection of the world. I reach out to across time and space to reach others touched also by my morning melancholy.

MARCH

*W*hat the hell is the water-table, Peter asked himself? People coming up to me demanding immediate answers. When I try to be evasive they call my bluff. If I plead ignorance, they look at me with pity. It's a game they play—taking the pedagogue down a peg.

For days it had been raining like the devil. The water scoring arbitrary channels wherever the surface was soft. From unexpected corners and channels and underground pipes a bubble, glug-glug, up she spills milk chocolate pale, up and over water flowing mercilessly. In a breadshop Peter had the unwit to remark that the country was deluged and a hillside farmer sharply said, "Townies know nothing about the water-table and care less."

"Like a briar that fellow," the grocer looking after him said. "He has sixty acres of golden land, never in his life has he set a drill of spuds! Himself and his bloody water-table!"

The lilac tree in the yard had begun to farrow. No other word would do to describe its buds shedding and preparing to emerge. The town goes slightly insane at this time of year. Peter reflects this craze. Bedlam in the head. He tries not to show it. *The bastards to the west have wiped out the salmon; beautiful bars of living silver, superb in shape, texture and courage and even when dead—in taste. Am I married yet? What the hell use in considering marriage nowadays when the very foundations of the institution are shuddering with parishioners subjecting their church to a severe cross-examination?*

*

When summertime was announced in the early part of the year, the harness maker refused to advance his clock by the official hour. Behind the thin glass of the mullioned window the ancient clock hung or clung, proclaiming on the broad rim of its face the virtues of Vanner & Prest's embrocation when applied to horses, its pendulum dourly swinging backwards and forward inside its circular peephole. The old man knew that later the timepiece would puzzle the 11 a.m. tourists, who having left the coach in the Square would wander around the neighbouring streets for a time. This would cause the old man to smile under his grey spiking moustache, and he knew that at the onset of winter, when official summertime was at an end and the clocks put back on hour, he could say as he did every year, "There now, they had to come back to me again."

To offset his temporary unpopularity in the matter of the bell, the curate called a folklore meeting to put the legends and customs of the parish on tape for posterity.

Did the diversion quell the ecclesiastical clamour behind the pedagogue's back? Temporarily only. Peter could scarcely walk down the street on a peaceful Saturday morning without the mutterings of insurrection. The voices of conflict reverberate in his head.

"Listen, Father, you and your fellow-curates are birds of passage, blackbirds that can be ordered to nest anywhere. Those of us who are into years have seen dozens of ye come and go, each one of you with his own breed of faldal notions.

"Our beautiful sanctuary and the marvellous mosaics! What do the priests want to do, make a balls of the House of God? Well, let me tell you the war cry is: not a bloody inch! No Christmas dues, no station money. Up-dating the church? What do we care about up-dating? What I'm going to tell you anyway, Peter, is that I'm an Archbishop Lefebvre man. All the way—an old timer. Isn't that the secret of the whole shebang. The mystery. The incense. The flowers. The candlelight. The winking gold. The vestments. And another thing, that little mollycoddle of a priest isn't fooling me with his folklore sessions. And his glorifying the great Dancing Masters here abouts. I see right through his little plan. He wants to make the changes . . . palatable."

Palatable? That's a felicitous use of the word, John—well done!

"Go to Newfoundland, Peter," advised old Paul. "The winter there is like one vast sheet of plate glass. And the women in the basement parties are as hot as the wood fires that crackle on the open hearths. Aren't they descended from Irish fishermen from Dungarvan and Dingle? The land out there is cold, but the hearts of its people are warm. What have you here? A Vanner & Prest clock and goms talking about Bingo dogs and musty candlesticks? And as I'm at it, I'll try to educate you. *(Everyone in this town is trying to educate Peter-me in that regard!)* What I'm saying is this: a woman can compress the whole world of meaning into a cough. For instance, it can mean this: I'm dying, you tyrant, and before the first coat of daisies is on my grave you'll have another hot arse planted beside you on our Odearest mattress. Or a cough can mean: think I don't see the sort of lascivious glances you were casting at Monica's knee. You're not fooling me, Mr Rudolph Valentino. But then again so many people like yourself are blind in this regard and illiterate as well. Like a good man, Peter, I'm for your welfare; hoist your sails this summer and hit for Newfoundland. If I had my life over again . . ."

Peter sniffed deeply: the smell of wood smoke was in the air. Another imaginative bone on which to chew at bedtime, for Mr Fantasy, Pedagogue, Hero Town.

*

A stranger could pass through Hero Town and say, what the hell happens here? Sweet bugger all, by appearances anyhow. A coach full of Virgin Mary blue past-their-best Americans, women and men, would wave out the window at the corner boys and have as little notion of what went on in the heads of those who smirkingly waved back as if they were Lilliputians or neomartins who led their existence on the outer edges of time and space. How to explain to these obtuse travellers that the citizens had compelling and even vital clones and zones of interest worthy of close scrutiny? Take for example indignation. Indignation with phones, communism, spouses, siblings, grave spaces, planning permissions, casky ale, bad mutton, poor schooling, lost football matches, appointments broken, letters unanswered, secrets selectively told. "He didn't attend our funeral, well he's shit out of luck if he didn't, for as long as one of you is left alive in this town let him bury his own bloody dead. If he hasn't the four bearers to take out his Da's Jordan box, I assure you it won't trouble me. We attended all of his and sent Mass Cards signed by the priest. We sent no duds. You hear me now, give him tit for tat. He had a cold so he had—hasn't he big able baiters of sons and barters of daughters that could show their faces or their rumps. Tit for tat."

Newfoundland, daisies on a grave, the water-table and indignation. There's richness. And people have the unmitigated cheek to say there's feck all to see and hear in a country town!

*

"Watch out for buzzards," Maria from-outside-the-town whispered to Peter.

"Buzzards?" he asked limply.

"The big bird with the moulted feathers that sits on a cactus or something in the desert and watches as the buffalo staggers and falls to his knees."

"I don't understand," Peter replied scanning her close-set eyes.

"There are people in this town who spend their time watching dying people. They look at faces closely. Experts on the signals of the Big C. As if they were collecting antiques. They rub their hands with glee when they hear of people with no relatives being shifted to hospital. They bring them grapes and Lucozade. They pretend to offer novenas. They'll sit by the bed for hours twiddling their thumbs and staking their claims: shooing off other buzzards. Without saying a word they proclaim, I saw him first!"

"Why do they do this?"

"So that they'd be left the spondulicks or the house or the roadside holding as the case might be. 'Twon't make you an hour older to settle your affairs—that's the clincher! Dr Taaffe says they're vermin—buzz-alcoholics; there's even a buzzard watching myself."

"No!"

"I have him like a dog on a lead. My couple of roadside acres are now prime building sites. He's handy to me so I keep him dangling. He's company too. I often feed him false clues as to my intentions!"

"You surprise me, Maria."

"I like hikers too."

"You do?'

"'Twon't be long now till the first of them come around again. I look forward to the beautiful interesting hikers from foreign lands. With their yalla cloaks and their rolled up mattresses and their clattering pots and pans. Whatever is in my place with its whitewashed gable on to the road they all stop and ask me questions. I give an odd couple I take a fancy to the run of the hayshed for the night. A young man and a young woman say, with or without wedding rings. The way I look at it, the maidenhead is well fractured before they reach my place.

"Thatch is a magnet, they can't pass it. I'd have knocked the caboosheen long ago only for the company. The last pair were from Hungary. I didn't understand them nor they me, but we had a gala time with the dummy language. I tell stories—Arabian Nights around the fire. Ah, but the buzzard gets cross and sits on the fence when he sees the hikers. No come in. They'll kill you for your money, he says. I have to laugh at that coming from him. They offered up the rosary with me before they went out to the hayshed. Jesus, Master, if I was eighteen again I'd hit the road! And I'd pass no foreign haysheds either. Between the buzzards and the hikers and my three cows I've a great old life."

"You have indeed, Maria. Good luck now. And God send you no worse company than myself."

*

The schoolmaster uses the backyard lavatory. His urine is golden yellow indicating that the distillery of his kidneys is running a potent product. Thousands of little men inside me, he thinks, working a twenty-four-hour shift each day, hoping to get a John Barleycorn of the body that's acceptable to the Connoisseur. The issue of a scalding systaltic liquid inclining to rust-red in colour can bring the management down on top of everyone. Peter listens acutely to discover if a hum of activity issues from the distillery within. Peter would like to have a chat with the Artificial Inseminator—that lusty rascal friend who was one of his first pupils and who now is an absolute authority on all matterts of animal activity, and women! Big black and randy as a stallion in May. But of course sounding him out is out of the question. *Instead of my teaching him, judging by the number of women he always has in tow he could teach me a thing or two, or three! Tempting to probe, but out of the question. Folly on my part to suggest it: or to even dare draw down the subject. Wait! Is that infernal migraine rumbling again like gunfire on the horizon of my consciousness?*

Jealousy, thy name is river! Don't tell me—ask me instead. This stretch of the turning year is by ancient custom dedicated to jealousy on the part of salmon anglers. They're like wasps. Here comes a disappointed angler about to vent the spleen of a fruitless morning, his fingers almost frozen to the rod—butt poised to tell a jibing story to disparage a rival angler and to console himself. Shall Peter pause to listen? Yes? No? Yes!

He too is on the periphery of this activity, conspiracy. He listens but doesn't comment except to say, "Is that right? Well, well." So on it goes. Jackeen killed. How is it everyone has killed except you—women are brutal when the angler returns with a sad slack satchel. There's Dominick, a man who never cast a line till pensioned, and he has ten killed. Change your flies and don't be making us a laughing stock. The powerful names of lures are bandied about. Thunder and Lightning, Bulldog, and Black Doctor. The women scold continually. "You're going downriver and the fish are upstream. All your antics with spoonbaits and minnows and nothing in the sack." Through all this fuss strides Strumpet Jealousy. Crouched over a pint of stout in a dark bar corner a morose fruitless angler dreams and drifts on the slow flowing water with coins of foam downstream from the big bridge's eye.

*

So it goes. Unending. The beauty of the disparate. The rag-bag of existence. A jackdaw's nest of a place. Queries and comments. Isn't it great to have a sanctuary row to tide us over the bad weather. The lilac tree farrows on into deep spring.

Watch the Jack Russell coming downstreet. I bet he lifts his leg and pisses against the Whey spuds. Get a hot look, perished schoolmaster, it might put a stir in you. There's breeding in the Prendergasts, even if they neglected their farm for books. Red winged thrushes on their way to Siberia—there they go. There must be a poetic way of arousing lust. So it goes. Buzzards and Budapest. Migraine and maggots, Jealousy River and the Skaters. No getting away from the skaters. They popped up everywhere!

*

Peter entered the butcher's kitchen. There he found an old woman of ninety, the butcher's grandmother, propped up in a sugan chair, her red-ink eyes wide open watching a flickering television screen on which the Winter Olympic Figure Skating was in progress.

Peter's eyes flickered from the screen to the old, wrinkled and wan stippled face and back again, as she watched a man and woman responding to music. The power implicit in the woman skater's thighs were fully in evidence as she thrust, accurately and confidently to indicate her mastery of the precarious surface beneath her skates. The pair, a contrast and complement, illustrating in sit spin, axel spin the harmony of complementary movement. The aesthetic swirl of Yes-I'm-female-and-I'm-glad-you're-male added up to as fine an exhibition of beauty as is capable of being projected this side of eternity.

The music gained in momentum. The old woman's eyes were still fast upon the screen. Peter stole softly down to sit on a chair in the shadowed part of the room. The woman skater's body proclaimed in its every movement that it was a receptacle for man-seed.

Faster still the music. Faster too the movement. The old woman's mouth let fall a web of spittle from her semi-protruding tongue. Her face was old parchment over which a rookery of ink-drenched crows had walked aimlessly. Light had stolen through the kitchen window and touched the old features with Inca gold, leaving the bulk of her body in darkness. Faster still the artistic coupling. The music grew in controlled abandon as the man skater rotated her balanced body above his head, his palm heel spinning her weight on her Mount of Venus. Movement importune! At the climax of sound and swirl the woman descending from a spin falls with a thump on her well cushioned bottom. A gasp of dismay from the audience precedes a full cackle of glee from somewhere deep in the belly of the butcher's grandmother. It's an odd sound which she repeats. Watching this, the old crone ever so slowly closes her mouth. One came quite close to the core of a mystery that kept eluding him, was Peter's reaction on watching such an exhibition. It takes a woman to make a man feel wholly alive. But all that's bloody terra incognita, Peter tells himself.

*

A time of change in Hero Town.

The eighties, a time of shuddering shifting shaking of swing.

So now Peter-he pauses to observe, to listen, to the crumbling of hitherto rock steady foundations, to the ominous creek of old timbers, to the creeping crack in the massive wall. "Things fall apart—the centre cannot hold." Questions unlimited and formulaic replies. Jargon, with the spectacle of power susceptible to and defenseless against jargon. Education cowering before "methodology". Irretrievable marital breakdown and elasticated disposable diapers. "And blessed is the fruit of thy in-vitro womb." Triumphalism out of fashion as the lemmings swim in a sea of simplicity. Meanwhile updating proceeds in the shifting of pulpits and the over-throwing of altar rails. Presently one may expect consecration in a tin can. For bread and wine substitute ice cream and Coca-Cola. Leer at the font, scrutinise the whisper box. How about the mosaics?

*

A voice is raised. Toughen a while, Father. I'd advise you to call a halt. You'll peg off one of these days to a fat parish in the south of the diocese and you'll leave us here with a sanctuary we can't warm to. Hands off the mosaics and the carvings of the pulpit. Do you want to leave our lovely church walls naked with bare-arsed spalls of limestone like the foolah of a priest did you know where, and its not a million miles from here. Those who went before us put their famine halfpence together and put those mosaics up there and when the morning sun strikes the length of the building we find them beautiful, consoling and nourishment for the imagination. So steady your horses now.

The Pope is it, Father, who came down out of the sky in his helicopter? I never heard him say a word about this simplicity you're talking about. You can be sure and certain sure that His Holiness won't attend my funeral whereas old neighbours will. Leave our church alone, Father. The bishop may be a nice handy little bible scholar parsing and analysing the Acts of the Apostles but like old King Laoire in Tara, when he faced Paddy Calpurnus in the year 432, I'm too old to be changed. So I'll put it short and sweet for you: I was baptised over in that corner a red raw infant howling at the cold water, and I took Christ on my tongue for the first time at that marble rails, and many a time thereafter my fumbling with girls was wiped out in that yellow box. And after I draw the last breath 'tis in there into that dead house my body will be taken. So like a good man, Father, we'll give you what's due to you in respect and in money but for God's sake let us peddle away in our own tinpot fashion. And whatever priests are sent here to us be they drunkards or not the full shilling in their senses, we'll cherish them for their altar and their cloth. But for Christ's loving sake, give up the idea of updating us. The truth is that we hate change. And because we're peasants, the last of that breed, we're also beyond the command of time. There now you have it now, Father, and make what you like of it—and of us.

*

On the Saturday pavements they pass in skeins of three, the Levi-clad maidens and their oscillating rumps advertising the advent of nubility! "Hello, Mr Mulrooney." The chuckle implicit in the salute inferring their conviction that it is a great time to be alive and that Peter is semi-dead. Peter looks up. The sky has floated upwards to the deepest empyreans. No cloud. Brittle sunlight. Good weather for cobwebs and the inner distillery. The memory of migraine and maggots now minimal. Ah there goes a Bingo dog, sniffing hopelessly at the passers-by, seeking the welcome scent of the master who betrayed him. *It is as if my biceps have never responded to the swinging hammer, Peter-he muses, it is as if I have never considered buzzards or Budapest, have never smiled at the memory of Shivers and other familiars.* Suddenly for the pedagogue the town is a cow and he is shouting, "Stop her!" "Head her off." "Take her aisy!"

Such a stubborn headlong cow of a town. That's it. Watch the gap: how out! I'll get you into the stall of literature if it's my last act this side of the grave. God'll mighty why didn't you get in front of her? A braddy old badogue. Let me get your head between the bails of a book then maybe you would mint money and respect for me. But no! Your own sweet way. You'll go scavenging through the countryside of future time picking a mouthful of grass here and there on the roadside, and maybe breaking into a meadow and getting a lambasting for trespass! Let her off to hell. When she's tired she'll stop. Off you go. And may all the harm of the year go with you, you willful, ungovernable, rebellious, gooky blasted and blinded cow bitch of a town. Not all the familiars ever dreamed up by the most fertile imaginations of mankind can save you now. Even the lousiest and most starved of the stray Bingo sheepdogs would scorn to growl at you now.

*

St Patrick's Day is at hand! It was exceptionally cold when Peter woke at the early hour of the morning to find the calves of his legs trembling with nervous tension. Notice of a general inspection of his work in school had arrived in the post the previous day. As a child Peter would take a rusty knife and a brown paper bag and go to the quarry, the river bank or the top of the graveyard wall singing "And the tear from his eye often wet it", insert his knife tip under the central stem of the sprig, prize it up from the clay, its outer tentacles dutifully parting in tick-tocks with the earth, the resultant sprig an object of loveliness. Old Darcy of the hills was never done describing the New York parade and McAnna's awash with drink, aroar with rebel songs. But the tear from his eye often wetting it is a bit too bloody thick in a bloody isle where it never stops pissing from the clouds; lachrymose effusions on the gentle trefolians is entirely unnecessary.

*

"Look at her down over, Master, my stupid bitch of a daughter. The one-legged pauper she proposes to marry. He'll get sweet shag all out of that Insurance claim—he was as drunk as Bran a'leanna behind the wheel. I have that on good authority. Will you give one look at the long hop of him on his metal crutches? And the lovely girl that I reared looking up into his face adoringly throwing herself away on that useless good-for-nothing idler. Stand back here a few steps into the shop, I don't want 'em to spot me. He's going to get £90,000 pounds? He is in his arse! I made it my business to enquire—he'll get sweet bugger-all! Let me tell you this, Peter Mulrooney—love is okay, passionate kisses and knees apart and the French thing, but money and a job are better. I've lashings of money now since I got the American legacy even if it came too late for me to enjoy it. But I give you my word that neither of that pair will ever spend a penny of it. Imagine my lovely daughter lying beside that fellah in the bed. For the rest of her natural life! Half a man! Sure if there is a fork to the woman there must be a fork to the man. That's sense! Blemished! Look at the stupid laugh of him! You might as well be talking to the wall as advising her. Money makes the mare go. I know that—for it's written in my blood. She's marrying for curse o' God love. A stupid, headstrong, deaf and blind bitch—that's what I reared."

Listen to this woman, labouring under a sense of impending disaster and doom. She may well be proven right—and her dismal prophecy in the matter of her daughter's mate and fate fulfilled, but again Peter considered that there was a slender margin of odds which may prove the match successful and the stupid bitch far more perspicacious than her overly concerned

Ma. The one-legged man may possess the qualities to overcome his handicap and may well prove to win the Blue Riband of Husband of the Year and his children adorable dolls.

Presently Peter is preoccupied with the more gracious than usual greeting from the lady chemist at Madigan's that almost counterbalances the bitter pill of inspection. When it's a question of accepting the tremendous risks involved in love, a woman can be ten times braver than the average hypercautious man! Still, to be rejected would be intolerable.

*

Life does not run on rails, nor can it be fully explained by reference to a pocket calculator, a table of Logarithms or even a Big Brother Computer. Granted, there must be something to be said in praise of the muddled, the discrete, the rawly poetic, the vernacular without grammar or syntax, the shorthand of the nerves, the language of gesture and the authenticity of the superficially disparate, but finding the link between the incongruent units in the context of a constricted community still subject to the sacred bondage of the sacred cow is the task.

*

At the most intense point in this train of thought the pedagogue meets Freddie, chief claimant for the title of Urban Bum. "Hello, Freddie. You're all dolled up."

"Today you are not to address me as Freddie. Today you are to call me Sir. Tomorrow you may call me whatever you like. Let me release you from your ignorance. Yesterday twelve months exactly I was walking around this town penniless to God and the world. Didn't know where the next meal was coming from. A wallet and yahoo—a fat roll of notes! God direct me, I said. I bummed and begged my way through England and I'd drink porter out of a sore heel. But I never stole a penny. My only pride, never stole. Draw the line there. I faced for the presbytery . . . say Sir!"

"Sir!"

" 'Father Hanrahan,' says I, such a thing. 'Lead us not into temptation.'

" 'Well done, Frederick, I'll put up notices, contact the Guards and put it on deposit, and if no owner turns up by tomorrow twelve months—a year and a day—the money is yours.' "

For Frederick time flies forward on slow wings. The summer passes. The Races come and go. Christmas is a thing of the past. "Then suddenly the shamrock is on my lapel. Today today—a year and a day, I knock at the presbytery door. 'Oh, the money,' he says. 'Is the time up?' 'A year and a day,' says I. Over we go to the immortal Bank of Ireland. Up the steps. A fistful of notes for Freddie—look I'll show it to you. Two hundred and fifty jimmy o'goblins."

"What'll you do with the money, Freddie?"

"Sir!"

"Sir!"

"No advice please! I stood to the Holy Man. Contribute to the support of your pastors. I staggered my sister with the dint of this big parcel from the delicatessen. Twenty years since I spoke to her—then I walked out. Bought a classy second-hand suit. Full rigout. I haven't touched a drop yet. I'm ambitious, Master. What I want to do now is to go on a booze in the company of my intellectual peer. That spells you, Pedagogue."

"Me?"

"Yeh, forget the Sir. Hire a car. Me and you. Round the county. Best behaviour. Be my guest. Killarney, Kenmare, Dingle, Park-na-Shaggin-Cilla. You never saw me in action in the old days. The best hotels. Wimmin—they smell money. I'll prove to you that I'm a man for all seasons. I'll astonish you—I promise. 'Twill do yourself a power of good. 'Twill liberate you. A memorable duo. Pedagogue and Bum. Cast me a kiss, Petronella! Action! Adventure! The women await us: Well?"

"No good, Freddie!"

"Not even if I begged?"

"No use, Freddie."

"That's that so! Die in your dismal soup. The offer shall not be repeated. Keep up your infernal facade and may the chalk dust increase and multiply and devastate you with Teacher's Catarrh."

I own to God, if Peter-I turn my back for a single moment those infernal lilac buds on the tree in the yard will have opened that little bit more. I think I could fix up a film camera in one cluster of buds and by clicking the shutter every ten minutes or so, be left with a series of stills which when replayed at normal speed would show the opening process of the buds with clarity.

*

But wait. Dear immortal God, wait. It was a year when shamrock was scarce. Papers full of the news of its scarcity. Peter buzzed off to early morning Mass here below hoping to see the arc of candle flame at the foot of the Caen stone statue of St Patrick the Gentleman—that and a patriotic sentiment—a sermon. Slemish. Milchu, a lighting whore outa hell. The wolfhounds on the ship, the congregation agog for the same kind of fare.

At the church gate Peter got half a sprig of shamrock provided by Philly so as to take the naked look off his lapel. *And what did we get from the Very Reverend Cold Nose? Not a spark of Paddy on Paddy's Day in Paddy's land! Not a spark! Updating the church. God help our renewed clergy.*

"Dearly beloved brethren, the message St Patrick brought was one of peace. It was the message of Christ. P-e-a-c-e. There are those in this parish that do not know peace. Instead of peace they sow discord." *(Sweet adorable deity, is he going to start this again?)* "You read in the local paper last week about those people in this parish who refuse to accept the divine authority of the church. And who do not hesitate to criticise God's anointed ministers in the columns of that sensational local rag?" *(Plough ahead, Father, I think I know who you're getting at.) Here I sit, a lark with my nest robbed. No arc of candle flame. Here I sit and my lower bowel bulging and bursting with the liturgical wind of peace.(Is this Mick Paddy's grandson who's addressing us or the Messiah in his second coming? Will you give one gawk at the face of Freddie the Bum!)*

"My peace I give you. Let us now offer each other the sign of peace—of true peace, not the peace that sets pastor and flock at each others' throats." *(That's the steel under the woollen glove.)*

Carry on Father—the man you're sniping at because of his objection to the removal of the altar rails and all of that—well his commonest cry is, "I have loved, O Lord, the beauty of thy house and the place wherein Thy glory dwelleth." And his twin uncles, both priests, carved out five parishes in the snows of North Dakota. Why should he be punished for an excess of sanctuary love? Carry on, Father, with your barren chat about peace! You're addressing fools! We're still secular Bingo dogs performing on our hind legs as we try to photograph cobwebs at daybreak. "Hic est Coca-Cola mea!"

*

For Peter, school grinds on into the opening year. Then, Laus Deo, a boy knocks at the classroom door and stands there smiling with a small bunch of throttled primroses in his little paw. A few green primrose leaves surround the thin legged harbingers of freedom. As the smile of gratitude lingers on Peter's face, it fades as he looks down the long corridor and sees the three women teachers deep in conversation with Earwigs Healy, the last travelling sweep who has come to clean the chimneys. "You're still a fine figure of a man, Mr Healy."

"I'm well preserved. I'm a good grubber. And when I clean myself up, I'm not the worst of them!"

"Listen to him. Mr Healy, behind that closed door is Mrs McLoughlin. She's for ever singing your praises. A widow—and lonely. We're women of the world, Mr Healy. You're a man of the world. Take the ball on the hop Mr Healy, the children are out at play. Play your cards right now, and. . . ."

The bitches are up to something Peter tells himself as he notes the way they stand and smile. Then with a last glance down the corridor he decides to keep out of it. When women are in that humour it's best to pretend to be idiotic or myopic, but never deaf.

Minutes later, raised voices. A loud roar. "The cheek of you!" Then—squawk, crack and whack. Healy stalks sootily past. "A feckin' madhouse!" he snorts at his tormentors. Healy now at bay turns and roars "Madhouse" at the scattering children and "Whorehouse" at the school windows where the laughing half faces of the women teachers are barely discernible. At last the sweep reaches the sanctuary of the gateway to freedom. This too he slams behind him. Instigators disappear into demure classrooms.

Who's that, Granny? That's the chimney sweep, my love. Why does he look so cross? Something must have upset him—must be the moon. The moon, Granny? Yes child, the moon.

*

The spring air is saturated with snatches of shattered semantic symphonies. The Pope's authority flouted. Madhouse, whorehouse or schoolhouse. Ah, the butcher has excelled himself in honour of Paddy Calpurnus in the embellishment of the half carcasses of firstling lambs. He has cut a crude shamrock design in place of the usual laurel pattern. "On Erin's green valleys look down in thy love." Colder and still colder the breeze as "Lord March blows through slanting snows her fanfare shrill." Night is here.

But "stall your whids." You must ask yourself, Peter, whether you have deserted the familiars or whether the familiars have deserted you? Where are the bombarding Buzzards and Budapest? The father of the town fool once referred to you as a castrated ass. The fact remains that you are unable to read the signals of women. I suggest that a youngish, ticklish widow-woman should take you in hands and instruct you. I daresay you'll go to God that way. Well, none of us is here to stay, as the Butcher's Granny is accustomed to remind all and sundry.

Look, Peter, that's Tim Darcy's Jack Russell bitch in heat—with a whole bloody fleet of curs in amorous tow. But Peter is only dimly aware of the conversation. He's in dreamland, floating on his back; he is being borne along a fast warm current in a river, and out of an eye corner he sees on the banks young women skipping on the banks in skeins of three or four dressed in scanty beach attire. Ah, but drifting is delicious. A distant weir roars in his ears.

As the roar of the weir grows louder the floating schoolmaster realises that he is drowning. Peter is constrained to shout, *"Help, Women! Leap in and release me! Earwigs, blood brother in the matter of our shared targetry of female hilarity, come to my aid, in my battle take part. I suffer now. Help! Help!"* A schoolmaster is drowning in the estuary of unfullfilment. Every outlet is barred. The last the down-hurtling pedagogue sees is the twin spires of Hero Town. Down you go. Down, down. Foam and final gurgle, that's that anyway. In finality—he hopes.

"That's loyalty for you," the familiars mutter in incipient revolt. "Always protesting how much we mean to him and with the very first distraction off he goes. He only calls upon us in times of stress. We'll keep that in mind. By God we will."

*

The pedagogue feels at the end of his tether. His legs shudder with the tremor of tension, as his school inspection is imminent. It doesn't help that simultaneously Margo is getting hot and bothered about the post-conciliar changes in the Sanctuary. Ah, Pope John from Bergame: you should have let sleeping dogs lie! She lost her husband Andrew to carcinoma of the bladder, her eldest son Andy to the Civil Service and Gaelic Football, her daughter Agatha to an accountant, her youngest son Petie to a bouncing lassie from Tonard with spikes of sex shooting out of her eyeballs. Margo wants the world to stop revolving. She abhors change. She has relied on the architectural permenancy of the Sanctuary and when it was threatened she was to the fore at the protest meeting. The pinnacled high altar to be overthrown, sanctuary lamp to be sidelined, the ornate pulpit to be pulverised, the shining communion rails to be dumped and, central to her obsession, the golden box that contained her godhead to be chiseled out of its place of honour and to be countersunk in what to her is the anonymity of the lower reredos. A bare table. Return to the Final Meal. If they carry on much farther they'll finish up with a hyped-up Wimpy Bar. No escape from vulgarity, Margo protests. Standards going down, down. But the same voice that with authentic harshness grates is capable of sweetly saying almost in the same breath, "But of course, Father, as you say, the Pope must be obeyed!"

*

"Let me tell you something! Hey you, Peter Mulrooney, listen to me! Stand here between two windows. Don't want to be heard. This is urgent. This town—I know you won't agree with me, you're so godamned straightlaced and pious—this town is pocked and pickled with Lady Macbeths. All of whom, to a woman, are capable of putting a knife into their husband's hands, not only to slay the King but anyone who stands in their way. There are those mad to be social queens, political queens, literary queens, even religious queens, queens of lust of body and mind, all of whom want to be the queen bee adored and fertilised, courted twenty-four hours a day, fawned upon, admired, looked up to even into senility. Oho, their ambitions are beautifully covered up, my good man, and they possess the ability to explain away their ambitions in the most simple terms possible and to put them across to those obtuse gomerils of bedmates—their husbands. Remember: hell hath no fury like a woman thwarted or denied a social or other sort of throne on which her mind is set. Don't look across now. The third window of Eager's up there. Neither sashes nor glass nor lace curtains. The wind of God blowing in through the rooms. You know the old Victoria Eager, the last of the line— she blesses herself with the left hand—was left the oval room for life by her father in his will, and also her meals in the house. She's bedridden up there. The house has gone through various hands for the past forty years, some of the parties good to the old lady, some bad. Well a new crowd from the west bought the house four months ago. A rough, tough and unprincipled gang. No mercy. Made money in England with a bowsy eating house. The woman the Boss. The clause still operates. Miss V's agreed meals? I have it from the Jubilee Nurse. They serve her catfood out of a tin, and soapy spuds at any hour of day or night—and they say, "Here's your dinner, Miss Eager." They put washing powder in her soup—a pinch only, and salt in her tea (they can say it was a mistake if copped on). The old lady is turning gooky—but she won't vamoose. These are the Reevy days—the days when the cold skinned the old brindled cow—and what did my hoboes do but remove the window of the room, top and bottom, on the excuse that the rattling won't let the old lady sleep and that the windows need to be mended. The windows are out now for ten days and nights. She inside—incontinent if you know what that means; she staggers to and from the commode, filthy and blue with the cold—the last of the family that owned the town. If she could get as far as the window she'd throw herself out. I have that on good authority. They hope she'll get pneumonia and die naturally—God bless the mark. The house will be worth a fortune. More if the old lady was dead and the place free of encumbrance. Is that cold premeditated murder or not? Under our bloody eyes. By a woman. Listen, Schoolmaster, you're a man of consequence in this community, and so I'm putting it on your conscience to rectify matters. I'm only an alcoholic—no one'd listen to me. You hear. On your conscience before God!"

"Wait!" Peter calls out in agitation. "Why don't you tell the Guards? Or the priest?"

"Because they'd laugh at me. It's your business now, Peter Pedagogue, shining knight. Do what you feckin' like with it. Don't say you weren't told. Spondulicks galore for hungry Ethiopians: buggerall for poor Victoria Eager rotting in an upper room."

*

It's all very fine, Peter tells himself later, to console one's self with thoughts about the intimacy, the loyalty and the caring neighbourly spirit of a small place like Hero Town. But the greeting after spending a Union weekend in the city, "You're a fly boy, moseying off without a word to anyone." Irritated—no need to tell Peter that he's back home. Above all to Margo, whose indignation at the leaking ballcock provides the perfect alibi for attacking the spirit of independence. Suffer, brother, suffer! Next time you'll ask permission before you depart. And give a full account of your doings when you return.

From the bathroom, scraps of Margo's sad song float down to Peter's ears. "We set out together, mate o' mine, We neither of us knew the road, How long the journey, Or how great the load." So that's what's wrong with her, Peter concludes. The water drip was a cover up for something else. Ah, well.

Who dat, Sam? Dat am a widdah woman, prettenin' she talkin' ballcocks.

*

The town continues to administer itself in traditional fashion. Tick, tock inside. It indicates a small spark of gaiety in response to the call of the advancing spring. Painted shop fronts and fascia boards catch the as yet silver sunlight.

Peter on his Saturday morning rounds remarks aloud to himself, "How dare I forget my familiars." Then—daring to forget them, he stopped in the windblown laneway outside a ruined forge and peered in the open window. The anvil stolen, its block hacked, the hearth overthrown, a cart wheel, its broken felloes and irregular spokes indicating various points of the compass, the once neat cobblestones of the forge floor show only a patch or two of their ancient pattern. Eight generations of the same family of farriers dating back to 1650. Here an end, a full stop, here silence and decay.

Is Peter doomed to end this quarter year on a note of despair? On the reiteration of "If only" which assails him from the lips of the old. Whichever way he turns he finds himself unable to face the dynamism inherent in the torture of spring. Spirit okay, body anything but okay. That's age. A—g—e. Age! On all sides, He is assailed by cries, expressed or implied, of "If only". *Maudie Quilligan set me off on this melancholy train of thought, he tells himself. But there you are . . .*

A woman then begins to complain. "The other day I went up to the graveyard and poked out Old Oliver's grave. They called him The Ram of Munster. And so he was! I was afraid of him when I was young—he was too blunt. "If I had you in a canvas canoe," he said, "sitting on the seat facing me out in the height of a gale with the waves going mountains high, and bigod, if the mind came on me, I'd say, 'To hell with the wind and the roaring sea,' I'd let go of the oars and I'd capsise you!" He frightened me, the devil. Ah! If only I got the chance again when I was more mature. So I knelt down on the wet grass of his grave and prayed, 'Eternal Rest grant to his soul, O Lord. And may perpetual light shine down on Oliver whom people used to call The Ram of Munster but whom I now call a fine natural man.'" *If only . . . if only . . . if only. Is there an "If only" involved in this Maudie Quilligan business? The girl at Madigans seems to be a non-starter. If only I could decide. If only I could ask advice from someone like Mickey the Rascal Inseminator—he knows a lot about these things. But he'd bullrag me all over the town. Let it rest. But . . . if only!*

*

"Life, is it Peter?" the old man moans. "I'll tell you what life is. It's a mixture of diarrhoea and sanctifying grace. Don't tell me what life is—ask me. It's what the poet called 'a series of inspired idiocies'. In the finish up it's a belch that turns out to be a mouthful of blood; then it's a scramble to the privy in the yard and the terror of a blood-stained lavatory bowl under a clanking cistern. Then, as the old women say, 'He made a good-looking corpse!' No trade to it: any fool can bring it off. Come up to my place and I'll give you a bunch o' daffs for your widowed sister. Both of ye letting your lives pour out the waste gap of existence. Take a tumble before you get senile. Go down to the travel agents and book a trip. Sun, sand and Swedish lassies. Go before you're senile like myself."

The voices continued to come through . . . *I'd capsise you, and to hell with the wind and the roaring sea. Does your mother know you're out, girl? Does she know that I'm about to steal yeh?* "Oh my, when I look in your eyes. . ." *There's a hairline crack in the record, Peter tells himself, it keeps repeating* "look in your eyes, look in your eyes, look in your eyes. . . . ." *Ad infinitum.*

APRIL

No one in the Council Estate would listen to the old man. "Feck folklore!" the youngsters said. The telly is here to stay. Boxcar Willie and Jessie Stuart—these are our heroes! The old countryman living with his married daughter in the smallest room in the house was bewildered. "I'm not from Ireland," he grumbled. "No one listens to me, I'm from Vietnam. I'm one of the boat people without a country to land upon."

So Peter thought it his duty to go up and listen as the old fellow galloped again into the telling of the old folktale The Brindled Cow. "Bó Riabhach", the cow, staggered out under the sky. Her hide was lit up in patches as a result of the long confinement. Great rhombuses of cowdung patterned her haunches and flanks, like the floor of the Burren only that that is in limestone. She mooed—the cow. "I made it begob!" she said to a small black Kerry cow. "That curse o' God March," the Bó Riabhach went on, "nearly crucified me. The stall was like a refrigerator with the wind of the Lord shaking the cobwebs." She carried on complaining and bragging for a while how she survived. High up in the sky, March not yet gone was listening carefully. "I'll quieten her," March began to whisper in the ear of young green April. "Give me the loan of three days," she said, "and I'll pay you back some other year!" April obliged, not realising what March was up to. So cruel March blew on the brindled cow. The blade of the breath penetrated the cow right to the marrow of her bones. Bó Riabhach could not understand it. She turned her wet nose to the razor wind. That first day her knees buckled, the second day she fell flat, the third day she died.

"The Days of the Brindled Cow—we have them now," the old man said, indicating the raindrops quivering on the outside of the windowpane. Boys-o-boys!

The weather grew milder. The lilac tree was almost fledged. Neighbours were getting generous with their daffodils and narcissi. "To hell with Long Johns," Peter murmured, but a cautious voice mentioned not casting a clout.

*

Peter, do you know what you are? Under the most respectable exterior there are all sorts of roguery going on in your head.

You're a contradiction in terms. You're always bloody well juxtaposing opposites in ideas and words. I've you copped. Go away and take a holiday for yourself. You're etiolated.

I might do that too. But meanwhile I'm happy mating opposites.

*

Cop this, don't let her see you, Peter! She's the last of all the female peasant independents, an old bent woman shuffling along the pavement dragging her foolish daughter behind her by the hand. They stop at the doorway of a small shop. As on a signal, they open their mouths and as if using the mouths as eyes, steadfastly look in. No one inside except the shopkeeper's wife. The old woman on the pavement swivels slowly to survey the street. The Guard had warned them. Ah, no spy from Strasbourg or Luxembourg to be seen. Satisfied she is unobserved she bends her body forward to conceal her hand as it enters a decrepit message bag. Her claw takes out two pale blue eggs which she passes to the outstretched hand of the daughter. Closing her mouth as if to indicate resolution, the younger woman enters the shop. She places the eggs on the counter. They swivel and come to rest. The innocent girl mutters, "Fresh duck eggs". The shopkeeper's wife pauses. She glances and nods to the old sentry outside the door. As on an impulse she goes to the cash register, clangs the button, and takes out a coin which she hands to the girl. The girl's face glows. The shopkeepers wife's walks to the cluttered yard and slowly but deliberately, lowers the eggs into a concealed nest of wastepapers. Takes all kinds!

Strasbourg! The European Economic Community in action.

*

To get the old fellow to leave his shop, to totter across the road and sit down in the kitchen to watch his first Grand National on TV was a considerable achievement and action on the part of Margo. Peter could not imagine what put it into his good sister's head at all. But without telling anybody, least of all her brother, she faced across the road an hour before the race and said, "Is it possible Shaun, that with all your knowledge of horses you have never seen the Grand National on television?" Margo said with incisive scorn. "I don't care what you're making but across that road you're coming if it's the last stitch you put in britchin," she sniped. With no means of escape the old man drew on his jacket and suffered himself to be led to the other side of the street and dutifully followed Margo right into the living room where he sat ensconced in a chair of honour in mid-floor with a glass of hot whiskey on a table beside him. "Well, well," he kept saying. "He'd be a long time waiting for you to ask him in." Margo was on the merry attack and the pair of men now placed at a disadvantage began to plead otherwise. The wide television screen showed the coloured tide of horses flowing over the jumps with jockeys pitching from their mounts or gallantly recovering their balance and setting off in pursuit. The old saddler's face that had been deathly pale and rigid now showed a brilliant red rosette on each cheekbone and as he leaned forward in the chair the better to view the Aintree spectacle, his thin lips parted in enchantment. Not a syllable did he utter in the face of this magic. The commentators, handing over to each other, kept up a continuous controlled yelping. The roar of the crowd was like the thunder of surf on a storm-ploughed beach. As three horses, rolling intuitively in the extremity of exhaustion, approached the final jump, Peter with a sudden glance at the old man's face was stabbed with the notion that Old Shaun would get a heart attack, pitch out like one of the falling jockeys and down on to the dining room floor. However the race over, Old Shaun sat back in his chair and began to breathe himself back to normal. His stammered syllables of thanks seemed inadequate to convey the turmoil of emotion that had taken and shaken his brain and frame! Murmuring "the same as if I was at Aintree", he left the kitchen.

Flowing over fences, a marvellously mad-sane river-in-spate of silk. But isn't it a wonder that the horses never cop-on? Killing themselves for the entertainment of bipeds. But then again, isn't it their nature to race? Even they feel the bugle call of spring.

*

"I hear you're going to the Canaries," the old publican, shoulder to the door jam growled at Peter on his way home from school. With eyes age-lidded like those of a lizard, he begins to act the philosopher. "Who said that?" Peter stabbed. By way of introduction he laughs as if at his own decision to share a secret enjoyment. "Be careful of the drink. It takes people in one of three ways," he says pseudo-profoundly. "It makes them either sleepy, foolish or quarrelsome. Me? I'm a sleep man. Laughter gives away the game when you're half shot. It spreads the alcohol all over your body. So if you find yourself tipsy abroad, keep your head low and your mouth shut."

"When I'm drunk," the publican said sternly, 'I'm a masterpiece. Of course on account of the years spent behind the bar and with plenty of models to go on, I don't deserve credit for bringing tipsiness to a fine art. You wouldn't spot my condition if you had your eyes glued to me for a hundred years. Everyone has it. You're going with a nice tuplip. Watch your virginity! Wait and see. You'll be either sleepy, foolish or quarrelsome.

"Ah to hell," said Peter under his breath as he walked away. "I'm gettin' quare," he snorted, "like the thermo dynamics of rotary squeeze."

*

Still in pensive mood, Peter now recumbent on the kitchen couch ponders.

A question I've often asked myself is this. If Margo, God forbid, were to die would I be able to endure the rarefied air of freedom? Or would I begin to live in the truest sense of this much-abused word? This is a thought that keeps recurring to me. As, I dare to say, it occurs to everyman. Am I living life to the full? Or am I an unpointed pencil trying to set down my personal story using a blunt writing instrument? What the neighbour keeps saying may be true! Here I am at the end of my days. And I'm troubled, not with the things I've done but with the things I've turned my back on.

Margo is for ever warning me against various damsels who keep trying to put the come-hither on me. "See that one? She's causing mischief between a man and his wife. Watch the strut of her! What comes by nature costs no money."

And here comes the big question! Why should she now be urging me to take a holiday for myself. She must know that if I go at all, it's to the Canaries I'll go with the Inseminator. God forbid, has she herself some notion of the Inseminator? After all, there's not much between them as regards age. Maybe she wants to show to Micky how broadminded she is by letting me go—and would be better still if he was hitched up to herself. Or maybe, knowing the rascal's reputation—he's a bit of a nationalist too—which kind of balances things up—she wants me educated or miseducated or even miss-

educated! Or maybe she knows that however much rope I'm given I'm incapable of being free. A parochial cut jack—terrified of a woman's shadow. I might show her yet! As regards our Margo, all I can say is, "Beware those who come bearing gifts."

Tickets, passports, traveller's cheques, light underwear, present and correct. So off we go on Holy Thursday, Micky the Inseminator and myself. Margo gave the pair a fancy farewell dinner on White Tuesday evening. All dolled up for the occasion, a new woman. If you saw her playful and prinking in the presence of Micky you'd get a weakness. "No nonsense now with the senoritas," Margo, giggling, said mock-severely addressing Mickey.

"Whatever you do in the Canaries, don't shout 'Up the IRA' even though the Canarians are looking for freedom too. I'm advising you, don't get the schoolmaster into trouble." Peter smiled wanly.

*

That same Spy Wednesday night at 3 a.m. in Gilly Halloran's a little boy of five came slowly down the stairs. At the door of his parent's bedroom he stopped, listened, then shouted, "I swallowed a safety pin!" "Christ, Mary, wake up. Theo has swallowed a safety pin." "A what?" "A safety pin. For God's sake—get up and see."

Thump, thump go the balls of bare feet on the floor.

"Theo, did you swalla a safety pin?" "I did, Dadda." "Was it opened or closed?" "I forget, Dadda." "Come out of the way, Gilly, you'll terrify the child. Theo, love, tell Mamma, did you swalla a safety pin?" "I did, Mamma." "Was it open or closed, child?" "'Twas opened, Mamma." "O holy God, don't stand there gawkin', you eejit, take him down to Dr Fitzsimons as quick as you can. I believe you, child. Gilly, will you for God's sake don't be acting the clown. Take him the way he is. Wrap a blanket around him. Stick on your jacket over your pyjamas. Your slippers'll do. Hurry, the child's life is at stake."

Clatter-clatter, flip, flop go the carpet slippers.

The child in his arms, the father stumbles down the street. "I'm fit to fall," he tells the boyish face in the blanket cowl. The moon watches from between the twin spires. Gilly staggers up the God-damned doctor's steps. Bang, bang on the knocker. Bang bang again. A light comes on over a tin box at the left of the door jamb. A Tannoy voice asks, "What is it?" Gilly stammers his story. "Was it opened or closed?"

"I don't know, Doctor." "Make him eat a sandwich of cotton wool." "Of what, Doctor?" "Of cotton wool." "I've no cotton wool, Doctor." "Tear up a sanitary pad or something like it. Put it between two slices of bread. I'll have him x-rayed in the morning." "All right, Doctor." Stagger down the steps. Stagger home. White face projecting from the doorway. "Wha' did he say?" "He said to have him eat a sanitary pad in a sandwich." "Are you out of your mind?" "That's what he said." "Did he examine the child at all?" "He was in bed. He spoke into the yoke." "I don't know who's the bigger edjit—you or the doctor. My darlin' boy might be dead by morning. Come Theo luv, to your mother's arms. Sweet Jesus," she mutters, after an initial fierce hug. "A sandwich of a sanity pad."

*

So off they went. Buzz-buzz. Margo's capable hands are on the wheel—she relishes being in command of two men as she drives to the Airport. She displays unsuspected resources of driving skills and continues to revel in the small but adequate audience. Peter has been manoeuvered into the back seat. As the vehicle passes a neat farmhouse Mickey twists his head searching for the red rag on a bush to indicate that the heifers need insemination. The rascal is equipped to read every letter of every word, every reference in the book of rural life with its accent on the essentials of mating, birth and death. The Brindled Cow rises from her ashes.

But now they were off on a completely new caper to be played out against an alien dropcloth; for Peter it's farewell for two weeks to sanctifying grace, to the familiars and the constriction of a country town.

"Who dat, Sam?" "Dat am the man with the bull in his pocket." "Who dat with him?" "Dat is a small town schoolmaster who now suffers from the delusion of freedom." "Who drive the automobile?" "The sister of the schoolmaster—name is Margo." "My, she got pretty fingers." "Boy, she shoh got pretty fingers."

*

Meanwhile back home, the town is aware of the saga of the safety pin. "Well, Gilly, how's that child o' yours? I hear he swalla'ed a safety pin." "I took him into the Bons. They x-rayed him. Nothing." "That's some consolation. But . . ." "But what?" "I don't want to upset you, but there's a new machine in the County Hospital that's guaranteed to find a needle in a hay stack." "Came from America. Scans the whole body. Responds to metal." "Is that a fact? I'd go farther!" "Would you?" "I would indeed." "I'll mention it to Mary."

"Hey Paddy!" "What?" "I'm after puttin' Gilly Halloran up the walls." "Do you know what I think?" "What?" "The child is takin' them for a ride." "Ah God no?" "Ah God yes. Taking after his Uncle Garrett. Small as he is, he has it in his eye." "Keep the fire under the pot." "You can depend on me. A talent like that should be nurtured." "Gilly and the wife are sieving his stools." "Never." "Yes indeed , that class of roguery must be nurtured."

*

So they rode a crazy coach from the Island Airport into that equatorial dawn. Towns were lighted up in harshness and brilliance. With the movement of the coach the lights swung so that to Peter it seemed that he was in a machine piloted by a madman. It was bloody awful hot. Peter was conscious of his thermal underwear. Volcanic gorges, a series of corkscrew moonlit roads, and always the cliffs veering and sheering around below and along the crazy coach. This will trigger off vertigo, Peter shuddered at the thought.

Now only the Inseminator and himself were left in the coach— Mickey was sound asleep, his sunken head lolling this way and that, a dribble of spittle fallen to his bare chest. A black bull and no mistake at large in a foreign land. The 6 a.m. apartment was brown-tiled and warm. As Peter sank into his bed, Mickey was already sprawled naked and snoring in a bed on a higher level of the apartment.

*

Meanwhile, the Sacristan of Hero Town was discharged from hospital to a church of postconciliar change. He was already old: now he was also wan and weak. Unsteady on his legs he took his walking stick from the hook under the stairs, tottered out of the house and made his way by the edge of the Square to the Sacristy. "Tck tck, why didn't you stay at home for yourself? If you fall you're finished," the Job's Comforter of a granddaughter told him bluntly. The old man leaned his elbows on the robing table and looked his fill of the raped sanctuary. Sorrowfully into the core of his eyeballs. All that was left was a plain-slabbed table with little dignity to it. The tabernacle lamp, indicating the Great Mystery, with its colza oil and the floating wick the silver glory of his life— where was it now? No rails to run his fingers along. The pulpit gone. On the old man's face the cheeks that had once been fat sagged still further. In his day he had been well-fleshed and quick tempered, feared even by the most authoritarian of parish priests. Now the old man contemplating the downfall of that which he loved, betrayed in his smouldering eyes the fact that the fire inherent in his spirit was consuming the final fat of his body. Fire and fat, two goddam incompatibles, that would burn him up some day.

The old man closed his eyes—in resignation or in reminiscence? He seemed to hear the irregular din on the tiles of the centre-aisle as the last remnants of the veteran IRA marched into the church to pay annual honour to the memory of his dead uncle. An Easter occasion of pride. The old man turned and staggered out of the sacristy.

What do you say, Father? This is Peter you're talking to now. We have to fall into line with the universal church? But what about the goddam tradition-bearers, Father? Does anyone care a thrush's shit? Easy now, 'tisn't the first time Our Holy Mother the church took a wrong turn. Okay, I get the message loud and clear. It's updating the liturgy and abjuring triumphalism. It's blurring the lines of demarcation between various forms of Christianity. Fine! Why not say that?

Bareness is a balls, Father! What's that? Do what you're told by the Holy Pope? Good on you! But when the Holy Father sent yourself and the diocesan clergy a bishop and told ye to accept him without fuss or query—what happens? Ye legged it up to the nunciature howling hieratically that ye hadn't been consulted. Who consulted us, the laity about the altar and the rails? Cuckoo, but we the plebs, generation after generation find ourselves gypped out of love, sanctuary and high black turbery, in this lousy Hibernian huddle. Hero Town! Hero Town my Royal Irish arse. There now, Father. You asked for it and you got it!"

*

"Cop yourself on, Peter. You're in the Canaries now, and not in Crocka-weerha. Put on your jazziest shirt and sally forth. No confraternity lingo: I'm not going to listen to it here. Spot the form. Jeez! You're not thinking of wearing those swimming togs. Forget Ballybucktawn and the A.I. station. I'm a cattle breeder— true enough, and you're a Professor and a historian. I've been saving up semen for this place for five years. Almighty God, you're not wearing thermals. You'll fry alive. Rinse out the fecking long johns—few minutes in the sun they'll be bone dry. Forget your shaggin' academy, your confirmation pledge and the roarin' Redemptorists! This is a sensual Shangri La! Buckets of Scandanavian talent. I've spotted two beauties, one of the women is so blonde she's like an albino; the other is a bronzed Latino. I'm having the white lassie: the Latino is yours. They're so 'civilised', that they'll go wild for a Baluba like myself. No problemo. You'll see. Hang the washing on the line—let them know we're in residence. Good on us! Yehoo! Ballybuckthawn!"

*

"Dadda!" "What, boy?" Back in Ireland. Scene as before. Early morning hours of the same day on which Peter was rinsing his long johns in the equatorial regions. "The safety pin com up!" "Don't stir, Theo, till I get up." "Ab bont!" "Will I put in my finger, Theo, and take it out?" "Here, Dada, take ib." "Thank you, Theo. Bold safety pin. Look, Mama." "Are you taking leave of your senses, Gilly? You've got nothing in your fist." "Lower your voice, you ape! Pretend you see it. Now, Theo, I'll drop the bold safety pin out the window. Watch. Go—o—on. Back to bed, child." "I will, Dadda." "Almighty God! What was that all about?" "Imagination, woman, that's all." "There was no safety pin?" "Neither now nor the night he thought he swallowed it." "Is the child normal?" "Of course he's normal! Didn't he settle the question by finding it?" "I don't know which is the dafter—you or the child. One of ye: two of ye." "All I'm saying, woman, is that oddness in my children comes from your side of the bed. Not from mine!" "Well, Jesus Christ, if you say that again—I'll split your head with this flower pot."

*

"Cuarenta y Tres—Forty-three Liquor, Hundred Pipers, Jamesons, Bols Crème de Caca. . . . .oo." Mickey roared this last word at the top of his voice as one by one he took the bottles out of the daffodil coloured shopping bags. Cheaper than bloody water.

"It's an Alladin's Cave for Alcoholics."

Mickey-Midas stood back and gloated over his hoard. Solemnly, "Must have firewater to jizz up the women if we want action. I am rearing to go, I could bull Europe this bloody minute!" Peter having discreetly pegged his long johns on a line, which stretched across the balcony, looked on apprehensively. "Where'll this end?" he asked himself. His memory had just regurgitated the ancient nickname by which Micky's forebears were known. "The Gullagoos"—that was it.

Up there in the hills and boggy valleys they were affectionately, and by the women, rather admiringly known as "right hoormasters" with byblows in every generation. The Gullagoos—inseminators long before the AI process was ever dreamed of. Strange how the nickname came up.

The question of the turbary came up too, this also with a shock. No doubt about it—Peter had been gypped out of two fine acres of what auctioneers called prime high black turbary by villains of the Gullagoos. "Give me twenty pounds, Peter, and when I'm dead and gone my two fine acres of turbary on Mings mountain are yours." A thirsty fellow, his uncle. Peter had lost count of the advances and subs he had made on his legacy. "Cut all the turf you want every summer and when I go to God it's your property. Word of a man!"

It was hot on the balcony. Peter was wearing only his pyjama trousers. A wind has risen outside. The long johns had begun to dance wildly and would be bone dry soon. No trees around to indicate the strength of the wind. Only the legs of the long johns and the waving flags down at the pool. Wind socks alfresco.

*

Over the waves the future of Hero Town was being determined over a game of cards.

"A bypass but that's not how we'll refer to it." "How so?" "Call it a relief road—to relieve the roads and the town of the heavy traffic." "I see." "I hope you do: you're set to benefit from it more then me. Your sites will treble, even quadruple in value if the road runs where I've said." "You won't do so badly yourself." "'Tis the last item on the agenda. It won't do any harm if you contradict me in the items that come before. Create a bit of tension. Our agreement on the relief road will then sound natural like. Have you got me?" "I have." "Avoid the word bypass like the plague; read another way 'twill sound like passby. The publicans will gang up against us if they hear the word. Relief means that they'll get rid of the big truck and trailer drivers. They only lower the tone of the town." "Keep an eye on that bloody schoolmaster; he wrote a letter to the papers about us before." "Yeh; declaration of interest!" "There's too much talk about environment in that bastard of a history book he wrote." "If he gets awkward this time I'll cork his bottle. Steam up the Peepee too about the Pedagogue's campaign against the removal of the pulpit and the altar, and his backing for the itinerants. I seen him chatting up tinker girls now that I come to think of it." "That little fecker is too lousy to flatter a woman unless the Gullagoo tutors him out foreign." "We have our Plan of Campaign." "We have indeed, Martin." "And the man to lead it." "My lead is it? Here I'll lead a club. Beat that if ye can. Oh you little bastard. You had the five o' trumps in your hand all along."

*

Peter was still brooding on the lost prime high black turbary, stretched out on the divan in the apartment in Tenerife. As regards ownership of the patch of bog Peter had nothing on paper. Neutral onlookers at home called him a scholarly fool. An innocent abroad. Then the claim jumpers, tutuored by the Gullagoos, moved in, so that when Peter tried to establish his claim he found that he was dealing with snakes, scorpions and barracudas. Turf that burned like coal, his peat-mine as he called it, was gone with the wind. Rural ranks were serried against him. "Gone with the wind" . . . WIND . . . was rising. The flags of the nations by the pool were flapping wildly.

Wait! Stop! Halt—beyond the spectrum of the bottles. Beyond the slavering head of the Inseminator. Beyond the now closed patio door that led to the balcony, the long johns had disappeared. Gone with the bloody wind. Peter sprang up out of the couch. The Gullagoo howled with laughter. He rolled and jigged like a man in an epileptic fit.

"Who dat there?" "Pair of crazy Irishmen who nebber was nowhere". "What dey do, man?" "Dey just lost some underwear." "On Good Friday?" "On Good Friday!" "Thermal?" "Yeah, thermal." "Some folk sure is hilarious." "

The voice waned. Gullagoo—Inseminator was eyeing him narrowly. "Are you going to look for the long johns?" Mickey asked. "When the wind dies down," Peter said meekly.

*

Back in the hometown, much against its will, cold spring consented to succumb to the first mild symptoms of approaching summer. Harness maker and cobbler stitched on, the discontented housewives bitched on, the pitch and toss players on the edge of the river cliff pitched on, the morning-after drunkard retched on. In other words, life there was abnormally normal and normally abnormal. Darkie, on point duty, at the corner of the Main Street, his eyes lidded, sprang stiffly aware, hobbled after and pinched the buttocks of the maiden passing by causing her to leap and shriek. No one takes notice of fine natural trading like that. Only strangers. And they don't count.

All change now! God spare us. And the fine houses in the Square—gartered into flats. Soon we'll have super-shops, they say you never get a taste off the food in that class of shop. No humanity to it. *You could be right there, Paddy.*

Darkie, housewives, roaring Redemptorists, safety pins, are all part and parcel of You Know Where. I'll not have a word said against them. They're the imaginative cement that binds the individual blocks of the community together. Is that Peter talking to himself again? That's right, I guessed as much.

*

However, there were complications in paradise abroad. Still lying on the shaded couch in the apartment and awakening from a doze, Peter was hauled from the deeper recesses of his mind by the excited voice and door banging of the Inseminator. "Christ, my body is burned alive," he shouted. The Inseminator indeed had a wonderful body. And the bugger knew it. "Ffff," he said wincing at the burns. The smell of suntan oil filled the room. He was red raw from sunburn. He'd peel to the bone before morning. You couldn't advise him. "Even my middle cut is raw," he growled.

"Where were you?" Peter asked. "Beyond the point. With the . . .? The naturists." "The nudist crowd?" "Aye. Nothing to it. Women should wear clothes. No bloody mystery without the rags." The hissing and splashing of water downstairs announced that Mikey was seeking solace and comfort in the bathroom. Peter too . . . seeking relief and long johns took the elevator to the high road above the hotel that wound into the cliff road which was bordered by volcanic boulders. High among the rocks Peter strolled indulging in deep diaphragmatic breathing. He was constipated but soon he was going to have a plenteous bowel movement, he told himself with a smile. *Give it plenty time. It's gathering since the Airport—three full days. I'm glad I got away from the Gullagoo. He's all tension.* Still, to watch him strut around the crowded edge of the pool with his flick of a bathing trunks rolled down as far as possible made Peter feel like an awkward pennyboy in his wake.

*

Tenerife, full of indigenous religious feast days that Eastertide, attracted and convinced Peter to participate but Mickey had other celebrations on his mind. As Peter still discreetly poked around in an effort to find the missing long johns, Mickey issued a warning: "You'll get arrested for peeping and the Policemen with the operatic hats will lug you off to Santa Cruz. Forget them is my advice!"

That same evening, Mick stalked into the Restaurant Paradiso dressed in his air-force light blue suit, white shirt agleam like snow, with Peter trailing behind. Sole Santiago? Micky enquired masterfully and went on to ask how exactly the fish would be cooked, as red translucent candle grease fell in a daft cascade of rivulets that congealed in the shape of coiled lava streams. "The Feast of the Snotty Candles," he said with a smothered guffaw. Seated at a table with solid rock behind them, Mickey ordered like a lord, then ate and drank like a ploughman. Peter who was feeling light-headed after a glass of wine was not as sensitive as usual. Indeed the ambiance in the cave restaurant seemed congenial. The long johns and the filched turbary receded to the background of his consciousness.

To this day, Peter-I do not know how the Gullagoo stage-managed the remainder of the evening and indeed the eventful, and for me distressing night and morning hours that followed. I'd rather forget the whole affair, and indeed am determined to postpone the telling of it to a later day perhaps when I am home and far away from the scene of the misdemeanors.

As I say, don't ask me how he did it, or even how he set events in train. It started smoothly. One minute he was grandiosely vetting the bill for the meal with the fat old proprietor seated behind his counter patiently looking up at him as the waves pounded on the black sand of the beach just outside the restaurant. The next we were outside in the cooler night air. Mickey was walking ahead with the blonde Swedish girl, with her Latina Americana companion mincing beside me as I tagged along. Timing is of the essence, he always stated.

Seeing is believing, I whispered to myself. Beneath the cliffs at sea the fishing boats showed brilliant lights. Loud laughter rang out fully and yes a little wantonly in response to something Mickey had said. On the shoreline in the darkness the wave caps came and went in whiteness. Glancing at the confident stance of the Gullagoo, I considered him worthy to wear the red rosette of a prize ram.

Yet despite the epic and awesome (The Inseminator revelled in them, did he not?) happenings of that late night-early morning, which accepting Peter-you were a normal person, did you at any time loosen the chain that bore you over-the-waves and still bound you to you-know-where! "'I doubt it,' said the Carpenter, and shed a bitter tear."

Physically I could get away from that kip of a place you mention. Emotionally, never.

Mulrooney, Pedagogue, this is all a diversion. You're trying to avoid telling of the sequel to the Festival of the Seven Snotty Candles. *How right you are!* So you're not going to tell us about the Gullagoo and the Swede? And your Latina with her spreading scarlet skirt with its appliqué design of orange coloured dragons! *Not for the moment anyway.* Correct! Let me tell you something. The bloody story will be home before you. You can keep nothing secret from the CIA of Hero Town. They have the bones of it already. The long johns on Good Friday.

Micky was chastened during the flight home. A dawn taxi took both men to Santa Cruz Airport. The place was shrouded in sorrow: an all-time record in loss of human lives was reached when a plane crashed on the hills above the Airport, three days before.

The shamrock-green plane nosed upwards and the volcanic and at times verdant island fell away far below. Mickie was quiet. Peter realised that the bloody bastard was terrified that the plane would fall down on the flight home and that he'd burn for ever in eternal fire. He could hardly wait to get home to confess his sins for the second time that week—to be as it were medievally shriven. Witness the face of the priest in the sun-desiccated church in the mountain village who the Goolagoo persuaded by gesture to hear his confession.

"No entiendo Español, Padre," he had begun to say. Linguistic variations present scant penitential obstacles to the resourceful Gullagoo. And besides, the old Holy Roman Catholic Church has the ability to accommodate the most bizarre of craw thumpers. Even an artificial inseminator—of cattle.

Margo was at the airport. She glanced sidelong at the Gullagoo and noted his mood. Accepted it philosophically or appeared to do so. She gave us all the news. "Some American letters came the day you left, one from a University." *Oh dear Lord, am I back to this? Same old rigmarole.* "I left them on the hall stand for you."

I'm dead but to stiffen. All I want to do is sleep. I'm de-bleedin'-well-flated. And de-ditto-hydrated. "Go up and have a sleep for yourself. You're exhausted. And I'll have a nice dinner for you when you get up."

Daring "James Marshall" mounts the stairs, taking not the Wall of Death, but the Wall of Life. It's surely a form of jetlag or advancing age. At the Final Spring Sale of Thoughts, he buys one with every tread. Familiars and voices flit in and out of the brainbox over the yawning chasm that lies between the reality and the fantasy in the matter of the Latin girl and the just now realisation of his lot here cast.

"I hear yourself and the Gullagoo had a whale of a time in the Gran Canary. What's the story about flannels, or was it flags?" *How much does this client know? Deny it simply. Straight up.* "Yourself and Mick the Dick must have had a gala time! You're lucky that the Inseminator didn't land you in the calaboose. Or in the Lock Hospital with you knew what! Is your sister gone off her head to let you off on your tod with that great black ox! P.M's two shoes tread the upward world."

After a long, long sleep of oblivion I'll sort it all out, he tells himself. Tomorrow May Day, delightful day I'll give it my full attention. And later, like the harp in the legend, maybe I'll recite it all aloud to myself or to some most discreet person I can trust.

Will I ever make the bed I'm that sleepy. And so . . . Y . . . a . . . w . . . n! and zzzzz!

MAY

Green green and again Maygreen. The vivid transatlantic day green around Peter is not the same shade of green as that obtaining in the nostalgic pastures and woods around Hero Town. The American letter Peter placed aside until the weariness of the Canarian return had ebbed from his flesh, bones and blood. Within a short space of time Peter finds himself magic-carpeted to an environment thousands of miles from his home. Has he hitherto been a chrysalis? And is he at last emerging as a large blue Butterfly name of Mulrooney.

Why is he here in Savannah land, Georgia, sitting on a weather-beaten rocking chair on the porch of an ante-bellum mansion, with pillars almost throttled by a large magnolia tree with blossom petals like vulgar slices of bread, home to the famine Irish who in the 1850s sailed here in great numbers, among them a number of the clan O'Connor. The magnum opus, his history of Clan Connor, has travelled well and has resulted in an invitation to address an O'Connor Clan seminar in the States where recently their famed writer, Flannery, had died. The seminar presumably to provide an Irish equipoise to the Halley Kunte Kinte saga called "Roots". Chance of a lifetime, Peter, grab it with both hands!

Gom! Half wit! You're off again, Peter. You've a grand life. But before you leave for the USA, I'll try for the last time to straighten out the kinks in your brain. I heard that the Inseminator did his stuff out there in Malta. But you did not. *Not Malta. It's too wearisome to explain.*

Hilda the Dressmaker is giving Peter pre-departure advice. It is still going round in his head as he sits on the rocking chair. "I know all about the Connors or O'Connors, my grandmother being one of them," Hilda goes on. "They have as many nicknames here as the Ryans have in Tipperary. Will you tell 'em about their nicknames?"

Let it rest for a while. "When you stand up in that University give it to them right between the eyes. Tell 'em about Cooker. Tell 'em about the Looricks, the Oily Britches, the Proddies, the Stallions, the Easynows, and the Booltems. And tell 'em that's only a minute fraction of the nicknames following the longtailed O'Connor clan.

"What else are you going to say? Kings and queens, I bet. You're a chicken."

"Correct! I'm going to tell of Roderick O'Connor, the last High King of Ireland, and Queen Maeve having the pillow talk in Cruachan and the epic, the Táin Bó Cuailgne."

"The what?"

"You wouldn't understand."

"I'd understand the pillow-talk and the pillow squawk and the pillow stalk and the pillow baulk—that's you! They can't be paying your fare and giving you a fee for talking bullshit history like that. A pity my grandmother, old Mary Conner-Borick, couldn't hear you. Borick means bandy legged doesn't it?"

Why does Hilda always chew the fat about sex? Woman's whole endeavour. It creeps into all her conversations like Kudzu, that invasive plant introduced to the southern States and hailed as a crop to solve everything. Took over completely—climbed trees and telephone poles, now it's up there swarming all over the railroad and camellias. Like rabbits it became a curse.

Might make a familiar. Note it, Kudzu!

This mansion in the deeps of the countryside is close to Dublin Georgia where on St Patrick's Day they burn the pitted and petroled 365 rattlesnakes to commemorate the banishment of reptiles from Ireland by St Patrick himself. Is this too a voodoo land?

Peter-I am fully aware of my unexpected metamorphosis and surprised that my employers, the Department cooperated in releasing me so readily. There must be a reader up there. Either that or a nest of O'Connors. It is as if I were transported across land and ocean by a genie in a bottle, to a civilisation as remote from Hero Town as if it were on Mars. Your whim, Master, is my command.

From the porch Peter views the scuffed grass of the yard, where a kennelled hound is howling as if warning of impending perdition. Clint, a powerfully built coloured man with the graceful movements of a tiger, tends the camellias, which grow in the woods.

Heat suffuses every aspect of existence. Li'l Old Dave, the host professor, yells the hound into silence. In the darkened porch he spoke of the almost complete extermination of fireflies. "The goddam insecticide I put on the pecans killed off almost every goddam one of them. I'm a polluter. I go around upsetting the balance of nature. People like me should be exterminated—not the fireflies who are doing nature's business. Some nights I don't sleep thinking of the harm I do." Piercing catcalls and perpendicular tails follow the foreman to the lone tree.

As for Hero Town, from this stance, Peter doubts if it is worth a tenth of all the gooey, mushy sentimental concern and even praise he has entertained and lavished upon it all these years. Every thought, word and deed of his has been smeared with the agar of its activities and its human projections in their many manifestations. Come to think of it, Peter, you are something of a mocking bird yourself. That bastard the Inseminator almost got you arrested in Tenerife. Himself and the bloody flag. Better not make a similar mistake here. Be careful not to be funny about Old Glory pendant here. There goes a Cardinal bird. Over the cats. Straight out of Propanganda Pro Fide in the Vatican. Bloody well brilliant.

*

As Peter rocks the chair here in dreamland he contemplates, like a holy man in the mountain villages of India, the intricacies of his own navel. From it extends a string of fine wire that serves both as a transatlantic cable and an umbilical cord stretching over the wrinkled afternoon spans of the Southern States squirming out into the seabed of the Atlantic, with its weighty swells of water, then snaking across the pig-brine wastes of ocean until at last striking the golden beach at BallyB in Ireland. From there it twists up over the grassy cliff top and over the bogland until at last it is suspended from the corner of a building in mid Hero Town, its end now becoming a sensitive microphone and indeed a camera lens to enfold the smaller square. These two pick up all sorts of sounds and images. By day and by night. Conversations from the past are again most sensitively recorded and replayed in the spinning tape of his brain box.

Just then the navel telephone buzzed. *As sure as eggs are eggs that's Hilda in the head. If I'm not careful she will complete my shamrock of confused thought. I'd better pick up the receiver. The word ectoplasm intrudes as I do so.*

"Is that Dr Peter Mulrooney, the famous historian?" (It's Hilda!)

"Speaking!"

"My dear retarded Pedagogue, prior to your leaving for the United States, you did not give me the chance of instructing you as regards the ramifications of the female psyche. So that armed with the knowledge you might seize the opportunity of reaching manhood during your sojourn in that great Republic of the West."

"You bitch! Who gave you my phone number?"

"Margo. She is one hundred per cent behind me in this conspiracy."

"Hump you and her."

"I'll ignore the muted obscenity. I'll just tell you what woman is like."

"Get off the line or I'll hang up on you."

"Don't ask me to explain things: I'll only tell you what way it is. Man is the key and woman is the lock. Then there's the sense of touch. In the climax of mating all senses fuse into one sense. T-O-U-C-H. Women are more biological than men. Figure that out for yourself. Woman is—hold on now, Paddy—Bladder-Kin-et-ic in her emotions and static in her limbs. She's a topper at religion, dreams and death, but not so good at drilling or soldiers—or things like that. With man it's the other way about."

"Are you reading this out of a book?"

"I have it written down. Let me finish. The male mind turns on nobility, nationality, integrity, scholarship and chivalry. Will you— I have this printed here in big block letters—for God's sake forget Your Shitten Chivalry! If you keep woman up on that pedestal she's going to slip down when you're not around and beetle off with the young gardener. À la Lady Chatterly. Now that you're in the US of A where young women ripen early like the fruit in their orchards, just find one almost at the end of her shelf life with lots of Rhino. Go about it deliberately. Wear your good gray suit, the white shirt and the dove gray tie. Speak slowly. From time to time look dreamily out of the window as if your hobgoblin of a mind is 6,000 miles away. Rompin' with the leprechauns of Coomafooka. Then, properly handled, you're in the mint for life. This town is only a privy. And you're the privy attendant. In the USA women are alive and emancipated. You're a bear and when you get the first taste of woman honey keep my advice high in your head. You hear me?"

"Are you off your nog?"

"I know what I am, a small town dressmaker. A well-read simpleton."

"Where are you getting all the money for the phone call?"

"Jack is at the seaside."

"Robber! Get off the bloody line. This will cost him a bundle."

"He has wagonloads of it."

"Hilda, before you go. Open the window, put the phone out and let me hear the sounds of the town. Then scram. Today is Thursday. Is that a creamery tanker passing?"

"Right, Peter. There's a man standing at the pillar box telling stories to the passers-by. Mouths open in guffaws."

"That's Tully Daw!"

"Right again, Peter. I'll have to watch myself or he'll cop me up here and tell Jack. Wait, a countrywoman approaching with sweets in her hand."

"Is she giving them away to the children?"

"Bullseye."

"That's Minnie Humbug down from Ballinwoodera. I'm going to cut you off."

"It does me good to chat with you, you're so innocent and gommish. 'Tis nice and cool here today. Is it hot out there?"

"Like a furnace. You owe Jack six or seven quid. I hope it weighs on your conscience."

"Hump Jack!"

"You too!"

"Good luck."

"Thanks for ringing, Hilda." Kling.

Back in the reality of Swainsboro, Peter is absorbed in the brilliant birds of the yard. Redwing blackbirds, cockers, hummers, peckers, thrashers and jays. There they are! Robbers, playboys, fashion models, prelates, carpenters with augers, consummate mimics like Marceau—to and fro—watch them go—weaving a tapestry with rich colours to its pattern. Keep them all, Peter would now settle for a humbug out of Minnie's bag of sweets any day. And how fares Gentle Child, and Maudie Quilligan? No, he has not forsaken you.

*

Peter trembles. A sudden shiver. He is considering the academic

Gethsemane before him. At the prospect of addressing an audience of long-established and affluent American-Irish, each unit of the attendance utterly convinced that he or she is descended from ancient Irish kings and queens. Peter is dressed exactly as Hilda counselled. All the elderly women present have blue or purple rinsed hair—how accurately Hilda visualised the scene. But Peter fails to spy even one unattached middle aged woman at what Hilda termed the "end of her shelf life". In an hour or so he shall mount . . . (at this word Hilda giggles from afar) the podium, advance to the lectern and begin his address, still assailed by doubts.

Heckler. For once in your life, Pedagogue, control the fecking habit you have of reducing everything to flippancy. And forget about your goddam familiars and your navel telephones too. Not to mention your recent obsession with rhynchosporium, that fungus disease of the cereal leaves, and rocks of musical words. *You're bloodywell right, chum* . . .

So Peter begins. "Ladies and gentlemen, and distinguished guests. Conscious, amazed even—that the small candles of research I have lit have cast their beams afar, I will now endeavour, imaginatively of course, to take you across the Atlantic Ocean to trace in small compass the Story of Clan O'Connor-Kerry, Lords of Ciarraí-Luachra, as mentioned in The Book of Rights, tracing their chieftains back to Hugh in 1067 to Brian in 1151. Though their castle stands slighted and their ancient lands are delivered up to the Elizabethan undertakers, carpetbaggers I believe you call them here, there are very many O'Connors still left on ancestral soil. At least 1,500 families bearing the surname still reside there. So widespread and repetitive is the surname that you will find it difficult to ascertain to which subdivision of the tribe you bear kinship, unless of course there is preserved in your family lore the name of the townland whence your ancestors came and more important still the diminutive appellations of affection which each individual family proudly bore so as to preserve the individual identity of each unit of this haughty clan."

Mulrooney, you're a prevaricating whore. Nicknames? You're not going to mention Pukes, the Cluas Mhors, the Jimmy-Jars, the Woodbines, the Fullstops, the Know Alls and the Mollycoddles. No doubt about it, you glossed over that neatly. Carry on, Brother, carry on. I'm listening.

Peter carried on less flamboyantly, but of course, the mind wanders back, back, and over the waves to a silly but pungent account.

⁎

What put this diversion into his head? Must be all the smells of the lecture room evoked by the heat. The smell of azaleas in bloom. Must go by opposites. Mind's eye: mind's nose. Hard to isolate the umbilical cord of memory. Someone in Hero Town talking. An incident to do with smells.

"Peter! Let me tell you something. The Circuit Court Judge is a giddy boyo. My garden as you well know adjoins the Courthouse. District Court judges are gentlemen. But that other bucko, the Circuit Court judge—oho wait till I tell you. I had Dickie Donovan pitching a couple of loads of manure across the garden wall for the cabbage in my garden. Dicko had to go up to the Courthouse Avenue to throw it over. As all belonging to me got it thrown in there since time immemorial. And no complaints from bench, bar or barrack. It slipped my mind that the Circuit Court was in session. I should have known about it because the flag was flying beside the door. A damn hot day. The Guards were all country boys and to them the smell of manure reminded them of home. But the pompous booby with the wig on his napper was from Foxrock in Dublin, a place without a fox or a rock, nothing but lawns shaved to the veins of nicety. Bowling greens and croquet hoops. Dick was pitching his second load of dung over the top when on the bench inside his Lordship started to sniff. "What is that odour?" he demanded of the Sergeant. "I believe it's farmyard manure, Your Honour." "Go out and see that this nuisance is ended at once!" (This intrusive interlude is recalled in the context of coloured birds, brilliant azaleas, musk and sherbet, and the room of composure wherein a visiting lecturer is given a half hour prior to his lecture to collect his thoughts.)

"Out stalks the Sergeant—a West of Ireland man squeezed out of all sorts of manure, chicken shit and rotten seaweed. By this time the smell, even at fifty yards range, was lethal. Dicko is on a teabreak in the lodge at the courthouse gate, with a mug of tea in his mucky paw. The lodge-keeper's wife, a mountainy woman, ignored the half-empty cart. To her the smell of the farmyard manure signified lowland loam and was as acceptable as the scent of 4711 would be to a jaded confessor in a hot confession box.

"The Sergeant makes out the bould Dicko. Dicko spluttered the mouthful of hot tea over the floor. 'Is this what we fought for?' he yelled—what harm but Dicko and all belonging to him wouldn't pull the skin off a tapioca pudding. He was referring to the troubled times and the Fight for Freedom. 'Keep your voice down,' said the Sergeant as he walked back with him to the cart, which was backed in against the garden wall. 'The judge is cutting figures up on the bench; the courtroom is stunk; remove the cart and cease the work at once.' 'I'll tell the bastard a few home truths,' shouted Dicko, fit to be tied.

" 'If you do, you'll get jail for contempt.'

" 'Contempt! He'll be the laughing stock of the country if he carries it one step farther. Cripes but 'twould look lovely in the papers—the Magistrate and the Manure. The Coadjutor and the Cowdung.'

"'The coadjutor has nothing to do with it. Shift your load now, that's all.'

'Is that what the Easter week men died for? So that I should be prevented from helping a man set a hundred of Enfield cabbage. Hey, you in there! You cocked up paycock in your gown and wig. Let me tell you the truth for a change.'

"They had it hot and heavy. Dicko looked a dangerous man

up there on the load brandishing a four-pronged pike, shouting up at the window of the courthouse. The Sergeant got as red as a turkey cock. A couple of Guards came to his assistance. Only for the woman in the lodge hanging off Dicko 'twould have ended badly. Dicko went down the town leading his animal by the head. He was roaring like a stuck pig, about Robert Emmet and Wolf Tone and Lord Edward Fitzgerald.

"That was a historic hundred of cabbage plants I tell you!"

*

But whatever Peter can or cannot do, he cannot get Fiddler's Hill out of his head. No matter where he goes, whether the destination is exotic or prosaic, mad daft or abandoned, any excess of tension sends him scurrying over land and sea, over hill and hollow, to the quiet asylum afforded by the fields and hedges around the foot of Fiddler's Hill outside Hero Town. No one knows who the fiddler was. He must have been a dab hand with the bow and the tunes. The hill is there, the road running almost die straight upwards for the better part of a mile from the bridge over the Gearach River with one of the finest views in all Ireland.

Stepping from the bridge to the hilltop view Peter, pace after gentle pace, finds solace, sedation and beauty in seasonal change. Here, now, as May draws its green curtain across the landscape, he can experience the tactile delight of drawing towards him a cluster of fat ivy berries in the palm of his hand and having admired their dark green matt finish can cast them up in the air and savour the pitter-patter of the berries falling like green rain on the nine-foot wide roadway.

Just now the whitethorn is breaking in abundant spray as the orange tipped white butterfly patrols the furze rich with blooms the colour of old country butter.

Thoreau had his Walden—Peter his Hero Town and hills.

*

On the late night porch, lecture over, tension released, Peter is proud. His host professor is easy and relaxed in his scholarship. The drowsy magnolia tree crowding around the black shutters of the mansion release their sensual scent on the late evening air. The seminar was his idea: he too had an O'Connor in his family tree and knew Ireland in the romantic abstract. The ice cubes tinkle in the whiskey glass, as Irish history is spoken of. No special sequence. Columcille's monks burying their currachs on Iona so as to kill all nostalgic ache to return to Ireland. And then again Peter's second telling of the story of O'Connor-Kerry proudly staggering ahead on the Retreat of O'Sullivan Beare, his ulcerated legs oozing so that he was forced to lean against a tree and batter his bare shins against the rough bark to rid them of pus and evil blood. And how with each frenzied thump he chanted in semi-rhythm. Because of his lineage, Peter could have told the Professor this particular story ten times a day without his growing tired of hearing it. I'm a true seanchaí, Peter told himself. Every time I tell the tale I make it a bit better. "Remember Limerick," the animated professor shouted so that the bird dogs barked madly in the yard.

But Fiddler's Hill was not yet finished with Peter, the Exile of Erin. The shorn scalps of riverside fields where the first silage has been cut pulled Peter back and above a swirl of water below the river bridge. All is seen in Peter's distant mind's eye. At the torrent's edge Peter walks the bluebell carpet and views a herd of Friesian milch cows, each beast with a glistening tag in her ear, munches and watches, watches and munches. Smiling, Peter recalls the description given by a scholarly labouring man of such a fruitful herd. "Slow lazy rheumy waltzers of cattle, their wonderful dugs legging them as they walk. Their paps powerful and priapic."

*

Powerful too and beautiful were the features of the Latina maid. Neat, remote, mysterious company, feminine. She took short steps as if her feet had languished in bandaged bondage when she was a child. She had never seen the tropics, nor her father nor her grandfather before her! She spoke English in low tones with a Cockney accent. *Try as I might I could not imagine her performing any of the erotic fantasies my timid mind flirted with and which I felt somehow could never take shape in reality! If I tried to bridge the chasm between imagination and reality I would surely fall into the pit of awkwardness, confusion and shame.*

Who dat talking? Dat am a foolish schoolmaster from Ireland shootin' off his mouth.

In step we walked away from the restaurant. The Swedish girl and the Inseminator had paired off into the darkness—as they moved away across the dark sand I heard the Swede laugh provocatively.

I was blessed if I knew what to do with the girl beside me. I was ignorant of the thermodynamics of Rotary Square. My mind was occupied with cotton wool and my lost prime acres of high turbary. There I was on that foreign shore with lascivious sparrows chattering in the bougainvillea, and beside me a dame of dames, every millimetre of her body proclaimed her a she and here was I, a cut cat unable to forget the roaring pulpit of my youth and the sonorous pronunciamentos of Butler's Catechism. (I'm confessing all this to the magnolia tree in the garden of the ante-bellum mansion on the other side of the Atlantic.)

Heckler: he's dodging this bloody issue of the Gullogoo and the Union Jack again.

Okay. That I may be as dead as my grandfather, I offered her rice crispies and milk sitting on my divan. She sipped the limp cereal like a cat. The dress with the appliquéd pattern was spread ornately on each side of her. She lay down on Mick's bed and to my surprise, or was that relief, she slept in a foetal curl. I tried to sleep on my own bed on the lower level in the apartment but I never closed an eye. Out on the morning sea when the lamps of the fishing boats were losing their gentle fight against the light of a new day, sleep came over me. I felt dismal at my failure to be a man "jumping into the sea", or into personal anarchy! When later I awoke, she had departed. I then recalled the remark the young woman had made as together we strolled towards the apartment the night before—this in an understressed throwaway tone—"you should learn to enjoy yourself".

Pondering the implications of her advice I stood on the balcony and looked down on the swimming pool, and on the flags of the nations that clung limply to their flagpoles on an elevation above it. My eyes then followed the course of a rope that had snaked into the light green water of the pool. I traced it backward to the foot of a flagpole and quickly scanned the colours of the mastheads. "Holy God," I blurted. Where was the British Flag? What was it the Inseminator said when we looked down from our balcony and seen the serried pennants, "that I may never die till I wipe my arse with the butcher's apron".

Behold the Gullagoo at break o' day in the lavatory of an apartment in one of the Un-fortunate Islands. He squats at stool amid, as James Joyce would have it, "his own rising steam". The Union Jack is draped about his naked sunburned shoulders as he bawls a Wexford ballad of future rebellions in an unfree Ireland

"God grant you glory, brave father Murphy. . .

In another fight for the green again."

Peter-I gasped in horror. My holiday was in smithereens! What possessed me to go abroad in the company of this Baluba? It will make the papers and my name will be mud at home. I'll have to move fast if I am to avoid a calamity. I dragged on my dressing gown, almost tearing it as I did so.

Give my mind its due, it moves fast in a case of dire necessity.

I thumped the guffawing Gullagoo and tried to tug the flag from about his shoulders. I soon realised that he was sitting on the greater part of the emblem which was as loaded as a baby's nappy. Sweet God! After a struggle I got the flag out from under him, showered and rinsed it with a garden hose—liquid fertiliser for the orange coloured bougainvillea. His chant followed me as I raced downstairs. Crouching at the pool's edge I began the task of restoring the cloth to

*its former glory. Seizing a stone from a miniature rock garden I beat
and plucked the cut ends of the flag rope until they appeared frayed.
Just as I replaced the rock the sound of footsteps approached.
Summoning all my sham sense of idle curiosity I stood at the pool's
edge looking down at the half drowned flag in dumb amazement. I
turned and allowed my gaze to follow the rope to the foot of the
flagstaff. Up, up my eyes travelled: my mouth was fully open as my
gaze accused the pulley at the top of the pole. The pool attendant
wearing a dark red blazer was now behind me. I heard his
exclamation as he saw the flag. Belatedly I prayed that there had been
even a minor gale during the night. He was now examining the
frayed ends of the rope. "Ah!" he breathed pointing upwards at the
pulley. "Ah!" I breathed as in revelation. He then smiled and, with
a twirling of fingers, mimed the act of splicing the rope ends together.
"How clever you are," my smile replied. As he fished the Union Jack
out of the green water I prayed that I had washed well. I sweated as
he examined the cloth. However he seemed satisfied. As he turned to
spread out the flag under the morning sun he flashed me a
conspiratorial smile. He then placed his finger to his lips as if asking
me to keep the affair a secret. I nodded my full agreement! I also
closed my goose's mouth. Halfway up the stairs, I leaned against the
wall to deep-draw a sigh of utter relief.*

An innocent abroad!

*

There were times during the days that followed in the States
when Peter was forced to lie still and ask himself in what
dimension he existed. Did he, like O'Connor, also stand at the
crossroads "Where time and place and eternity meet"? The critics
saw only the freaks and the grotesques, but Flannery's scalpel
went far deeper than the superficial and drew wise arterial blood.

*Do I too in my small town see only freaks, grotesques? Peter asked
himself. Only I choose to call them familiars: the words, phrases,
incidents, idiosyncratic personalities, navel telephones, even sniffing*

magistrates that occupy the bedlam of consciousness. Peter resolved to keep the phrase "time, place and eternity" in the forefront of his mind in the hope of achieving a personal epiphany, a dividend most welcome indeed in an island of imitators.

Meanwhile, removed from the natural scene of his activities and having an unusually long distance perspective on home, Peter realised that there were items to be recorded prior to his eagerly sought flight home. Peter slit open the green-and-orange edged envelope from his sister Margo. Out popped Hero Town, its grief and its humours, its smells and sounds. Margo was shocked, but Peter laughed.

"Hey, Tull, what did ye do to Malcolm Darcy last Sunday at Mass?"

"What are you talking about?"

"Come on, Tull! You're not talking to a fool. Spill the beans."

"Just took him down a peg or two. That's all."

"At Mass?"

"Yeh. At Mass. He got on our bloody nerves. The way he walks up the middle of the church every Sunday at two minutes to ten, dressed in a grey overcoat with the velvet collar, his grey silk hat dangling from his fingers and it swinging. Him and the big belter of a missal under his oxter. Here, Almighty God, comes Malcolm Darcy. Looks around—superciliously. About ten seats from the altar he stops. The person at the end of the seat who has been there since twenty to ten has to shove in. Looks down his nose a second time at these around him. Takes up the missal. Cleans specs. Looks over rims at the priest. Sniffs as if it is a curse. He's a Pharisee—he'd give you the gawks. My bloody mock squireen. His father a fish jowlter from Traheen. His grandmother sold seagrass and periwinkles."

"But what did you do to him?"

"I told you we took him down a peg."

"How? There are all sorts of rumours going about."

"He has all the standing up points in the Mass measured to a

T. Stands up before everyone. Glares around at the ignoramuses. So I got Holy Jimmy to mark the points in a missal and I got right in front of him. And I bet him to the draw. Every bloody time. Everyone around us copped on."

"Had ye the ends of the seats blocked off?"

"The lads manned them. We made him go inside for a change. His nostrils were quivering."

"What about his hat?"

"It sort of fell down under the seat. The lads booted it back. All very respectfully of course."

"His missal?"

"Full of faldalls. Mortuary cards and aspirations. That fell too. He was an hour picking it up. 'Twas my standing up broke his Melt."

"Did the Dean throw a fit?"

"Huh—no. He burst a gut laughing over the dinner table. The curate too is as wide as a gate. Do you think they haven't Mr Darcy copped on? All very respectfully of course. A stranger could be right in the middle of us and he wouldn't cop a thing. People blowing about a classless community. Who'll be next on the list?"

"You'll hang yet, Tully Daw," Peter whispered from afar on reading the account.

"Crucified, not hanged," came the quick retort. "Up there on Ballysynan Hill. Two dark crosses between Yourself Peter and Arsey Darcy. One on each side o' me. Leave off schoolmaster, we have you under observation too, Krrrck! I'm off."

"You're a rogue, Tull."

"And you're a knocker, Pedagogue."

From his distant foreign perch, Peter looked down on the town where in the presbytery, off the Diamond, the parish priest had just shifted the hour of the Eve-of-the-Sabbath Mass so as not to clash with the broadcasting of the Eurovision Song Contest.

Time and place beckoned Peter back home to Hero Town.

JUNE

L et us wipe the slate clean. Let us begin the beguine all over again. It is said not much happens in a small country town but what you see and hear makes up for it.

The sixth month came in cold. The bullfinches have built deep in the recesses of the blackthorns now deep in foliage. People in cottages and rooms turn into mirrors and cry out, "I am lonely." A woman of thirty-three, the shyest and most shivery neurotic in town, cries out in the morning hours, "Why am I not being fertilised?" A monstrance displayed in a haberdashery window causes a storm—it's an advertisement for a play *The Real Presence* to be presented at the Drama Festival. Arguments raged. It wasn't a play at all. It blinded by the sheer shining of its technique. A strenuous knock up of verbal tennis. Where was it in Hero Town that Peter saw soup in a saucepan on a sofa?

"When I'm dead, Mary, go to the islands where you won't be talked about. Stop your crying, love. Is it love to decree that your lovely beauty should remain unenjoyed? I'd turn in my grave if I thought that would happen to you."

The piercing town siren blows its top. The citizens with a rueful smile at each other are holding their fingers to their ear holes.

"Fire on the mountain, run boys run,
You with the red coat follow with the drum."

The golden farmers who pay neither income tax nor rates because their income is alleged to be negligible and their valuations too low, walk along the pavements heads down, faces locked in a grimace. A fabrication of fat lies. The same farmers who draw the dole and get creamery cheques the value of which would stagger a wage earner are again setting fire to their boglands and mountain flanks, and the rate payers are paying through the nostrils to send out the urban firemen, sometimes three times a day, to prevent the flames from spreading.

Peter-he is still awaiting the imminent General Examination of his progress as an educator and he can almost sense the sediment of terror setting in the well of his brain. The houses of Hero Town seem to tighten him up, squeeze and compress him, body, brain and spirit in spite of his recent excursions. Margo is only temporarily pacified by the present of the silver broach with the inset turquoise. It's that time in her life. In bed at night Peter is uneasy, tossing and tumbling, fearing that he has left weals on a disruptive boy's palm. Later in the morning he watches with apprehension the entry of boy after boy into the classroom and finally emits a deeply drawn sigh of relief as the lad bounces in with a cheery grin on his face.

But is this the real Peter-you? Brother, Peter, are you not an onion? Layer after layer of memory, emotion, reality and fantasy, pretence and sensitivity. Contrariwise also. What is the criterion of truth? Verisimilitude—a plausible air? The power to occlude the everyday world and create a world of the illusion that is endowed with a new form of reality. Real in the sense that it can be made most truly to exist in the Kingdom of the Imagination where a mare can be decked for service by a snorting locomotive and a Volkswagen be born? Are you not now oscillating in fancy between two poles? Did anyone ever attempt to equip you so as to cope with this mighty polarisation? The hurried whisper in Peter's ear, "This girl is very fond of you," does not rule out the admissibility of your head wearily resting in the lap of the woman who through a go-between has declared her overpowering infatuation for him. There it is. Or is it all an almighty delusion and the only reality that occurs to you is the sight of that infernal saucepan? Eh?

*

Hero Town staggered out into the prime of year that Peter abhorred. How to make enemies and out race people? Now the time of the General Election approaches. It makes a rattle and din like that of a runaway stagecoach.

Beware, Peter! Dare, Peter! The candidates are rabid dogs even scarecrows. Go ahead and make enemies, Peter. He who lacks the qualities to make enemies also lacks the qualities to make friends. Fortunate is the election candidate whose mother dies two weeks before the polling day. Her funeral, her dead body even as David used a sling can overcome the Goliath, that is his political approach. The formula is, "We won't forget you. Leave it with me, 'tis in good hands." Rabid dogs carrying in their bloodstream the deadliest of all poisons—that of pride. "Is it our Mick to be beaten at the polls! Bechrist no!" What will you do when in their turn each group stands begging at the table outside the chapel? Subscribe to each party in turn! And learn to smile in a way that conveys "We". Okay, do the other thing so: tell the candidate that he knows nothing about the Irish language, which is very dear to you. Know what will happen: for the next decade of years his mother, his wife, his sisters and all belonging to him will have the following vituperative dispatch sent to you by ingeniously circuitous routes. "The Curse O' Christ on the cracked Schoolmaster." Ten years penal servitude at Church Bazaar, at Whist Drive and Dramatic productions locally organised. You're trying to save the four laburnum trees and the laurels in the Diamond: they'll get the Council to have them condemned, felled and eradicated. They'll have it rumoured that you can't teach C A T, only that blasted Irish, conveniently forgetting that for three solid months Peter vainly tried to have one of their sons replace his deliberately torn English Reader. Brave Brother Peter, aren't these the normal hazards of living in a small intimate community? In the larger cities the beasts that lurk in the undergrowth are loneliness, frustration born of assembling with a DIY kit a neighbourhood viable as a whole and in each of its parts. Speak out your mind when the candidates come knocking at your door. Say, "Your party dragged down the noblest head of state we have ever had and wishes to destroy all that is dear to our people." Act now, or live for ever a coward in your own esteem.

Talk up, Peter, politicians are cowardly too.

The argument gathers momentum. The traffic-choked town howls its Greek chorus of shut up. A prompter off-stage, a female, prompts, "Kinder . . . Kucke . . . Kirch." (Children . . . Kitchen . . . Church.)

Peter savouring the words tells himself, I too am involved first with Kinder, in as much as I am a surrogate parent in loco parentis.

Kuche, to me a mystery, a conundrum, the Secret of the Innermost Veil, the beacon on the horizon of my desire for as couch it holds a reclining figure not yet a nude, but seductively draped.

As for Kirche, only for my equals, the Irish schoolmasters and schoolmistresses, there wouldn't be one iota of faith passed from generation to generation. Look, I'm a nun's man and a priest's man too but it was late in the day when they gave us credit. So the clergy, jealous of their privileges and our position, sent cheeky boys to the United States and to catechistically pernicious Holland to see what was afoot and to bring home what in essence were transferred experiments. Dangerous buckos to be sure. No wonder the sacristan almost got a stroke when in his hospital bed he heard that his beloved candlesticks had been removed from the church and were even then in a greengrocer's window advertising the local production of that play.

Almighty God, the priest surely isn't going to start preaching again about the men standing down at the church door. They are yelling about that for a full century. Give it up, Father. Didn't my big eejit of a Dean here long ago run down the steps of the pulpit and racing at the men at the door their arms folded across their chest, gave one fellow a clout in the nose that put him spouting blood. Do you think your man took any notice? Spilled from one leg to the other and taking his time about it stuck a snotty handkerchief up his nostrils. Do you think it "fluttered a Feather o' Flutter"? Not bloody likely. Every likelihood that the fella bleeding was a sheep hill farmer accustomed to slitting the scrota of a young ram with a knife sharpened like a doctor's lance, or lacking same, biting off the testicles with his teeth, before cooking the rare titbits to determine whether or not they could thenceforward be reckoned a delicacy after a day of merry castration.

If that querulous foaming priest, the Dean of St Michael's, thought a drop of blood would make them abandon their posts at the doorway as a result of a couple of rebel yells, superstitious threats or a farty puck of a fist, his Very Reverence had another think coming. So he had. The Toms hereabouts slow to approach the table of the Lord do not readily succumb to threats, blandishments or even pucks in the gob.

Ah, the cut scrotum and the cowardly buckoes of Hero Town, they have mousetraps to trap the red, green, brown and blue paper money. Trapped old greasy treasury notes, gotcha! They have forgotten how to use the money imaginatively. Convulsion makes everything as bright as day. Ah well, Peddah told himself, this place for me is my personal crossroads to eternity. Nothing else for me to do except to pull this tarred rope which I find close to my hand.

*

Peter's dreaded school inspection came and went; it wasn't so bad after all—he got a good report. The cardboard giants of the night were laid to rest. Hard on the heels of this came a notice for the annual Christian Doctrine Examination. Peter spent four days from nine to three cramming the children. A cramming session that had nothing to do with Christ, His Father in Heaven or the Holy Ghost. The proofs for the existence of Limbo and Purgatory. The various creeds, Athanasian, Nicene and Apostles'. It was, Peter brooded, the final dying kick of the learning by rote system, senseless in its idiotic assumption that the I'm-Sitting-On-the Stile Mary's and Paddies would be theologically equipped to encounter H.G. Wells at every twist and turn of the English Road. The class crammed with profundities and parables were marked excellent. Such was the transference of charity which is at the core of Christian belief.

Almighty Father who created butterflies and tigers, piranha fish and prime primroses, forgive me the trespasses I have committed in teaching the news of the Kingdom.

Meanwhile the town was going to hell: Peter winced when he saw one of the teachers in the school using the Division One English Soccer League Table as an example of averages, and when the same teacher some days later brought to the school playing field a cricket bat and wicket, he didn't sleep for three nights. "Was cricket not played in the local classical school, Peter?" The reply, "Aye, by the flannelled fools of Hero Town."

"You never know, it might make a comeback."

"And so might the great British Empire," he curtly replied. Of themselves the games didn't matter, he told himself, it's just the abject surrender to the influence of the mass media, the downgrading of the native, the mimicry factor. Presently we shall become a polythene people, living in easy-assembled houses delivered in huge kits complete with the domestic dog or kitten. Please indicate sex and colour, all assembled in a single day. What's that noise in the street? The election. Vote Number One Monkey Gibbon. The finest politician in south-west Ireland. A topper to do a turn. Become the fifty-first state of the Union. Be a star? To hell with Niamh of the Golden Hair.

Summer came galloping in remorselessly thudding the turf of time behind it. Peter was up to his eyes in schoolwork and was at times fighting a lost cause. "My mother said to gi'me the money," he said. "She found the reader Mary Anne had at home."

"But I can't take it back now, son—it's soiled." Loud talk in the corridor as a consequence, the parent pitching on the word "soiled".

"You'd swear he wiped his arse with it! Soiled! I'll have my money back, if you please." Still it all toned Peter up. Freedom and the islands off the west coast were at hand. Now that he had got a taste of freedom at Easter he found himself slavering to go. Whenever Peter, his nerves jagged after coping with the devilment and tormentation of horseplaying pupils, heard such comments, he found himself tightening in cold rage. "Half a day, half a week, half a month, half a year." Suffering such asides, "That's right, Ma'am," Peter said smiling, but under his breath, with the tendency to migraine manifesting itself once again, he muttered, "You bitch!"

*

Knock. Knock. The canvassers rattled on Peter's front door knocker while he and Margo were out. Later one of the canvassers put out a rumour that Peter was a cowardly dodger. They said that he was inside all the time peeping out from between the slats of the venetian blinds. Too cowardly to refuse his vote! Watching the canvassers drift in a knot from doorway to doorway Peter-he realised that in a small tight community allegiance was a coat of many colours. Each allegiance true to itself, political, business and cultural allegiance. Equally ingenious intrigues were formed with other perpetual foes now blood allies in a different sphere of activity. Certain versatile intriguers were capable of carrying on three or four different intrigues at one and the same time, all with the prospect of power as their final goal. This evidenced itself across the table at the local council meetings: a meaningful glance across the plain of polished mahogany could sign and seal a treaty as firmly as if it had been contracted in blood. A glance could be interpreted as follows: "If you don't back me up in this, you bastard, I'll phone and ask matron why your lousy father-in-law is kept beyond his time in the local hospital." Power! Peter whistled to himself. Is there any other roadway to govern people? Even the town fool knew on which side his bread was buttered and jammed. He was parrot trained as a consequence by the gift of a few pints of beer to repeat, "So-and-so is my bloody man! He's no imported sonofabitch like Hairy Mary's git. Yahoo! I'd cut that fella's gad before I'd give him Number One!" No billboard was in the hunt with propaganda of that kind. Yahoo! Where do you leave your saucepan on a sofa now? While these events were in train, the old shop fronts were being crucified. And lots cast for its seamless robe. Clinker built be damned. The craze now was for copper canopies in updated pubs, all this in the name of progress. The plastic storks croaked their agreement on the tidy shaved lawn in the suburbs.

The weather turned cold. The whitethorn blossoms have rusted off and the lantern tree is opulent in its balance of red and green. Each spray a blossom admirable and weighty against the sky.

Pay heed now, Peddah, to what Hilda had said, the thin voice whispered. "It was a woman's nature to seek out emotion. Catch her in an emotional environment and if the chemicals of attraction are correctly and sensitively pestle mixed, the job is oxo. If you get a letter from a woman and she uses the word love in any context—well, move in there right fast, you blind fool of a pedagogue. The women who pass you by as if butter wouldn't melt in their mouths, they come in here and tell me their confessions. You'd get a standing weakness sitting down if you heard what some of them say; for the last time, Master Mild Mannered Mouseen Mulrooney, will you stop the shittin' chivalry. Br-oo-oo-se'em the teasing butcheens and they'll lick your ankles. Dominus vobiscum is fine. I'm all for it: the other is part of human condition too."

*

*Dear Madame Bovary: Peter was whispering to himself every book
in literature open seems to mention your name. Dear dear Madame
Bovary. I wonder who is it in this town approximates most closely to
you in character.*

"Come right in!" said Miss Delamere, the retired librarian who
spent most of her life in Halifax, Yorkshire.

Peter had given the regulation three tinkles on the almost secret
doorbell which was sited at the top corner of the left hand door
jamb. Miss Delaware always wore a hat and was the quintessence
of courtesy. "I'm just entertaining my international friends," she
said entering the living room and taking up and clasping to her
boosom a new paperback from the top of one of the neat piles on
the stools. "I've just been introduced to a marvellous friend," she
added with a youthful laugh. "I love you, John Fuller, Oxford
don," she said pressing the book to her and swinging left and
right adding, "even though there's an echo in your work of
another sweetheart of mine. I've thousands of sweethearts," she
said archly. She thrilled with laughter as she pointed to the
stacked bookshelves.

"I suppose you'd call me a censor when I worked in England
as I got all the naughty books first. Going home on Saturday
afternoons to my flat with a little attaché case full of . . .
sweetsmelling fresh print, all brand new off the presses, many of
them . . . what would be called por-no-graph-ic-al today . . . I
didn't need any social contact. Bridge—pooh! I had lovers galore.
Some of them refined and gallant. Others . . . well. Axel Munthe
from the palace in Stockholm. Arnold Bierce—he comitted
suicide.

"But I like to keep up to date. Molly Keane is a beloved old
rascal—I am a sort of a Molly Keane myself. Australians too—
Patrick White leads me into the outback. Some of my lovers were
beautifully rough.

"I do wish you'd take some sherry, Peter. I must appear

positively tipsy here while you get more—dessicated by the minute. But you needn't pity me, Mr Cautious Mulrooney. On the contrary—'I am replete with Love'."

These are her familiars, Peter told himself. What a range this woman has. Is it any wonder she'd press them to her bosom. Her fire, her lamp, intimacy, silence and the imagination. All with her ritual drop of sherry.

The middle of nowhere: the centre of everywhere. Hope is a something with feathers . . . what is the quotation? Love is a whole aviary of birds from everywhere. And what birds!

At times the roar of the traffic, mostly creamery stuff, pounding, grinding, roaring, bellowing past her little window, interrupted her tale. Storytellers par excellence, the Arabs and the Irish. Milk thundering past, drowning the drone of the tellers. The town's economy depending on a cow's udder. City cows titty. Ballylactation. Ville La Leche. Ballybonyanamo. Madame, can you milk a cow? There was a cold sting to the wind. No growth. No grass. No milk. No cream. No casein. No milk powder. No ice creams. No blancmange. Fiddle-de-dee.

*

Singing "Polly de Lool de Doodle Dol de Day", coming on for half past six o' clock at the Polling Booth, Carmody shouts, "I'll put a stir on these bastards!" He was looking across at the other crowd who represented the rival candidate, moneyed middle of the road, well-fed buggars every one of them. In any country of the world you could pick them out to join the equivalent of the Monday Club Crush. You'd know what they'd say before ever they'd open their mouths. Carmody calls for the station wagon and says that it is time now to lift Polly Hanrahan. "And bring her the long way round the town," were the instructions issued. They lifted old Polly, bed ridden with a spinal disease for years—they had a loan of the Red Cross Stretcher—and they brought her out in the street fully robed in her brilliant green dressing gown. Polly raised her hand and yelled, "Up the Republic", setting the whole of Cathal Brugha Street on fire. Neighbours who hadn't yet voted echoed the warcry, pushing their hands out through the sleeves of their coats, felling for the courthouse. Polly on her makeshift throne half in, half out of the station wagon paraded down the street. The sight of Polly's pale face and her brandished fist and the soul of her rebel yell roused out the town with memories of ambushes in the Troubles fifty years before.

"Up the Republic." Now she was moving though the grey cut-stone cottages of Arthur Street and these she set on fire too. The canvassers heard the cries approaching! Her partisans grew animated and the old lady was carried in triumph into the booth. Deliberately (though she was a great reader) compelling the presenting officer to shout out the names of the candidates so that she could comment cogently on all except the man she meant to plump for. There was a side issue to this little tragicomedy too for Jurr Mahony, an old ex-soldier of the First World War who had been given seven pints of porter to vote for the Conservative Candidate, succeeded Polly in the Illiterate Stakes. She tried to stay on but was expelled together with her ardent camp followers. "Read the card," "Up the Republic" as the animated Jurr footed a plumper for the extreme left wing Republican Candidate. His aides deserted and disowned him on the spot. Polly and Jurr left the polling centre to loud cheers, a blow struck. Well you can't make a mistake in extremism.

It will be an ease to us when the damn election is over. The politician is a breed apart, never underestimate him when his back is to the wall; he is taken by obsessional pride, pride of family being paramount, and he wouldn't be averse to a timely family funeral cortège demonstrating what an important place he occupied in the affections of the people. Fear of the power of the politician exists too, similar to the power exercised by the priest and doctor (a hang over from witch-doctor-druid days), to that power exercised by the writer or even the simple satirical ballad maker who could on a bitter whim resulting from a slight, scarify one's self and one's descendants by a single apt line of marked song. Fear, overcome only by the bawdy humourist, who come to think of it was a type of high priest in his own right since being mythofacient by instinct, he could preserve you for good or evil in the formaldehyde of an anecdote; and when the passions of a people were roused, when their emotions were engaged, be it at election time or on wedding morning or law case, one needed to remember that the shutter was being clicked open on a highly sensitised film in the brilliant sunlight of vivid experience and that what one said or did at these times was for good or evil most highly memorable.

*

Take the case of Old Donovan and the salmon at election time. Salmon were a sore subject out by the estuary. Traditional fishermen there were agitated by two recurrent considerations: they considered an earlier opening to the season would benefit them, and the mark defining the point beyond which they were forbidden to fish was an irritant. Infringement of this mark was a recurring source of prosecution by Bailiffs with field glasses hiding in the dunes overlooking the estuary. Now Old Donovan, a seasoned wily ex-County Councillor, was asked by the Conservative candidate to help launch his campaign and speak in the little fishing village, this since Old Donovan's grandfather was a native of the place. A Republican law clerk heard that Old Donovan was on his way out so he decided to steal a march on the opposition and went out to the estuary the night before and addressed his own meeting there. The law clerk standing on the sea wall said: "Hard working salmon anglers of the estuary of the river Deen, two matters I know are causing you concern. My mission here to you can be expressed in two sentences; if this man beside me is put into Dáil Éireann the mark defining the fishing ground will be fired into the Atlantic and ye can fish from where

I spit into the water here, right across the Atlantic till stopped by the tall walls of Manhattan." Cheers! "And again, if my candidate is put in he'll see to it that ye can salmon fish from New Year's Day till New Year's Eve and the devil take the begrudgers." Prolonged cheers!

So this was the situation that Old Donovan faced and he detected hostility immediately at the river wall when he arrived in his car with his candidate as innocent as yesterday's lamb. Things got off on the wrong foot. The fishermen were closing a haul and one of the fishermen stepped down, took up a pool salmon by the tail and threw it at the candidate's feet, then crouching and rising he threw a second one at the feet of Old Donovan. "How much?" Old Donovan grated. "Ah, sure we couldn't charge you," he said, but Old Donovan lobbed a note on the wall and paid for the two salmon there and then. As they walked to the lorry to make the speech Old Donovan muttered, "The dearest thing you ever bought was to get something for nothing. That bastard would come into my shop next fair day, order groceries galore, and could I charge him? Wake up, Sonny Boy, if you want to make a politician. Wipe your mother's milk off your mouth." Up with them on the lorry. The crowd began to heckle them; defined mark and opening and closing days. He hadn't done his sums so he depended on Grá-Mo-Chroí, plamas and genealogy. No good! The heckling got worse. When someone imitated the release of wind from the human vent the whole bunch broke out into a loud sustained jeer. Old Donovan paused, then said wickedly. "There's more votes inside in Martin Street in town than in the whole of this scabby village. As far as I'm concerned ye can stick your votes up your arses."

It worked! As he was getting down off the lorry in high dudgeon they pushed him back up, apologised, said they'd listen in peace after all; if only for his Da's sake he should get a hearing. And the burliest net man present growled that if there wasn't silence he'd ram his fist down someone's gullet. Old Donovan recaptured a fair share of the votes. Anything for an anecdote, was the fisherman's cry. Old Donovan is a mythofacient kind of fellow and no mistake! Caught salmon this time, not caught trout. The tall walls of Manhattan. Tessarae of incident, anecdote and myth placed in a neat pattern adds up to an acceptable mosaic. And let it be known that if the truth is told every man jack in this burgh is mentally hammering out a bastard on the body of a beautiful but imaginative bawdy anvil.

*

That blasted siren! When it goes off no one can speak a word. Is there a second recount inside at the Courthouse? This place is always in trouble. A bundle of fifty votes noted under the table. Krrck, krrck. Saucepan on the sofa. By the way no harm. Not half. The slitted scrotum.

Round and round. Where shall I go? On the physical level, on the spiritual level, on the imaginative level? Countrymen and their sayings. A salmon by the tail. Chuck—chunk—the sound as the salmon hits the gravel at the candidate's feet. No matter who wins the election, saddler, you'll be stitching and I'll be scribbling on the board. Fine for some people. The sea trout are in the river—see the flag iris is in flower on the Inch. Do you remember the mill wheel, and the thousands of trapped trout when we knocked the floodgate and the iron wheel rumbled to a stop? Slash, slash with the wire sabers as we snatched the silver bars from the limestone passage behind the wheel. Oh boy! There is an urgency in my loins.

Hero Town paces onward to the summer solstice and still no sun. Henceforward alas the days will be shorter by a cock's step.

"Myself shocked," said Brigid McGrath. "Burned out by a blessed candle. Full of capernosity and function at 6 p.m. Homeless at 8 p.m. And no insurance. Husband in danger in hospital."

Dahlias appear on the altar vases. The priests push on regardless with the annihilation of any trace of emotionalism, remoteness or triumphalism. The introduction of the vernacular into the literature may mean the spaying and castration of Miss and Mister Mystery. Poignant guests these but doomed, male-like to a future without progeny.

How am I to come to terms with Weirdo-Town, Peter whispers. "Life is a jest and all things show it, once I thought it, now I know it." Where indeed do I stand?

"And as for you, Peter Mulroony, standing on the threshold of forty, the biblical two score: where are you headed for?" At least the Inseminator undignified in the small hours, blind and blotto, had some kind of a cockeyed ideal, inverted and perhaps perverted as it may have been. He did indeed possess some idea of introducing a solvent into your life. With every day that passes you can trace the trajectory of individual human breeding, seeding, feeding, being repeated over and over especially in the case of young women. You try to fix them in your memory as winsome toddlers, with deeper inflated rumps and before you know where you are, hey bloody well presto, the instant the last paper in the Leaving Certificate is finished up goes their hair, out go their boobs, back goes their rumps, and yipee, they are ready for the market, via the festival marquee, the giggling in the telephone booth, the "stop it, I love it, you're hurting me", lovely muffled scream of wantonness in the first of summer woods.

Dear foolish fond rather plaintively idiotic schoolmaster, children in awareness of human relationship on several levels, most of all on the awareness of the possibilities of the body, race past you, laughing over their shoulders in compassion, pity, mockery and provocation. What under Christ am I to make of it all? When that rich cousin of my mother's, his Rolls Royce at the door, looked at Margo and myself and asked, "Say, would either of you like to make your fortune in Pittsburgh?" you were both struck dumb. The hot nights of the American city would have broken that steel kennel somewhere inside of you. And would have set you free. Hot flushes would have singed you and set you growing luxuriantly. Is it any wonder I'm unable to

understand the semaphore of women and instead seek the comfort of
familiars?

Fingertips. Beloved pulpit. Snotty candles. Hilda in the head
and Madame Bovary, to mention a random few. Do these
imaginary more-than-friends, these straws at which a drowning
man will grasp, these masters of the imagination, indicate
psychosis? Of course they do. But the word psychosis encloses
such a vast variety of human behaviour that the label is
meaningless. For Pedday-you the condition argues that neurosis
is perhaps a better term to use in your case. And again, you must
never forget that the man who put his arms lovingly around your
neck at the consecration and said in a hoarse voice, "Peter, I am
stone mad but I'm pretending to be drunk," at this moment his
case provides a comforting parallel to yours. A dry out-of-season
north-east wind races through the midsummer sunshine of the
west side of the street and thereby deters people from visiting the
sea for oxygenation of the blood.

What other task did Margo ask me to do? I do my best to please her,
Peter mutters. Might as well be married as the way I am; all the
disadvantages of a woman with ne'er an advantage except a few
boiled potatoes and Limerick ham. I am lonely. I am a key of that
limited section of the human race that comes within my conspectus.
Half are women. Half therefore are locks, with none to fit my key. The
town is pounding down around my ears and stinks to high heaven
and low hell after a few hours under the summer sun. It's a whey day.
Giant tankards dribbling accidentally on purpose a black track up the
roadway near the great creamery dominating the western skyline and
the clear river pool where I learned to swim. Burrum, burrum, the
traffic throbbed. Hero Town, post post electionem mortem is salvaged
from ennui when a sudden frying pan fire almost trapped and grilled
three of its bestloved citizens. Hurray for the fire! We almost died of
boredom.

Stagger on, Hero Town. "You weren't at my father's funeral
then?"

"I never heard a word about it till I came back from Dublin."

"You were missed."

A reprimand. An unreasonable reprimand. The crime against society, against friendship, against compliment, against protocol will not be readily forgiven. Stay where you are, girl! He wouldn't bother his bones attending my father's funeral. Vote for him is it? He didn't vote for my dead father the day that he was burying. Not wishing her harm, but I hope she won't get that job—how could she be good and her old fella asleep, moryah, and my father's corpse passing the window. If he drew the blinds itself! Maybe now he has an allergy to incense. The sun blazes and boils! AH! The heat. The heat we are unused to. In the God house fine coloured gladioli blades plug rusted arum lilies. In Hero Town an old man complains. The most depressing feature of old age is impotency. Never again to be able physically to respond to the stimulus of rounded buttocks is a dire situation to be in . . . Ochon—O!

Escape! Go to the islands. Boffin. The Arans—set sail, to where the environment imposes intimacy. Last chance saloon! The islands.

Why so, Sir, tell me why you didn't promote my son? *Good Christ, not that again!* Go, Peter, like your namesake to the "Holy Land" of Peterborough in Ontario. Push out your boat like Robinson. Stray into the woods and desert Hero Town taking bag and baggage with you. Go Mulrooney, you cutjack.

JULY

*H*ero Town. *The wheel, the wheel, the wheel. Round and round. The Tumeltys always defied the town planners. Write a letter to the paper about the addition to their sprawling house. Call it a mockery of the Town Planning Act. Nothing stopped them before. Money talks.*

Are you stone mad? Do you want them to kill you? To batter in your head and leave you for dead in a sand hill to be found like a lost golf ball in the marram grass? Sshh! Play tough. Like a good man ignore them and don't mention the trees. Don't be rigorous, Ireland, an island, is insane. Hero Town. Bastard town. Snake town. Wicked bitch town. Florence Nightingale feckin' town. Fox town. Bull/bitch town. Benedict Arnold town. Slave town. Why do you begrudge a modicum of insanity to a small inbred community like this?

Peddah hearing that there was a brown flood in the river blundered out into the fine bright July morning in Margo's car to the upriver Castle Strand. With a rod and canister of blue headed worms given him by the last town farmer ploughing the adjacent school field, Peter was back in his youthful days when he fished with spillards. The floodwater yellow brown looked fruitful. Down the rutted track with its lodged water he went deliberately crushing cow parsley underfoot. The resultant smell was wonderful. The gurgling river lapped the beach stones in the glade. A perfect retreat. The baited hook waited on what the river had to offer. From the cascading falls downstream the spires of Hero Town came into view. Peter read the river well and Margo marvelled at the four speckled trout. On the dusty streets of Hero Town the current too ran deep. Peter knew the eddies, rocks and pools where other interesting fish lay watching and waiting. They in turn had to be reeled in gently.

"Give in that book you promised to old Joe when you're passing," Margo instructed.

"If I do his bloody half-bred hound-terrier will take the shins off me. Home rule—himself and the hound."

Knock, knock. "Is it me to marry and lose my independence?" muttered Joe, as he unlocked the door. "Are you daft? Tied to the likes of Bessie next door, coming back at 4 a.m. pissed drunk to God and the world, effing and blinding as she is lifted out of the car, and yet at 9 a.m. on the dot she is in her boutique, superficially the epitome of feminine discretion and suave sartorial elegance. I'm blind if she hadn't a love bite when she passed up yesterday, Peter. Sure what do we know about the feminine mystique? Female of the species. Marry? I'd rather my greyhound. Yes, in the bed. What the hell about it? Spring sleeps with me every night on top of the bedclothes. Except when the night is very cold, then I bring him under. He curls up and looks at me. He is a narra head. I daresay, some people would prefer a more warm natural dog but I wouldn't swop Spring for all the pedigree dogs of the Royal Kennel Club. Me get married? Well now, if Spring died I might give the idea a going over in my mind. At least I have company, unlike some! Thanks for the book."

At the corner Peddah meets Josephine, alert, untidy, yet gregarious. "Ped," she says, "open confession is good for the soul, and I'll admit that I have no fecking gift for housekeeping. Nor for scouring pots, nor emptying chambers that stink of ammonia, ugh, nor for sticking up rosy wallpaper, nor for pouring piss-coloured tea into dying aspidistras. I tolerate the very minimum of cooking and my culinary achievements rarely go beyond the boiling together of hairy bacon and green adorable cabbage. But, brother Ped, refined scholar, my too-tamed boyo, when it comes to observing the lonely, the hurt, the bewildered, the terror stricken who are walking straight into the net of craziness, I'm a bloody dinger. I'm whatever is the female equivalent of a maestro. In that direction, listen to me now. I, Josephine Prendergast, elderly spinster about to be crippled by sciatica, perform a most important civic function. I try most gently by a fingertip to direct, advise, assist, tip off a priest, maybe even a relative, to offer a deeply thought out word of praise to the lonely one. I am an expert diagnostician of emotions. Christ, I hit the jackpot every time! You'd laugh if I were to tell you the truly magnificent intuitive coups I have brought off.

"Tim? Tim and the parson? No, you never heard! That's because I'm discreet. I'm only telling you because you're tight. Up at Parson Gordon's making adjustments to the ballcock when the Parson suggested a nip of something warm and strong—he had a weakness in that direction—Tim as good a neighbour and plumber as ever you would find was missed in town. Up I went and found him spread out on the sofa, crooked to God and the world, a whiskey bottle in hand. The Parson no better, with a dirty boiler suit on him, down on his knees, trowelling cement into clock beetle holes at the side of the range and Tim shouting, 'Parson you might be able to pray and give sermons but you can't trowel for nuts.' Hushed it up I did and now Tim is back on the wagon, hasn't touched a drop in months. Took some doing. Bull's-eye, Pedday Boy. Jackpot! On the outside, tell the God's honest truth, I'm feck all good-looking. Don't bluster or apply cream to the cat's paws, leanbh bán. I'm too long in front of the looking glass to be deceived by the likes of that bastard of a crow with the skelp of cheese in his beak. But inwardly I've an accurate beautiful heart and a percipient old brain box. Up here. Look, I've told my fortune. Cogitate upon it. Tooraloo."

Peddah standing midstreet in the noonday heat viewed himself in the shop window with cautious optimism, white cotton trousers, safari coat, straw hat purchased in Puerto at a provocative angle, to the accompaniment of jibing Ha Ha! "Hot in your mate, Pedagogue, a proper Yank. You're looking summery, 'twould take little to have you throw off the balance of them." *Ah to hell, ignore it. It's all of a piece of the patchwork quilt of existence in Hero Town*, Peter thought as he walked deeper into the heat haze and sunglowed streets of the town convincing himself that he was again in Savannah, Georgia. "By God, this is what it feels like to be a native," he said to himself. Sweaty, dazzled and lazily ripe for natural mischief. Good Lord, am I never to dodge the bold Josephine? She approached again and stood abreast and with her shoulder against the red wall she let her eyes move slowly up to the jaunty tilt of his straw hat.

"Hmmm," she said by way of introduction to a tentatively lugubrious theme, "rakish is takeish! Sorry for interrupting you but what I often meant to ask you, Ped, supposin' only supposin' that you encountered a gamey young one in a back way of a warm night and that she indicated beyond a shadow of doubt her willingness, her eagerness even, to be as the old people put it taken aside, taken off her path, her willingness to sing a duet, to exchange taypots—to play hide-and-go-seek, what would your attitude to same be?

"Are you heeding me at all, or are you contemplating taking up music, gawking at the Jews Harp in the window? It might be the only thing you knock a tune out of. Answer?"

"The backway scutterises it, Jo. It deromanticises it. 'Twould want to be a sylvan glade before I would venture a decision on same."

"Sylvan shit, Ped."

"Now you're being vulgar, Empress Josephine."

"No, I'm being curious, Petereen. And curiosity is the biggest part of sex. How she'll squeal. How she'll surrender while shouting 'no' at the theatrical top of her voice. Out with the answer, Pedagogue. This day when cows udders are legging them as they run with the heat, this day when young maidens surrender their most precious possessions as a direct consequence of the subtle ministrations of Farenheit. Am I expressing myself with rectitude, schoolmaster of the hamlet? Feckin' well answer me directly even with brutality for I am consumed with curiosity as to whether you harbour in your pantaloons a round tower or an extinct volcano."

"Well, Pheeney, when an old native of this town at the biblical fourscore was asked the same question he said, I'd rather an egg, but if a blonde were to put up a proposition of an intimate nature to yours truly, perhaps with certitude I wouldn't disappoint the blonde."

"Good bloody man, that's all I wanted to know, Peter. I'll leave you now with your musical notions. Toorlaloo, ould cock, and I stress the appellation cock—and me neither illiterate or educated."

"No, Josephine, you're what is vulgarly termed One Quare Hawk."

"Second the motion, bastard."

"Seconded, Josephine. Progress reported, eh!"

"Progress reported."

*

Dearly beloved brethren. I have come amongst you married people to preach a new doctrine, to found a new joyous movement designed to reach the fuller life through the full physical enjoyment of Christian marriage—the Joyous Intercourse Society, Sustenance of Marriage—Jissom for short! My theory is simple: not even a fraction of the full enjoyment is being experienced by men and women bound together in the unity of marriage. All sorts of inhibitions keep them on a low level of understanding and carnal knowledge. It is my mission in life to offer them new vistas of enjoyment within the framework of Christian marriage, as we understand it. Jissom. Why should such an important part of the human experience be left to the porno rats, to the lice of the lewd? I am not ashamed to speak on a subject that has been traditionally a taboo.

Rrrats! Sketchem, Springboy.

A proliferation of sects. Cautious optimism. The Jehovah's Witnessess, and three fine scroungers of boys from Salt Lake City, are this minute whitewashing Mick Flanagan's yard. Up down! Up, down, dip, up down! All in the name of Yahweh or some such. The joyful society. Jissom. Empress Josephine. The quare hawk.

"The grace of Our Lord . . ." The priest turns from the lectern in the half empty church and continues the Mass. The offering of Peddah's particular sacrifice was tinged and tinctured by her presence, her slim presence, her graceful slender neck supporting her poised head, the way she entwined her fingers while praying, her lovely bold but fine features and above all by the smell of her perfume which he kept drawing in through his nostrils. Had she accidentally on purpose positioned herself next to him in the church? It was all so vague and involved acts and attitudes that could be denied covertly or if necessary overtly.

On the other side of him he sensed that Margo was aware: he was vaguely conscious of her barely detectable tension. The Mass went on. The first time he made a response aloud, he found he had a frog in his throat and he suffered the small shame of having to begin a second time. Did he detect the faintest flicker of amusement in her tightening of her entwined fingers as if she were quarreling against laughter? He made the other response in a low mutter or growl that if he were successful would have warned her against even the minutest flicker of hilarity indulged in at his expense. "Hmm!" he said inwardly. At the Consecration she was demureness and piety itself. As the moment for the exchange of the sign of peace approached she became fully aware. Margo joined them in awareness. It was not easy to define how

Margo indicated to Peddah and possibly to the girl the knowledge of her awareness, but all three of them, Peddah knew intuitively, were now in a state of keenest anticipation. When the priest skipped or forgot to extend the hand of peace, the tension ebbed. Out of an eye-corner Ped watched her narrowly file to the rails for Communion. The sign of peace? How would it have been, the touch of her hand, the texture of her finger and palm skin? The pressure—how would he have translated it into her emotion? How good an interferer would he have been? Or did she station herself there to disillusion him. To dismiss him, to rehearse a wedding ceremony with him as groom and her as bride. Let's pretend! Her light summer clothes indicated a certain measure of holy wantonness. Who had said a woman's mind oscillates between the altar and the boudoir? "Go in Peace. Amen." In the streaming sunlight of the open Diamond Peter is dismissed as groom.

*

Knock. Knock. The knuckles of the small hand whiten on the oak-grained door of the house on the edge of the town. "Who is it?"

"It's me, Father."

"Who're you?"

"It's your daughter Minnie, home from Minneapolis."

"Shit off!"

"Now, Father, listen. This is your daughter Minnie with her four children, home from Minneapolis for the first time in twenty years. My married name is Johansen. I've four lovely children outside in the car. Open the door, Father, let me in."

"Shit off. I don't want any of ye."

"Now, Poppaw. This is my home. This is where I was born. This is where I left to go out to my First Communion. This is the house in which my mother died. You must let me in, Poppaw."

"I told you to shit off or I'll give you the contents of this gun."

"Poppaw, what are you saying? You're my father. When I was small you had a nickname for me, Bitter Ball. My first time home in twenty years. It's not the money, Poppaw. I've got enough money to stay in the best hotel in town. I've got more money than is enough for all of us. Take the bar off the door and please let us in. You hear me, Poppaw? I'm tired after the plane. One of the children is frettish. The taxi is watching. Please, let me in. Don't shame me in front of my own people.

"That's no way to carry on, Poppaw, I did nothing to you. You were a hard man on us but that was your nature, and whatever happened you're still my father. That can't be wiped out. You hear me? I'm your daughter and I have your temper too. Are you listening with your ears? I'll get a rock and smash the window and break down the door. I've been thinking of this for twenty years and no one is going to come between me and my home."

"Shit off or 'twill be worse for you."

"All right, Poppaw, I'm now getting a big stone off the fence and here it is—right through the window."

Crash! "Fire now, you cowardly bastard. Fire if you like, you mad whoor with your rusty gun. And here's another, and another. . . . by Jesus Christ I'll pull the throat out of you. You don't know me. You don't know me. A nice homecoming . . . That's better. I knew you'd open it. Put down your gun, Poppaw! Let me put my arms around your neck. Don't cry, old man. I'm still your flesh and blood. You . . . you twisted over on my mother like a cock'd treat a hen yet you wanted my mother. A 'stail'—a moment aware. And out of your seed I was conceived. Oh Poppaw! Kiss my open mouth. Dear dear dear and beautiful Poppaw. Tell me I'm welcome home. Oh, Poppaw, Poppaw."

The voices drift in the gallery of Peddah's skull.

"Peddah? Where are you going for your summer holidays? Abroad again? With you know who? You're a glutton for punishment. No? Let me tell you so where you're going, Peddah, old son. You're going as far as Sweeney's boxes, the yellah whiskey boxes that are put out in front of the pub. And you're going to take your seat there, side by side with the old publican who thinks he can sing, a voice like an onion fart struggling to be free from between two fat arsed cheeks. And that ex-railroadman back from the States who has more years than sense watching and sniping at all the passers-by."

"What age would he be," she asked? "He'd be two years older only his father was bashful. Let you be making up that on your fingers."

"Menfolk! Spare me."

"What hurry is on you? Sit here, girl, and let the world pass," Peter voiced as she went off in a pure conundrum.

*

"Cuckoo, Peter, Cuckoo."

"Hello, Bat, sit in here beside me on this box and tell me all. Christ, I nearly forgot, how's herself now?"

"Oh, yes. La Leche! The breast, Peter, the breast. And the sense of touch that is bloody well primal. The delicate innocent, unhurting, nails of an infant, idly curled on the hillock of the mother's breast. I have a tendency to stray, Peter. There I am in the hospital. A routine job for Mary—the wife. "I've a class of a lump there,' she said, pointing to a place under her arm and to the front, what you'd say in the foothills of La Leche. The man over in Fair Street said too innocently altogether, "Next time you're in Dublin show that to the doctor just to ease your mind." It didn't register with me high up or low down. Someone mentioned the word mastitis: what heifers have, Peter, you know the old radio is never done giving out the pay about it in cattle, cures for it and all that. So there I am in the ward standing at the foot of the bed, class of ashamed of the gallstones woman in the other bed, proud as punch showing off her stones in this cellophane packet to all and sundry. Blood too like you'd see in a white enamel tray after it had been used for showing liver in a butcher's window. I couldn't bear to look at the fecking things. True for the man who said that women are more biological than men. Urine, blood, phlegm, pus, bowel motions—the waters breaking before childbirth—all that bloody jargon is right up their alley. I'd run a mile from it. In that class of situation I can stand back and see myself as plain as a shagging pikestaff being supremely awkward, a fish out of water, no idea what to do with my hands sort of wishing they were cut off at the wrists. Herself Mary looking fine all dolled up in the bed in her cash-and-carry yellow nightdress, as gay as a noinín when the two doctors came in. "We've done the broosy,' they said in quiet tones, 'and the tumour is malignant.'

"It didn't strike me for a minute or two. Benign malignant, malignant benign. Carcinoma, cancer. Conquer Cancer. It was a long time sinking in, Peddah. We looked at one another, Mary and myself. God help her she had always been terrified of it but she went to great pains to cover it up, to lead me on false trails. She'd admit to any pain on God's earth except to one that could be understood as that. Jesus. A while to sink in. Mary's face twisted in a way I've never seen it twist before. Like a house falling. The tears came. She began to cry out brokenly. She wouldn't be mutilated. Not go to the incurable ward. To be bombarded by radium. She'd let it run through her. They brought her niece."

It was hot, boy it was hot in the sultry afternoon haze of the Twelfth. No Lambegs here, only the clop of the hooves of the horses drawing the caravans bearing pseudo-gypsies from Montmartre echoing down the quiet streets. The locals knew the tourists liked to be saluted so they saluted and benedictioned the passers-by most lavishly. International and national sets of summer strangers, families on holidays, street strolling in Hero Town gawking upwards at shop fronts. The striding man in the coloured sweatshirt and fringed shorts led the white horse, child astride, as the wife perched on the stool in the caravan doorway guided the reins. Clop clop. "God bless ye," said the voice at the corner—"they like that ould shit." But some of the salutations were sincere. Later in the welcome shade of the church the family pointed and whispered, "Why they change? Why they tumble down the high altar? Only a slab is needed."

"In the hospital she put her arms around her and cried for a while and said, 'Aunt Mary!' The niece—she was a doctor in the maternity close by. 'It isn't such a terrible thing. We have it every day. You'd be troubled if it hit you when you were younger. But now it defeats itself at your age.' It was strange to see the young woman drop her professional self and become her crying domestic family self. La Leche. I left them there, the screens drawn, their arms around each other. After a time she came out into the green corridor with the statue of Luke and said, 'It's all right now. She's willing to go through with the treatment.'

*

On reflection Peter concludes that the inconsequentiality of life could be magnetic in an impish kind of way. Always on the outskirts of communities there are insane pockets of humanity. Four or five households of what the world would stigmatise as deprived people, but who in their own eyes are confident of immortality because they keep finches, make bodhrans, have skills at poaching, and harbour eccentric individuals. Shards of humanity that glinted in any light, these were special cases of course. They too responded to the heat of summer, each in his or her individual fashion. Just then the ultimate fiddler of the Glaise, which was a huddle of cottages once thatched now oversheeted with galvanised iron, took to his bed and refused to get up. Ever a gambler on horses, he complained that there was an outbreak of coughing in his stable and that he and his old grey mare of a sister who occupied a separate stall under the same roof should now be marked Aged in the race card of Life!

*

Peter passed on smiling a little fearfully through Hero Town. Fearful of the reception Margo would give to the clutched goodies in the paper bag. A marble cake. Margo eyed it quizzically when she unwrapped it and placed it skeptically and disdainfully in the bread bin. Peter reflected that a woman priding herself on being a housewife can clearly convey contempt, amusement, tolerance, pity, hatred, love, disdain, even jealousy by the manner in which she places, hurls, casts a bought or brought shop cake in her bread bin.

"Hey! Hey! Mutt."

"Me, Babe?"

"Yes! You, Peter! With each day that passed you are descending into the nethermost galleries of eccentricity."

"Would you say so, Babe?"

"Would I say so? I know so. I'm not blind. Christ man, go'way and get interested in The Thing."

"An rud?"

"An feckin' well rud. There's nothing else in life except an rud. Listen, schoolteacher, who can teach but cannot learn: the male like the female is subject to hormonic—is that the correct word, Scholar mine—hormonic cycles. I represent what is called the vulnerable sex—you the Masterful. Oh Holy Jerusalem—what a miserable specimen of that same you are. Peter, you're a hypnotised hen—with your head under your wing. Snap out of it. Flap your wings. Take flight. Buzz like that wasp on the windowpane. An Rud!"

"Lower your voice, Babe."

"I'd tell you what to lower if I feel like it."

"Touché!"

"I have an idea what that signifies; don't think that because you shout two twos are four that the rest of us are dullamoos, boobs and simpletons. An Rud! Slan leat and indeed as the vodka said to the cocktail mixer, you're no great shakes."

Swish! Hit! Felled! The stunned cruising wasp fell down over the

check white and blue haunch of a horse's collar in the saddler's shop.
Peter beaten and bested in a verbal duel was now in imagination the
last white Anglo Saxon Protestant lying not flying, stunned in the
undergrowth of a century of a saddler's tackle. Fly to the islands Peter
told himself, if only for sanity and peace.

Peter strolled away the mid-July days with families on holidays
struggling on the warmed streets, his mind repeatedly engaged by
the word peppermint. Engaged? Surely the word he sought was
obsessed. Peppermint—An Rud. "On the point of the
peppermint," an expression the Victorian lady used describing
adolescent males. The Hypnotised Hen. Pepper-mint. Taste-
smell. Smell-taste. Peppermint.

If he were to leave Hero Town, Peter cogitated on what he
would miss most. The daily minor entertainments, incidents,
confidences and the soothing comforting familiars he called his
own. He didn't delude himself. He refused all substitutes no
matter how exotic. He rejected all imitations. He would accept
nothing except the real product.

Am I not product myself? The blacksmith had fashioned me on his
anvil, the farrier's red iron shoe was smoking on my hoof. The harness
maker had cut me out of a half-hide of leather, the joiner had taken
me as raw tree trunk to the sawmill, had turned me into planks half-
planed, dovetailed and mortised me. I was stone under the masons
chisel, wet plaster under the plasterer's trowel, clay under the spade of
the peasant, the grain of wood decorated me as the painter plied his
oiled rag on the door of my personality. I was wood, stone, clay, milk,
water in its thousand alibis, to be shaped, carved, cast, woven, fitted,
branded, frozen as ever since infancy as the environment had insisted.

How utterly unspeakably lovely it was to be able to trudge for a
few hundred yards and meet the comicals of another human being.
Words and images that wing on a flight of fancy without any
conversational frame of reference whatsoever.

I was born on the side of a street, Peter told himself, and there I'll
die. Well, well old Hero Town, with your corralled menagerie of

ponies, wasps, hens and hounds, you never cease to cause me pleasure,
interest and astonishment with the pattern of behaviour you form.

"Where did you say you have the shingles, Oonagh?"

"Up along the inside of my right thigh and up to here, herpes
zoster or some such."

"You must give me a closer look at them sometime, Oonagh."
Off she goes gagging with lascivious laughter, the mildewed lust
overcoming the sense of annoyance engendered by the diagnosis.

It was all part of life in Hero Town even if at times unbalanced.
Stripped to its essentials it reveals a hilarious insane human
beauty.

Humanity—hilarity—indelibility!

Whatever you do, don't bring up the felling of the trees by
those brutal politicians, that's barbarism in civic affairs. "You
know something, Peter, I think you're clean gooky."

"That's your privilege, friend."

Before Peter could develop the theme, a cobweb of
conversation and prayer, the rosary at Fennells' encircled him.

*

"In the name of the Father, Son, . . . kneel down, Sonny, we'll
offer up the Rosary for Uncle Mick, he's in some part of America.
I couldn't tell you where, Peter boy, we didn't get a line from him
in the past fifteen years, so whether he's dead or alive it's hard to
say. . . and of the Holy . . . Almighty God will you catch that
child before she falls headlong into the fire and we'll have to shift
her to the Bon Secour, . . . and of the Holy Ghost, Amen. . . . I
believe in God the Father Almighty . . . Almighty Father who's
that east in the vet's white car, would the Jersey heifer have slung
by the fellah above, Good God we don't know what's before us
from day to day, like the year '54 when my mother died and our
fine cow was lost in a bog hole that same year."

*

"Oh Jesus Christ, who suffered sore on Calvery's cursed hill, what will they do with the flesh itself. Cuckoo! The actual flesh that comforted me, that excited me, that consoled me, that made me sane when I was stark staring mad. Is it against all laws, Peter, to ask the surgeon where it had gone? Is it put into the incinerator? Mary's breast. Breast of the Mother of God that comforted and fed the Infant Christ. My Mary's breast. Or did they bury it in the nun's graveyard at the back of the convent. Where will she find it, Peter, when she rises on judgment day. I walked the shaggin' corridor, Peter. As true as God. And my own inadequate or shameful man's breast winced vicariously when I thought of the knife slicing off such loveliness. Such a source of entertainment. Some said it would putrefy. Putrefy on her body or off it. That's the choice.

"Will she miss her power to console? The comfort. To make sane. These are the things that bother me, friend. I drove the car home in a dream. May Christ comfort us in our hour of need. She lay mutilated, my most beautiful of women, Mary. Well named after the little Jewess of Nazareth. Blessed was she among women. Pray for us. Up to this the forays of death were wan and inadequate, horsemen on the horizon of the imagination, no more. Now I hear the deafening thunder of hooves. And now the riding boyo grows more arrogant with each moment that passes. Le Leche, the peppermint, the early morning laughter of lust. Chances missed. Don't miss a single chance, Peter, or when you're old like me you'll regret it. Every hour of every day. The image of the severed breast continues to intrude. . . and to think there were Amazons who cast them off entirely lest their pendulousness impede. Ah. Weren't the Celts obsessed by the image of the severed head? All this while a Virgin somewhere sighs in anticipation of the advent of a tall seducer.

"Mark my words, Peter, next thing they'll do is go floggin' the sanctuary lamp. As sure as God it's solid silver. Could be it's worth thousands of pounds. Down with triumphalism they shout. 'Hey, Father, hold on there. Five years ago if you ate a black pudding on a Friday or asked why should a Mass be in musty Latin you were excommunicated. Now if you don't guzzle meat, profess the authenticity of Protestant baptism you're an outcast. Didn't Father Keating standing on the altar steps strike a saintly pose saying, 'Pope Paul is carrying his cross of dissention up the Calvary of Renewal. The pastor of this Parish too is carrying his cross. Dissention over the updating of the altar.' Hell, who's crucifying the Pope but the clergy? Oh boy, good old fashioned lovely lust masquerading as dogma. Create animation. Cry, 'I've been robbed, come on Mary. Let's go sweetheart to Prince Edward Island.' If he goes on like this I'll stand up and shout. 'Leave our bloody altar alone! Hands off it you barbarian. What do you know about it anyway? Remember the Mass Rock and the beggar priest? Boy, who needs renewal? You!' "

"Glory be to the Father, and to the Son and to the Holy Spirit . . . Amen. Now, that didn't take too long, Peter."

*

Hero Town lived on. Peddah wearied, the black ghost of vertigo flapping his wings on the murky horizon nostrilised the oxygen at the seashore wall. "I'm getting languish in the head. I'm sighing all day. No energy," Peter told himself. This infernal heat would prostrate a horse. We're not used to this. The sun does something to us here. At the base of the cliff walk in the recessed bathroom, Seán prepared the seaweed bath. Green, green, green the walls. The "dúlamán" seaweed robbed of its virility is now a bathfull of hot viscous vaseline solution. Peter toe-tests it. Watch the step. In the old-fashioned metal tub the raised cow mouth fingers drip webs in the air. The seavite solution snots the steaming water. Lave, lave the body with an improvised loofah of seaweed. Massaaaage . . . Lave . . . Sensual! Oh Lady Chatterly's mother! Massage the trunk all over. Lean back. Sink deeper into the iodine pool. Peter is now truly a hypnotised fly. Life begins in the sea and nature is born again.

*

Stories still sieved through Hero Town gathering momentum in the heavy summer heat.

"You're sunburned, Maggie Mary."

"Why wouldn't I be with weather like this?"

"Anywhere a bus is going I'll hop aboard it. Any place where no one knows me."

"And then you let your hair down."

"We'll let that hare sit for here's down a bastard I must give a telling off to now."

"Don't get me involved, Maggie May." .

"Stand your ground, Peter. Excuse me, you, Mr Bobbet."

"Me, Miss?"

"Yes, you."

Under breath Peddah mutters: "When Christ shall come with shouts of acclamation, and take us home, what joy shall fill my heart. Don't involve me in this slagging match."

"What do you mean by coming round that corner the night before last and touting for other people in the town? You're a stranger that's just after walking in here and taking on the airs and graces of an old native."

"Touting? What do you mean by touting? Explain yourself, woman, I never touted in all my life!"

"If you didn't do it before you had a promising beginning. Those four Yanks had booked into me for bed and breakfast the other night and you collared the last one of them and said under your breath, 'Don't stay there; stay over at the hostelry across the Diamond.'"

"I did no such thing!"

"Are you a liar along with a tout?"

"Neither one nor the other. The woman going in your door

turned and said, 'Where is a good place to stay?' And understanding you were full she asked me. And I just mentioned the hostelry."

"Of course you did, you just . . . and if you give a repeat performance I'll just fix your bloody wagon, mischief-maker, touter, upsetting decent old stock of the town.

"Look at him go! That softened his cough, Peter. Tell me now, Peter, did I make a holy show of myself at the Miss Normoyle dinner last week? I'll tell you this, and I mean every word of it, there wouldn't be half the mental breakdowns in Ireland if certain backward individuals would only come out of their cubbyholes and get pig-arsed drunk for a change. 'Tis true for me!"

Lord my God, when I in awesome wonder consider all the Universe divine . . . What misfortune I had to stop to talk to Maggie May!

*

The year tiptoes out beyond the halfway mark in the march of life. The gun lap has gone.

Take stock, Peter. The thing is. . an rud . . . the thing. Identify the enemy. Not the church, not the state, for these the enemy seeks to influence or neutralise. The enemy is the progenitor of pseudo-progress, the destroyer of the loved old and beautiful, the feller of trees, the uprooter of old pavements, the closer of old pathways, the eradicator of salmon, the breaker of sanctuaries, the filler of walls in the name of updating all who do not crown graft on to the stick that is old. Beloved church turning treacherous in Hero Town. The noise engendered by the milk trade in our fecking cow stall.

The exultant summer strides on. The church row hots up. The medieval pulpit is again invoked. It will leave scars, deep half-healed parochial scars, the dust off your shoes formula and routine. As you said, there's too much democracy in Ireland. Indeed, Father, amend that to say there's too much pseudo-democracy in Ireland. Mazarin, His Eminence arises. A meeting will be held at the Community Hall on Tuesday night next to consider the various plans for the architectural reorganisation of the sanctuary. (Formelum, formulae, formula.) So that the parishioners will feel free to speak no one of the parochial clergy will attend. Trapped. The meeting was of the following opinion, Father. They don't want the High Alter removed. Trapped. Here comes the long lash of the pulpit across our backs. Crack. A vociferous minority sensing dissension in a peaceful parish. The Pope now bears the stigmata boom of dissension. Hold on there, Father, who objected to the appointment of the last Bishop? The laity? Cripes no, Father, but the clergy. The bishop bears the stigmata of dissension. Did you hear what I'm after saying, Father, 80 per cent, that a majority. Polish up your Maths, and weren't the other 20 per cent instigated by your white mice lads that do be whispering phone messages to one another all day and all night. Jesus, this is gas!

Arum lilies on the altar. They mean death. Burrum—that's the altar down. They portended the death of the altar. To some it was a portent of the death of trust and faith. Father, you're a counterpart of the Empress Josephine with all your ecclesiastical duplicity.

Sir, I condemn this attitude of yours, bell, book and candle.

No doubt you do, Father. But tell me, isn't your bell automated, your book out of print, and your candle still has no stick? What are we but hypnotised hens pecking at coloured marble cake! Off with you now, Father, and examine the faeces of your lean greyhound so as to determine his evening form on the track. Short odds I hear— but if he is baulked on the bend?

Dear Dean,

While you were away in Peru a couple of roman-collared tyrants made flitters of our parish. Do you know what'll be the end of updating the Church? The Eucharist will be on sale in tins in the supermarkets. Ochon O, the lovely altar which we were brought on to after being baptised, where we made our First Communion, where we were married and where our bodies will repose after death, gone, tumbled down. Bollocks the tradition bearers! We're out of our noodles, off centre, not the full shilling nor the full round of the clock, each man jack of us clear and clane fully insane, squatting for ever on a rusty Egyptian Elsan portable lavatory gazing down over our semi permanent eyelashes at, An Rud, with a Vanner & Prest clock strapped to our severed wrists toying with the idea of love biting a virgin. Tick, tock goes the clock of eternity while we endeavour to establish a veracity of sorts. Tick, tock. The tradbearers, hump 'em. The Knights and their likes worm in wood.

Christ is taken down from the cross.

Christ is taken down.

Concerned Parishioner.

*

Beloved Brethren, tonight we will offer instruction on how to make a 20 per cent minority appear as a majority. Nothing up my sleeve. Dial Hero Town.

"Is that you, Mick?"

"That's me, Sir Brud and Dear Knight."

"We missed you from the meeting. We wore the bibs. About the bother in the place below. The fellow who came down advised the following. Put out the word that the stone is decayed. Might fall on some priest or even somebody at the rails. Let it be known that a German architect said the sanctuary was a monstrosity . . . don't mind the buts, didn't he call meetings off the altar. Oh for God's sake, they have to be made think they are being consulted. They have to be allowed to let off steam, to vent the cask, pass on the word. By the way, that niece of yours, she's past the post for the school job, as none of us trust that historic schoolmaster. Pull the snaffle. Is that the term? You're on the Library Committee. Stir it up for him."

"I'll go with anyone anywhere," says Maggie May. Solid silver the sanctuary lamp but mark my words, you'll see it in a Grafton Street window one of these days.

Get interested in An Feckin' Well Rud, Peter. An pillywilly. Or you'll be whipped a cripple. I warned you, scholar. Allow me to remain your humble and obedient servant.

AUGUST

The year is waning fast. Stop, galloping horse of time! My boot is caught in your stirrup and I'm being dragged along the rockstrewn road of the advancing years. The photographer in Peter pulls back and views in the zoom lens the manifestations and activities so as to examine town and self. No flowers now on the alternate altar. The emotional florial gem-encrusted sanctuary is suddenly become Protestant-bare.

"Look, you begrudging begrippin' bastard that wouldn't give in and admire or admit, I say that the cleared sanctuary with the high altar vanished into the thick air of parochial recrimination is not as bad as you had anticipated. Now now, admit and concede begrudgingly."

The world is a series of vibrations. Vibrating waves of sound, light and pulsing ripples of tiny particles that pound "Napper Tandy" on drums of seeing, hearing and smelling.

Ah, but the women stakes, how shall I enter, how shall I win, Peter asks himself. The power resident in his fingertips, if only he had the courage to use them as intuition tells him to use them, to stretch out his hand and with those fingertips to caress the side of a girl's nose, gently, gently as one would caress a restive young mare.

Whoa, filly, whoa!! Stand still! I mean nothing; I mean everything. Whoa—that's the girl. There in the north of that island with its lava flanks Garachico took my fancy. I could have shacked up there, if

that is the correct trans-Atlantic term, with an understanding
woman and that suitcase of disparate references that produced a
history of my area could have been dumped into the sulphuric
cauldron of Mount Teide.

Weariness suddenly takes over in the neighbouring town
festooned with visitors, out in the open air of race time with its
galloping hooves. The most tiring game on God's good earth with
its recurrent excursions at half-hourly intervals. Every post a
winning post. The trudging through crowds to the tote window
to place a bet and, if lucky, to draw the resultant winnings. Like
a fall into a chasm the early walk to the car and there to encounter
an independent fellow sitting on the bonnet.

"Is this your car, Sir? Any chance of a lift to Hanrahan's Cross?"

"Okay. Hop in. Bang the door easy. Shove that stuff aside.
You're a country man?"

"That's right. But I lives in the town now. I was taught by
Master Abbott, did you ever hear tell of him?"

"Cleandrahan?"

"The very place. I was the dunce of the class but I am well able
to make out now."

"Expand on that."

"You mean for a living, what I does in the round of a week say?
Sure amn't I a man for all seasons. That's the name of a fillum. I'm
a gardener, a handyman, a dishwasher; I can turn my hand to lots
of things."

"Start with Monday."

"Yesterday I went up to the new bungalows in Casement Villas,
picked stones and concrete out of the lawn, that and a bit of
digging, heavy gardening they calls it, child's play to me. Pays
well, with the best of grub thrown in. That's the first go-down.
The digging stands me a few quid too and at night-time I go
down for the Pines of Nevada, the pop group that plays in the
Dunes Hotel three nights a week. I unloads and sets up their gear
in the Function Hall. They know I'm not a drinking man so they

tips me. The Manageress doesn't see me short at the end of the night either when I cleans up after the crowd. It all adds up. It would be a poor day I wouldn't clear thirty pound all told, even if it stopped at that.

"Have you relations here about?"

"I have an aunt a widow in Ballylyne, if there's slackage in town I goes up to her. She has two and a half acres of land. Building sites. Her family forgot her but she's good to me."

"Tell me this, you needn't answer if you don't like. Do you draw the dole?"

"Every Thursday as regular as the clock. I'm not regularly employed you see."

"I see."

Almighty God, education how are you. This iron fool draws more than myself, free of income tax.

"One last question. Do I have to pay you for riding in my car?"

"Not at all, Sir, sure it's a pleasure to be with a man like yourself! But you must admit I'm well able to make out."

"You are indeed. Is this Hanrahan's Cross?"

"The very place, Sir. Would you be wanting this old football cap on the back window?"

"Not at all. Take it with you."

"Good day to you, Sir."

A great man to make out! He deserves the George Cross so he does, for bravery in the face of life.

*

Stuck together, our lives and our dwelling places. A benediction, a malediction, valediction, this is Hero Town. We live in one another's pockets, urban marsupials, squirrels in a cage, that's what we are here. The telephone exchange knows all things, lost, hidden and to come.

"When we want a holiday, Sir, we go off to desert places or big cities like Birmingham where no one knows us.

"Mark my words, now that they're nabbing all the salmon in the sea you'll see that river below, for which hundreds of fine poaching gaffers were transported to Van Diemens Land, without the fin of a fish in its waters before long. And, if you breathe one word about factory or sewage pollution the cry is raised, 'It's making money for the town isn't it?'

"You have your fine job, Peter Mulrooney, talk is cheap, and you don't give a rambling damn whether my son is in the Bronx or in Pimlico. Or my daughter but as little.

"I can't stand talking here all the evening.

"I have to go back to the convent to mind old Sister Scholastica for the night. Ninety one, as old as a bush, but she's like a baby to me. I kept her alive for the last three years. And what harm but she refused me the Child o' Mary Medal thirty years ago and I a girl in the Fourth Book. Said I was too wild. And I'm the one left out of them all to feed her and clean her. And those she held up as models to me felt uneasy if men weren't in the saddle. At times when she snaps out of her dotage she's ready to piss poison and fart fire. Now the same bitches are having bastards by the new time. It's a queer world. I give up, Oh Holy Catholic and Apostolic Church, and by the same token, Master Peter, the sanctuary isn't so bad, is it?"

Blast you woman, it's vile!

*

In church an American priest reads a florial Mass on Sunday: beginning in Our Lord Jesus Christ. In the sermon he refers to the government you are rejecting in the current election. Who is he, himself and his florial Mass? He's Joe Tagneys son from Awnahowen. Back from Florida. Florida Mass—ha ha. Listen: if he read a quiet sleepy Mass like that in the States, he'd last a week and they'd pack him home to the Pope's green Island. Is he the fellow who was caught last year illegally netting salmon? The very man. When the case came up the Super said he had gone outside the jurisdiction of the court. Could they serve him with the summons now? That's not the way things are done in Ireland. Come here till I tell you: I think he's swinging. What's swinging? He's about to leave the church. Getting married? He came home to make up his mind. I have it from the stable—his mother is throwing off the clothes. Wouldn't you think the women'd leave him alone?

Black, black yet aromatic saucepan on a sofa. Eh? Eh? Kuche not Kirche. Madame Bovary rules again! But not in the parish in one of the villages in the hinterland of Hero Town where an eccentric priest is addressing his flock.

Dearly beloved brethren,

I wish to call your attention this morning to the fact that a new maternity nurse—midwife is a term you'd understand better I suppose—has been appointed to this parish. Stand up there now, Mrs Jackson, until everybody sees you. That's right! All see her? Turn around, Ma'am, and face the people—let them have a good look at you. You can sit down now, Ma'am.

Mrs Jackson will take up duty on next Wednesday morning, the first of the month. I hope that her services will be fully availed of by those lawfully and morally entitled to call upon them. To go further, I hope that the good lady will be run off her feet day and night by the young matrons of the parish. The population here is falling; the schools will likely be amalgamated if the averages fall much further—ye all know what that means. I was appointed to this Godforsaken mountainy parish as pastor and Shepherd which in diocesan circles is reckoned a penitential station by the man with the tall hat and the sheepstick, with instructions "for God's sake try and rouse 'em up. They're the most backward crush in the four walls of Ireland."

Insulted is it! God love you! The congregation was delighted. The old fella was in rare form today putting on a special act to impress and bewilder the new maternity nurse whose business is to deliver infants into the world leaving mother and child sound in wind and limb after confinement and delivery are over. The Gospel is silent on pre-natal and post-natal care extended to a certain child born in a stable or whether the foster father of the child who was present was of the slightest assistance in the very intimate and miraculous occasion.

Um—bi—il—icus! That's the Latin word for the navel. Laugh away! It indicates the standard of intelligence I have to cope with here. I judge a midwife by the condition in which she leaves an infants' navel. I want no more laughing now—I'm deadly in earnest. If the midwife knows her job, the infants' navel should not protrude. Nor should it resemble the entrance to a rabbit burrow. Keep laughing. The reason I bring up this subject is this. I was unlucky in my time. When I was born my mother was attended by that medieval survival which I am doing my part in routing out of the parish—a handy woman.

"Handy", Krrk! Prrp! Awkward woman would be a better name for her. If ye saw the navel she left me! Laugh away! I'll prove my case. I'll strip off this chasuble. And lift up this albe. There it is now. A navel you could hang your hat on!"

Peter-son, the authentic story of the Holy Roman Catholic Church in a remote rainy, mountainy parish in South-western Ireland has yet to be recorded. Don't get me wrong; I'm not being derogatory—complimentary if anything. What would the unfortunate benighted parishioners in such an environment do without their beautiful entertaining eccentric parish priest?

Without diversion of some sort the people would go stark raving mad. So the sermon on Sunday is a One-Man Show. The priests in the neighbouring parishes are jealous—they haven't a good word for this man. Let me tell you this . He's my bloody man! He's a champion! He's a masterpiece! He's lost out there! His likes couldn't be found in any country, in any clime. He's an out-and-out winner from trap to line. Snap, crackle and pop. A masterpiece. Yahoo!

*

Later en route to the bank, the booming voice of yet another US cleric, a former classmate back on holiday, beckoned Peter.

"So you never got married? Well, well. Here you are by choice, a total abstainer in the sexual lounge bar while in the States it's reckoned an enormous deprivation among us clergy. O my Gawd, keep me continent for this day! Young women, especially when the first hot days of summer arrive, intuitively sensing your weakness as a man come into the confession box and whisper, whisper, whisper, all the while watching your face for a betrayal of your inner and tried self. 'This will give him a sleepless night,' and 'Oh Lord be merciful to me a sinner' at one and the same time.

"Nature is funny. One of our guys ordained the same day as myself in Our Lady of the Woods outside Chicago left the priesthood and went off with a big-arsed blonde. Christ man, I told him, shack up with her but don't marry her. Didn't take my advice. Now he's broken and alone. He writes to me, complaining that the life he looked for has evaded him.

"It hasn't evaded me, I told him. It's a struggle but I'm holding out. Pitching good-looking young Irish country lads newly ordained into complex situations—O my God what a crime! The priests are on the green. They march along the deep. Strange to say they are playing a role and living in reality at one and the same. They seem to be a way unto themselves. What are we all but great men to live."

*

If ever the schoolmaster thought of school during the holiday period, he did so with a mounting sense of unworthiness and trepidation that the twin summer courses he attended for the secondary purpose of gaining six extra holidays to be taken when he wished did precious little to dispel. And why? Because nothing would do the Irish education authorities at these gatherings but to introduce and transfer the wackiest theories and ideas of

American professors that were often failed experiments in their own educational terrain holus-bolus into the Irish context. Peter listened to the outpouring of educational heresy, scholastic gobbledegook and to the regurgitation of words and phrases like the skewness co-efficient, ethnocentric blindfold in the company of the twins Homoscolastic and Heteroscolastic Error, all bastard sons of the linguistic company born of an incestuous relationship. What in the name of God the Holy Ghost this has to do with a snotty nosed or pampered child looking up to Peter for education disguised as entertainment, he could never fathom. Peter-he went along with it of course knowing in his heart that the story was king thus denying in tacit approval the valid presence of Christ in the Eucharist of his educational day. Even denying the holiness of the child shouting out why the Emperor is naked . . . He did worse than tacitly approve, for as chairman of a lecture he introduced one of these phrase jugglers in terms profound, erudite and lavish in flattery. Et tu, Petre? Before the cock crows thou wilt have denied me thrice. Which he did.

In the street outside the lecture hall in Hero Town, a tall Swissman led a restive procession of six horse-drawn caravans up through the traffic in the narrow street, holding in his clasped fist a string of mushrooms. A clasher of perfect cup mushrooms standing in green, green grass that has thrust upwards from an old cowpat was one of the loveliest sights possible and marked a delightful peak of summer for Peter.

*

Was life passing Peter-me by? Inexorably by. Feminine mystery continues to remain a mystery. Intuition is of course a series of leaps from stepping-stone to stepping stone. Peter the Petrified. Remember, base coward, how when the young woman in the midwest, high on champagne, who acted most lovingly towards you, moaning subsonically as her head caressed your upper sleeve was challenged by you to say something, O my fine brave man.

A man who in an empty house will prance naked from room to room in the free summer morning throwing himself on the flat of his back on a bed in sham abandon, answered her bitterly saying, "That's only the champagne talking now." Her wounded eyes. And then, Peter, you were pulled away by a young woman in a dance dress so bare that only two lace cups of love upheld her memorable breasts.

Prime betrayed. Has life passed by?

The Square of Heavenly Peace in Peking, China. Peter considered what it would be like to be a schoolmaster from a Chinese rural village on holiday in Peking and strolling in the Square of Heavenly Peace. *Exotic when considered from this scabby Irish burg but I'd bet my pigtail if I had one that my comrade schoolmaster doesn't see anything exotic about it. Hey, he might have Tiger Balm, the great eastern nostrum and cure all which Joe Minihan's son the P & O Steward informed me of on his last visit home. Tiger Balm! But I was absent-minded and didn't take it in. So that the Square of Heavenly Peace might be a misnomer and might well be called the Diamond of Hellish Turmoil. I daresay that if some tyrannical monk went to change the ritual of song in a temple or shrine on the perimeter of the Square of Heavenly Peace some traditionalist Chinese would kick up a fuss too. Would say, I'll never burn a bloody joss stick or let off a friggin' fire cracker if they change one stone in the Shrine of the Divine Lotus. Life there undoubtedly possessed a skewness coefficient too. One would need to be a great man to live to endure it.*

*

The view of the headlands and the stretch of foreshore sea not a million miles from Hero Town is suddenly revealed to Peter as being delectable. The quasi dunes sloped down to naked sand, its ravelling controlled by a fortress wall of railway sleepers. Tourists aren't such morons after all. The pounding white breakers were good, they warmed the schoolmaster's blood. The minimum of clothing, boy and girl hand in electric hand leaped discreetly before the waves. Youth was now free-rolling on the aromatic grass of the cliff top. Guitars, tents, pints of beer, fresh air, ballads, freedom—a new generation was upon him.

Passing me by, life. Beaten into the cowardly clay by the roaring Redemptorists. The Inseminator inseminating in the hotels at nights; whenever Peter saw him his eyes were bloodshot and deep-sunken.

*

The caravans went clippedy clop and trundled out until word came through the streets that one of them was upside down at the foot of the Vicar's Height. Peter-he rushed down to see the excitement. There was the shivering horse with the woman and two children sitting on the windowsill of a gate lodge bloodied and tearful and so utterly lost and crestfallen in the mysterious wilds of Ireland while the father was lying unconscious on the road edge with a small cluster of people observing. The doctor and priest crouched over him as the weary stethoscope and the shake of the doctor's head pronounced the man—a Swiss—dead. Standing apart, his mind wounded, Peter-he could imagine— hear over the airwaves the wellbred family discuss the adventure of the caravan holiday in Ireland. Clippedy clop the horse had run away and shied, some one said; the caravan went headlong as it banged into the animal's hind legs going down the hill. How did the priest know the man was a Catholic? "Hush, child," old Mrs Smyth of the lodge was saying to the stricken children as she took them indoors. The distraught wife has clasped her children to her thighs and looks in a daze at the sprawled caravan with crockery oozing from a rent in its green canvas roof. A dead husband. The height of hellish sorrow for a Swiss mother. How often would she tell of the incident to others most civilised in her villa by Lake Geneva, where old Miss Hopkins boasted that she had hunted the great Paderewski from his piano. "Will you be soon finished with the piano, Sir, I have to finish the dusting?"

"My dear Irish girl, if I were to give you this recital in Covent Garden it would cost you one thousand guineas."

"I know that, Mr Paderewski, but when may I dust the piano?" The laugh approximated to what one hoped were the beneficial effects of a liberal application of Tiger Balm. Good man to live. Good man to die.

It was night in Hero Town. The morrow is a Patron or Pattern Day in nearby seaside Bally. The year, that is the summer, is bunched when that feast day is over. If Peter does not attend the 15th will he in fact extend his personal summer? Before honouring the feast he considers telling his sins to a priest. Yet he ponders. Hell is being denigrated. Confession is on its way out and the white flag is out the top window of the Vatican. New and far-fetched interpretation of the rules. Isn't it a terrible thing to be delivered into the hands of the Living Dead. Garabaldi rides again! The old music hall song of his long dead father is now recalled,

"Mary Ellen at the Church turned up
Her man turned up, her Dad turned up.
And the parson in his long white shirt turned up.
And they found him in the river with his toes turned up."

The Reverend Gentleman with his long white shirt indicates the reduction of the ministry to the level of a subject for a McNeill postcard. And that's what'll bloody well happen the Holy Roman Catholic Church in the Pope's Green Island if the tradition bearers are outraged and made to feel superfluous. The Parson a stock type in current fiction—hope he proves to be a great man to live. But brother Peter is doubtful. So cast a cold eye on grace and faith. Ass man, pass by.

*

The dulled senses by the sea. The beautiful baleful glitter of the broad ocean. Aromatic airs. An onshore wind and the eyes gritty with sand. How renewed one feels after a swim. The life-giving ocean, was it out of it we crawled to eventually evolve gigawatts and the calculus.

End of summer. The skin prickly. The ooze goes real deep into the
diaphragm. Should last till Christmas. A nearby woman with her
lips curled around the thigh of a chicken. I'll have. . . woman on the
rocks. "Three wheels on my wagon . . . Cherokees are after me, but
I'm singing a happy song." "Get back in the wagon, woman."

Who's this befuddled rogue squatting in the woodbine-scented
hedge by the shore, who greets and bandies words with the
countrywoman approaching. With a wink at Peter the rogue says
loudly, "You should give me that daughter of yours, Kate."

"I will in my arse; you're fifty-five and she is nineteen."

"I've money and there's only a few years left in me. I'm a fine
natural man, well preserved, no more no less. I'm in dead
earnest—with this fellah, as a witness. God blasht it, woman,
she'd be a nice damn little party for me in the bed for a few years
and won't she fall in for everything?"

"I'd drown her in Poulnanny first."

"I'd make a few thousand over in your name—this honest
man'll be witness—won't you, Sir?"

"I will indeed."

"Good God, girl, d'you know what, thinkin' over it again that
daughter of yours is good arable ground and I might get one crop
off her."

"Don't draw me on you, you whoremaster. Fitter for you be
fingering your rosary and saying the Act of Contrition for
yourself."

"'Tis often an old chimney caught fire. I'll tell you what,
Kate—some young fellah will take her into the sandhills of
Skullawirra and scooptossle her and then skedaddle, and leave her
with a spinaker sail in her bow."

"A dirty ould scamp—that's what you are."

"All right keep her so. Katie May—held it from the boys and
gave it to the clay."

How far is it from here to the Divine Square of Heavenly Peace?
This here hedge-squatter is a good man to live. The caravans clop by

back in Hero Town. Tiger Balm burns bright in the forest of the night. The aromatic air. Any mushrooms up round your quarter, Ma'am? No. Very well so. The banjaxed sanctuary of Hero Town, ora pro nobis. Ass man, pass by. Woman, get back in the wagon compartment. "Sure don't we live in one anothers pockets hereabouts, Sir, is it any wonder we'd be cracked."

*

"A man needs friends. A man needs relatives. The trouble with you, Peter, is that you do not know how to cope with the knot tightening in your head. A man is so constituted that of his nature he must perforce explode. With one man, it is alcohol: with another it is movement, a new panorama, a new set of references, new food, new attitudes on the part of new people."

Bssss! "I'll be away for a few days" *and Margo's eyes flash fire. Because he dares leave her apron strings. Because of the esoteric fear that he will come under the spell of another woman.*

Bssss! What time does the boat go out to the island? Dolphin's in the Sound. The yeasty smell of the pub while he waits: the jigs, reels and slides on the pocket tin whistle. Then down the cast iron ladder to the oil smelling cabin.

Roar, engine, roar.

Over the sea.

Puffins.

Cool enough out here despite the heat.

Ah, the bowl of sand. He's making allowance for the tide—for the skewness coefficient of the tide and sea of moving water.

Where on the island in that blinding white cup of sound is Peddah sleeping? The bed near the wall? The roughly plastered wall of the old and largely disused house, with its bucket lavatory in the old porch. Yes, Ma'am. That'll be fine. Beidh an dinnear againn sa chistin timpeall a sé. Go maith! Slan! (Grubstakes at 6. . . . . Grand!)

The man of the house is mooching about among the hollyhocks peering, gaping through leaves at the invaders of his island home and experiencing a vague uncrystalised ache of unease at the sight of his wife being solicitous for the comfort of total strangers, the belated memory of monetary reward arriving in time to banish sheer resentment. The stone-tilled fields with their tilted catch-rain platforms which provide a measure of water supply for the milch cow, and above all, the boot-clutching trudge through sand, to the nightlife of the pub. The two girls seated at Peter's 6 p.m. dinner table are now in the corner of the pub; their eyes most bright indeed. Their eyelashes coming in useful to mask sex-eagerness. They asked demure questions.

Peter-I was addressing Peter-him. Now is the time to get drunk. To see what it's like. Two ripe girls. I'm too old—don't be a blithering idiot.

Never stopped the boozer in the corner with the captain's hat—a greasy article. The melodeon in the corner marched Roddy McCorly to the Bridge of Toome again and again, while Peter with his lemonade drink wondered if he should have ordered a Coca Cola. It would pass as porter in the half-light. Steady drinking.

"Do you mind if we join you, Mr Mulrooney? There are a couple of rough-looking fellows trying to force their company on us. We're a little uneasy."

"Certainly. Peter is my name."

"You're staying in our house, out in the old part? I looked into it once: there was a coloured man, a kind of an Indian doctor, there last week; he wouldn't talk to anyone. It was strange and exciting with the candle lighting on the table. Last man in quenched it.

You're alone there, Mr Mulrooney—Peter, I mean?"

"Yes, I'm alone; for tonight anyway."

"Hear that, Mary, for tonight anyway! I'm Orla and this is Mary. It's an experience to be in an island off the island of Ireland. It's like being marooned with you, the two of us, Mr . . . Peter. Will we write a note and put it in a bottle and throw it in the sea? Yerra, we don't care if we were never rescued, do we, Orla?"

"We don't, girl."

"You'll have another, Peter. . .?"

"It's my turn to . . . but I really think I should be getting along to bed."

"Sure the night is only starting. What's your hurry?"

"This stuff goes to my head: I've a poor tolerance for alcohol. Great! As a matter of fact and I hope you won't blab my secret, this is my first real visit to a pub."

"Still got your Confirmation Pledge?"

"What are you two so amused at?"

"Nothing at all, Peter, sure we were only smiling at a jackass we met today, isn't that right, Orla?"

"That's right. Mr Mulrooney you're in safe hands. You won't get rolled over by a car for there's none on this island. A kick from that black ass is about the most dangerous thing you can experience. And if you get a bit tipsy itself, won't the two of us carry you home."

Easy now, Peter Bawn. They're handling age, each of them. Are they out to make a fool of me? Arrah, let yourself go, you dumbbell. But what if they carry the word home to Hero Fecking Town? Deny it black and blue. Say the bitches were blotto themselves and 'twas you helped them home for fear they'd fall over a cliff. Drink on in this beautiful adorable pitch black island of oil lamps and concertinas. Here and now you are no longer P.M., respected schoolmaster of your Community. This for you is Last Chance Saloon. See the way Orla crosses and uncrosses her legs.

Today, my dearly beloved brethren, is the 15th of August, the Feast of the Assumption. Our Blessed Lady is assumed into Heaven. You may recall your parents telling you about the occasion when this glorious mystery was declared an article of faith. It is indeed a source of parochial delight that for the first time in a century Mary being assumed into heaven can now be seen, in glorious mosaic in our church window. No longer obscured by the wedding cake encrustations on the old altar.

Were it not for the tenacious stand made by the majority of the parishioners (20 per cent = majority) it would still be concealed. A victory for the simplicity of God's house.

Oh no, not again, I beg, beseech, we want to hear no more. Wouldn't he give you sanctified diarrhoea, your man. I daresay that this will go on and on for the next century or so. The after-Mass people came up to Peter-me and, knowing the form, switched topics and said, "I daresay you'll be at the Match" or "Is Tom fighting fit?" If it's not one thing it's the other. The Match! That's all right but if he plays a bad game this curse o' God huddle of people will avoid me like the plague. Poor Margo will suffer with her one and only, that he's no milksop on the field of play.

"Once the fifteenth is over you can be bidding farewell to summertime. Is there such a place as Madeira? That's where the Inseminator is gone to this time. Tingaling—you're the last bellman in the whole of Ireland. You won't feel it now Peter till you're back with the scholars again. I'll tell you the naked truth when I was in my prime fags or drink never bothered me but women their bare hips as armrests for the insides of my forearms, they kept me tossing and tumbling all night long.

"The traffic is mad in this town and the shaggin' Council has gone to sleep. The fifteenth is out—still it wasn't a bad summer.

"Do you know what I'm going to tell you? The tinker's girls are so dolled and dickied up nowadays that you wouldn't know them from doctor's daughters. Mutt, get this into your head. If virtue wins we're bunched: if vice wins we're bunched. It's the polarisation that counts. Hail Mary full of grace I wish I was in some other place. The white flag is being unfurled. When you're past forty don't jump off the fence. You'll rupture yourself as quick as a wink."

*

Peter on the island now began for the first time to experience the natural sway of the world and smiling he yielded to its amiable rocking in space. Orla crossing and uncrossing her legs. The drink steaming up all three. His eyes swinging still more closely in understanding of spirit, of mind, of body, to minds, spirits and bodies of the bright-eyed oh so understanding and oh so natural women. His middle cut began to protrude, to thrust forward, that is whenever he stood to order fresh rounds of drink, or when one of the women left them for a few minutes to whisper an order through the aperture left by a drawn shutter in the timber partition of the nearby snug. He smelled their sweat. The familiars crowded him round. The Parson with his long white shirt was there blandly tolerating the coefficiency of this temporary moral skewness. The Tiger Balm had evaporated in aromatic vapour that swirled round the Pedagogue's head with a smell like fermenting yeast mingled with the odour of burning joss sticks.

East was west. More, more! They are plying me with drink, Peter shouted at himself. Who was this new familiar: why hello if it isn't the bold Lord Thomas Babington Macaulay himself. Here in Inis Thiar. What'll you have, Babington, Millington or Harrington whatever your name is. . .

Can a man desire, but to sit him down by an alehouse fire, and on his knees a pretty wench.

Orla had stood up. Peter grasped her and with a cry she plumped down on his thighs. And to the red belly of hell with Hero Town and all its works and pomps. Peter from afar waved his handkerchief to Hilda the dressmaker who can see through walls. A gigawatt of electricity confounded his loins and genitals. *Hurrah! I'm a great man to live so I am.* The dumb bell is letting himself go . . . go man go. The metamorphoris of spaven mule into Inseminator Supreme. After the feast of the Assumption the year is banjaxed. *One final fling. This is really the Red Rose of Life. And the devil take the begrudgers, Bab-bing-ton Mac-aulay, here I come! Brandy in the system can generate gigawatts of electricity.*

*

So Peter travelled up to Dublin for the match with the county colours twirling from the bus aerial. His heart was in my mouth for fear Tom'd play a bad game. All along the roadway as he drifted with the others his heart thumped. Remember that he had to face the folks back in Hero Town and bear the brunt of it if he didn't come up to scratch. The stadium was now a vast sounding room and the noise sent the galvanised roof of the stand trembling in metallic echo. It was excitement sharpened to a fine point of exquisite suffering. The anthem was defiantly and resonantly chanted. *"It's ní fhagfar not ní fagfar,"* you illiterate *bastards the locked out schoolmaster in Peter yelled!* Tom is transformed. On the field he appears now to be a cold-blooded tiger. *Is that tiger locked up in his uncle?* Has his nephew as a result of prowess and fame with a ball been catapulted from bondage and fear? The ball soars. The home crowds roar as they call upon Darcy. *Does this courage he now displays crashing, leaping, accepting knocks even yet lie asleep within me, his uncle.* The voices pelt in upon him from the seats behind and above. "Christ, young Darcy is a topper." Peter finds himself yelling like a lunatic and screaming bloodily as he is fouled. *Do the obscenities streaming from these lip indicate the integral Peter? Is this how I would behave in drink or in great grips with a woman?* Scores are notched. A forest of flags—the papers will read a forest of flags and all the beaten words will be employed. *We yell him to the goal.* No, yes, no, yes. He parts, he feints, he jinks, he boo-oo-oots, the stricken net trembles . . . livid hell reigns on earth. *Da-arcy. He is king! He is god! He is the potential I. His name echoes throughout the land. Tom is the Messiah of the Bag of Wind! And I, God be praised, full blood brother to his mother, shall bask in the reflected glory on the road home.*

*

And on the other starry road home from the island pub; they have plied me with firewater. All three of us combining to make some sort of a triple centaur moving—swaying—as one, my fingertips, my fingertips, experiencing delectable watts of power, the smell of their bodies now truly the scent of aromatic red rose of life. Each a virgin Mary Ellen about to turn up at the church as mock, meek victims.

A nest of robins in the hair of each of the three of us. I am a great man to live and each each each . . . I now hear beside me the integral laugh of woman amused at the awkwardness of man. Oh at last I am patrolling the Square of Heavenly Peace, past the grassy beauty-smelling night field rooms of the island where the cover of the grass bed is already thrown back and in readiness the epithalamium is softly and seductively chanted. And I sway the pair of women to a stop outside the graveyard the focal point of sanctity of the whole western world where deep in the sand, deep under the cockeyed crosses and mottled graveslabs the holy patrons sleep (sleep me arse they are deader than the dodo). There Peter-I stop and begin to shout: their breasts even now resting on the low aramament wall, their love mons flat against the holy stones. Hey, Saints o' Holy God . . . help me to appreciate the gift of God. The clasps on the bras. Ah what am I saying? South of the border down Mexico way. Aach. The whiskey valour is draining, draining, away, away, away. Now, now . . . I have the opportunity to have a double woman on the rocks. Yes, bartender, that's what I require. A double woman on the rocks.

*

Ecstasy is the fodder of fools. Racketta, racketta, racketta, will the bus never get home to where Peter can hide? Margo must be suffering, though she will be too proud to show it. Why to hell do the Irish take this football game as if it were a matter of life or death? Why in the name of all that is high did Tom, just when he had victory at his feet, haul out and strike his opposite number a blow in the mouth that caused the other man to buckle and fall down as limply as an apron falls from a peg. Off! Off! Oh Hell, what a change two minutes could make in the life turn of a family. Hero Town would curse him. Sure, a few more bellicose would back him up, say he was right to do what he did, but the rest would say, "Darcy fecked up the match!"

Cheers and jeers in passing towns. No familiar ever conceived could help in such a situation. "Too bad about Tom, eh Peter. The winners did not relish their victory either . . . not a whole lot of glory in beating a team of fourteen men." Acre of arse in the paper again. Arsey-Darcy. Ass man, pass by. A bad day's work for local football. Darcy is it? Arsey-Darcey. He made right shit of us in Croke Park. The Square of Hellish Faction Fighting Crap! Do you know what should be branded on that bastard's forehead with a red hot poker? "Walk aisy when your jug is full."

And to overtop all bitterness there was the memory of the two women on the rocks moryah, who heaved me into the bed in the cottage and as I clawed helplessly into the dark den, ran laughing hysterically out into and under the prickled blue canopy of the night heavens.

Blast it, will this curse-o'-God bus ever get me home?

Burrum, burrum. The sky is glinting silver with a school of paleness in the early dawn streets. At last wearily, silently, Peter-he is home. The elms in the schoolyard—its leaves are rustling like brown paper. Change is in the air. *And my true love I have lost . . . Arsey-Darcey, will Peter-he ever live it down?*

SEPTEMBER

The tar road led southwards into what the map told Peter was the valley of the River Brad and before he had gone far he began to appreciate the unusual silence. No confusion in the accurate appreciation of where he was. He was, well not in a Square of Heavenly Peace, but in a line of ditto. . . Here the whitethorn hedges were high with a strong and parasitic undergrowth of briar and dogrose. On the sunfacing lower hedge the brambles bore vivid clusters of ripe blackberries, beneath which the dock leaves mimicked the green tongues of prehistoric monsters. Where there were gates Peter stood to watch grazing rabbits squatting tall-eared in the good green aftergrass, ever ready to hop to the sanctuary of the nearby bracken. There were no animals in the fields. On the road the traffic-squashed body of a shot crow flaps as the gentle breeze lifts a single wing of feathers apart as if it were the sail of a small dismal yacht that had survived a gale. In the wild crab-tree the tiny fruit were infant heads that possessed the power of looking down curiously on him.

The drone of a plane light and lost over Cooleybooley Wood was indeed as far as the umbilical island cord stretched in the case of the schoolmaster. Peter had pulled up the car on the roadside—he was on his way to see the perfect round tower which stood on a sloping field above the sea some miles from Hero Town. It was marvellous to be free from all bonds, he sighed, as he opened the rectangular box of Tupperware and took out the salmon sandwiches. This was the final salmon of the year for the angling season closed on the morrow. Hadn't he seen Jackie Mangan standing outside the fishmongers the morning before with a crescent bulging fishing bag, and in response to a request by the passing postman, he exposed the salmon and held it up by the tail for the meagrely populated street to see and admire. The silver of spring (me too, Peter thought) had been qualified by the red gold of autumn—so after nodding to Jackie on impulse Peter purchased the last legal salmon of the season. It will help Margo to heal her wounds after that bloody ould match. With relish Peter drove his teeth through Horrigan's bread, Lahy's lettuce and Jackie Mangan's salmon. An al fresco meal all produce of Hero Town hinterland. The tarred road led deep into the valley. He walked a mile observing the contrast between the wealth of the land and the paucity of the population. Not a house. Barley whiskers galore ready for the reaper but no human dotted the landscape. It was at this point that the umbilical cord came adrift in its eastern hitch, and despite the love of a genuine Round Tower in a fishing village to the west, Peter was jerked suddenly home to the congenial monotony of Hero Town. For like Jeanie in France, he too heard voices.

*

"What's that, Granny?" "That's a po, Lily darling." "What's a po, Granny?" "It's p-o love, short for pot." "Is it a pot for boiling potatoes, Granny?" "No, it's a chamber pot my love." "What's a chamber, Granny?" "It's an old word for a bedroom—'Come into the chamber, Maud, for the black bat, night has flown.'" "It's 'Come into the garden, Maud,' Granny." "I believe you're right, my love." "Why is there a pot in the chamber?" "It's too far to the bathroom, little girl." "What's in it, Granny—lemonade?" "It's u-rine, girl." "We've a boy at school called Hugh Ryan." "Not that, Lily! It's u-r-i-n-e, love. Bold people call it pee." "The letter

P?" "No, it's short for P-i-s-s but nice girls don't say that word at all." "Next time I see Hugh Ryan, I'll say, 'Hello Mr Piss!' "You'll do no such thing! You hear me?" "Why haven't I a chamber pot under my bed, Granny?" "I forgot to put it there." "Will you put it there tonight, Granny?" "I'll see about it, child." "Whose pee is in the pot, Granny?" "Mine, love." "Too far to the bathroom, Granny?" "Exactly, love."

"That's the worst of having city grandchildren, Peter, they haven't the faintest knowledge about bodily functions. Removed from reality—that's what they are. Those big estates in Dublin have hundreds of children who know nothing about decay and death. No old people die in estates. Shifted off pronto. All one ages in the estates. England is worse."

"What's that hanging from your nose, Granny?" "I've got a cold, girlie." "Yes, but what is it?" "It's mucous, child." "Music?" "No, Lily, it's mucous." "You keep it, Granny?" "You blow it into a handkerchief, child—you don't keep it." "But I saw people putting the handkerchief with the music—the mucous I mean—into their pockets." "There's nothing else they could do with it at the time." "They couldn't throw it away?" "They could, but it's kind of awkward." "Not if you had a tissue, Granny." "That's true, Lily." "I saw Hugh Ryan one cold day in the schoolyard with a mucous below his nose." "Did you, darling?" "I did: and when I went to look at it, it vanished—you know where it went, Granny?" "I'm not sure, love." "Up his nose, Granny." "Well, well!" "He didn't call it mucous, Granny." "Didn't he?" "He said it was an ould shnot." "He's not a nice boy, Lily." "I think he's nice, Granny, but he does peculiar things." "I'm sure he does, love—oh there's Mammy looking for you in the garden. Off you go and don't mention our conversation." "About the piss and the shnots?" "Sush, love." "Do it again, Granny, before I go." "Do what?" "Snuffle the mucous up your nose!" "Up my nostril, Lily dear." "One, two, three. Going, going, gone! Hugh Ryan might like you as a grandmother, Granny." "So he might child!"

"Peter, my grandchildren are skydivers. Did I ever think in my wildest dreams that I'd be a grandmother to a skydiver, parachutes at Farran Thomas! Butterflies they do have—they tell me. Is it how they carry them in a jar or what? The beautiful silence when the parasol opens. Down, down, down, down, down, just like that, Peter."

Prosaic things. Fragments. Items. Quiet planes of feeling as opposed to mountains of adventure. The priests, the younger ones back home on holidays from their American parishes. Among their own they draw breath. They gather themselves on Sunday and mention a strange being called Almighty Gawd, but for the most part we who squeezed these lads out of our street football leagues and smelly classrooms understand their stresses and when they step up to the hotel bar, well we make allowances for abroad you are tested to the ultimate in moral resolve. So, young priest, when you chant Almighty Gawd, we vote you perfectly entitled to do so.

*

Brrr! The first ground frost of autumn greets the last of the late Yanks in evidence at cut-price, end-of-season rates. Phenomena, recurrent phenomena. Peddah-he abhors those who express patronage for what they lousily call blue rinse Yanks! It is a form of blasphemy, for each no matter how aged, no matter how desiccated, is absolutely beautiful when looked at in the moonlight.

Brrr, the cold wind blows out of the icy north and bronchially terrifies the person it chills with its innuendo of old ailments. The Californians, like swallows, will fly to a warmer clime. Would that he could too, like the swallow . . . but alas we are northern Europeans. And over the centuries our blood has become conditioned to a certain span of temperature on the Fahrenheit scale.

Moo! Moo! The last stalled in town fine herd of cattle milked and fed in the urban area crowd the street. The shrivelled ashplant prods and taps the cow flanks as the youthful chargehand whistles and shouts in turn, not giving a fiddler's curse for the watchers, as the cows dam up against a combine harvester creating a traffic snarl. The milch cow herd of cattle is gloried in by its nearby owner, who insists on having the lazy waltzers given priority, as they are driven through the end-of-season tourist traffic rejoicing if they evoke a poisonous retort from the final one beshawled woman in the almost ultimate ass and cart. The owner of the cows proudly walking on the pavement disowns and accepts ownership for the steered steers as befits the occasion and deriving, as witness his poised countenance, a volatile glee from the changing scene. The young drover spies and shouts at a preoccupied Peter now roused from his contemplation of a far more appealing female standing and viewing herself in the mirror of the boutique window

"Hi, Peter! You want to know the cows' names? Big Head, Windy, Sully and Diana for starters, she has a big head, explains itself. Well, how out, blast you," slapping the flank with his open palm. "This brown one is always getting up wind and the White Head leading was bought from Johnny Sullivan of Deerpark. Diana? She's out of a book." But the mind cross-pollinated and Peddah considered that a woman can never view herself except she tiptoes out of her body, crosses the room and looks back at herself. Let her be in full gorse blaze of anger. Let her romp and shout in fury. Let her be convulsed with the ultimate in grief and if she chances to pass a mirror she'll glance at her reflection to see how her countenance is forming, whether it still possesses remnants of attractiveness. How does she look in the mirroring faces of others? Does she draw their attention?

Peddah, the town scribbler, so as to bear witness subjectively must constantly be pulling back the lens, and like the woman zoom in close to examine the many attitudes in which the woman views herself, her special and feminine way which is supple and strong and not at all squeamish, for with woman squeamishness is a pose. How often has Peddah seen slim frightened looking slips of girls cowering in bedrooms? "Please, Dada, don't quench the light?" And then post-Leaving Cert when transferred to Whips Cross Hospital in London proceed with aplomb and composure and ungrimaced features to wash bodies fished out of the Thames or earth from a collapsed sewer. Bodies with yellow transparent bags slung merrily across their shoulders in the final defiance of their kidneys challenging them to do their damnest, which is just what they have done, and bloody well goosed them into the bargain. You couldn't frighten 'em now with an atom bomb exploded under their graceful boondoons. Woman? Timid? God help your innocent head.

*

In the evening time, the first harvest moon shows its full face over the dusky steeple illuminating the approaching figure who huddled past. "Are you over the shingles, Sheila?" "Blast you, you great bastard, and little pity you had for me." "Honest I thought you were joking." One would need to be wholly indigenous to realise the subtleties of the vernacular in Hero Town. One who is called a "thundering hoor" does not take offence, but rather accepts it as a compliment conditional on the epithet being uttered in a certain admiring tone of voice. What is a "great bastard" but admiration simply standing on its head. These remarks or comments are only by way of finger-posts to a vast range of subtlety in the use of the vernacular. Now throw the thought away and give ear to the troubled whispering voice.

"Pssssh-wssh, psssshwassh, Peter."

"What are you saying, Molly?"

"I don't want to be raising my voice, Sir, shove in here against the wall. I'm a show to God and the world since Johnjoe died and I let the pub. Almighty God, who'll I face to tell my tale?"

"What's the matter, Molly?"

"What ails me, is it? As you know I stipulated that I'd hold a room and get my dinner. But Almighty God, the carry on."

"What carry on?"

"At all hours of the day and night, boys and girls. If Johnjoe could only come back and see our lovely sweet well-run respectable public house turned into a common whorehouse."

"You're exaggerating, Molly."

"I'm neither adding nor subtracting, sure how would you know anyway. Hold till this fellah passes. I came down last week one morning at four o'clock and there were girls being toppled in all parts of the premises. Oh, I'm shamed before all. And them foreign appliances making their appearance in the chaste lanes of our sweet town. Don't let on a syllable, my dotey schoolmaster— do you know how many compulsory full ages have come out of that place in the year since Johnjoe died? Six! And a seventh waiting on tenterhooks for the moon sign. Out of the six, Peddah, four of them have been rectified at the altar rails in white. Blast it, but in years to come it'll be argued under the head of nullity what the solicitors of the future are going to fortune their daughters out of. Psssh-wssh, nullity! I'm in such a state of nerves that I can't stop shivering. It wouldn't surprise me if Johnjoe's nephew is one of the hoormasters. There's rumours about him having a girl up the pole. A public house is the last of all. For a conscientious woman it's hell on earth. Cripes wouldn't you, Peddah, be in a nice fix if you got into a jam like that! Huh! The unmarked knight would be a thing of beauty."

Diana the cow. The woman flitting out of her body to watch her ga-mees from a distance. Whips Cross. A suppurating penis. Well, well. The red, yellow transparent suture . . . worn like a scapula— with his blood thrown over her shoulder tied up "with a piss yellow band". Diana of the uplands. The yellow cereal selvedges of the roads glistened with September corn bulked to the grinding mills. Leakage bequeathed by farmers to the clean intelligent rats whenever they glanced up from masticating to observe the passing cars. Sparks, mirrors and nullity, the zooming lens of woman on itself.

*

In the church as he knelt there with the priest using Almighty Gawd as a shillelagh, not that he had ever seen one outside of Killarney. It occurred to Peter with unusual force that the horizon of age was now galloping towards him and that the chance of an amorous adventure that would prove safe and noteworthy in retrospect was diminishing with every second that ticked by. Was he growing impotent? It was a while since he had experienced stirrings.

He looked around him: every second person in the church was female and thus possessed within certain defined limitations of age, of course, the ability to bestow upon Peddah a marvellous cornucopia of three dimensional delight. "Ilka laddie got a lassie: ne'er one has I."

The horizon of age gallops towards him, and though a part of his mind orders him to rejoice, to blow trumpets, to beat drums of self-congratulation that he has not been buried like some of his schoolmates, he cannot yet reconcile himself to the bitter prospect that lies on the wrong side of forty. Even if he had a store in the treasure house of his imagination of adventures of the fingertips which he could take out and handle so lovingly in the drab unmarked ahead, he would have been satisfied.

Already the leaves of the undergrowth begin to noise, the noise acting as herald for the winter. The roads are strewn with fallen fuchsia blossoms and there is little need of his long dead mother's Ouija board to project his wretched future.

He could still feel his mother's hands deep in his armpits from behind raising him high over the advancing wave and whispering, dulce et decorum —it is noble and proper to live—before ducking him down on the mad mathematical wall of attacking foam.

Alas, for Peddah has not been exposed even to the love born of propinquity, the nearness to woman in an environment that would artificially bring about a certain congruence or fusion of spirit and imagination.

Meanwhile, the operative word is meanwhile, several secret wars are in full swing in the community, some with tentacles, that extend like the roots of old trees, ranging far and wide through the relationship exercised by person upon person. Some of the wars are personal and on the level of major or minor apprehension regarding disease: e.g. the war against cystitis—it being the boyo calculated to advance the cause of matrimonial nullity or even constitute the goal called divorce! Here too the war of the batter is being fought out bitterly among dance teachers and dance lovers as to whether in competition at county, provincial or national level the batter in the polka should be allowed or outlawed. Likewise political wars fought out with fair face among smiling wives and sisters of the elected or the ambitious to be elected.

Dusk in the porch of the church. The ranked saints in stone. The Please Pray board just inside the porch is the agony column of the church. Peddah screws up his eyes to read the vicarious pleas.

Loud and raucous laughter now in the billiard room of the Clanmorris Hotel, one of the old dames is sending out messages. Frantically! Or does he dream? Too late! Too late shall be the cry when the men with the bargains pass by! But not too late for Margo's son the footballer who is being married on Saturday. Does Uncle Peter have to make a speech? The horizon of age gallops closer and Margo's son on next Saturday night will be sexually wiser than his dumb uncle. Still colour blind as regards the signals of woman, and illiterate in body language. The tide at its somnolent edges began to squirm as a sleeper experiencing a painful dream tosses uneasily in sleep. Dream on.

The reek of yeast from nubile girls in a convent boarding school assailed his nostrils. *Pray for Peddah who is obtuse, woman scared, migraine scared, you name it and I, Peter Psycho-somatic, has it. The Council for Illusionary Illnesses: secretary of the local branch. Who needs the Ouija board? My future is mapped out. And there proclaim, my God, how great Thou Art. How about getting elephants-drunk at the wedding and no one will dare ask me to speak, lest I put my foot in it. Punch in my days, is that my lot? Senior Shaggin' Citizen. Retirement gratuity. Is that my ultimate of achievement? They pleaded with me to stay on. I had enough. Heigho! Shall I break free and become a maggot breeder? Wheel me out spouting history for the fully fledged tourists, each one funny and daring in his or her own way. Peddah-I, my footsole on a Guinness barrel of sterling silver in deep conversation wave. A parting wave. They respond. From behind the glass they respond. The parting glass—"For you must go and I must stay".*

Peter smiled as the horizon of finality veered closer to him, comforting himself with the thought that with the first fart each infant begins as it were to die. The horsehair in the old auction house sofa began to pinch the backs of his knees. The secret war against death. This footballer nephew would experience mating, the fullest sense of the word, long before his Uncle Pete. What kind of a sexless bastard am I, he asked himself. Diana the Cow. The cold winter approached. Brrr! Brother—will I suffer now, he murmured.

"Are you married, yet Peter—no altar no halter?" *Rural rhymers . . . feck em!*

*

Peter ruminates, unable to follow the missing stepping stones across the ford of consciousness and subconsciousness in his mind. Familiars, words, images, repeated over and over till some solid is created . . . are these the hidden steps, Peter asks himself. You bring them to life, the life of words, greet them with a shout of welcome as one moves through the day. Look, there is a fibreglass skiff. Or a ventilation cowl. Or a manorial bell. Peter— you're a dunder-head. Nothing has an existence in words more firm than its real presence.

Though weary, Peddah decides to abandon all such thoughts and like a tethered goat move from point known to point loved.

Known and loved, groping dutifully as he goes on the herbage of religion, education and ethics and resolving for his caprice peace of mind never to pull too hard on the rope that has cut deeply into the flesh of one of his hind legs, for if he were so to strain who knows but that the peg might come up out of the clay and he would then have to experience the exquisitely painful sensation of being free. The only answer to this conjured up problem is to chant in a tone indicative of crude hypnosis, fibreglass skiffs, ventilation cowls and manorial bells. This Peter proceeds to do. Later Margo apprehends his chanting and smiles at him, thinking that he is rehearsing yet another historical lecture he is to make at the upcoming visit to the medieval castle.

Dear citizens of the tall corn state whose bird is the wild canary, whose flower is the wild rose, within these great walls on Shannon banks that have stood against the storms of nature, and would-be conqueror, I welcome you to Ireland and home . . .

With the mead and claret in the perfumed air the woman next to Peter at the table giggles. She could scarcely wait for her husband to swing around in his seat to watch the pageant performance in the great hall, before she whispered in Peddah's ear.

"You don't say," he replied *blushing unseen in dimmed hall of the castle.*

"I do," whisperingly she smiled.

With the audience engrossed, Peddah wonders in the darkness if he dare explore the inducements of this giddy giggly narra-back daughter who is playing her role to the full. Peddah rehearses, and with a sudden spurt of bravery born of the certain knowledge that after the medieval banquet is over "We are scattered to the ends of the earth. . and we shall never lay eyes on each other again." And she, he is convinced in his bones, is equally aware of the imminent ending and is prepared, even wine-eager, to be a participant rather than a dreamer.

She grabs his left hand as if to say, "Behave yourself! But I hope you won't. You'd better make a prisoner of that hand or he'll wander all over the castle!" An epic giggle now and a drawing of the hand in closer to the centre of attraction. What with the sensations arising from the fact that his sweaty hand is in sweeter stocks, what with the fingers of admonishment raised by the censorious Piano Tuner, French Polisher and the Egg Tester, a most pedestrian trio back home in Hero Town, the veritable stallion of black terror which reared up on him has suddenly become a trembling man. Incipient erection fades to full limpness. Peddah the cowardly bastard is unmanned. Mr Strong becomes Mr Wilt. A few minutes ago he was indeed two men: now he is no man at all. Poor hoor! The Ouija board in the window, it readvises from the past, advice he didn't take. "About wimmin, Peter, they are attracted to emotion as a moth is to flame. Get them in an emotional environment and you have woman with her most female tendencies on display. Then she's weakest. She won't run away. A different side to womanhood. One never seen by the censorious three."

Tell you what: we will leave Peddah-him with his hand imprisoned as indicated in the dark chanting castle. We'll place a pause to his activities at the point of agony and we shall allow him either to retreat from that position or to advance further to the junction. Serves him right for the cowardice. O Jesus! here comes Robert Emmett the darlin' of Erin, strutting the stage. "Let no man write my epitaph. . ." With the help of God she'll fall in love with him now and abandon the Pedogogue's Paw. Don't allow it. Screw him to the cross there and now.

*

In the woods, the crooked wobbly carpet of acorns crack softly beneath Peter's shoe soles and he curses into the pit of hell the pinhole nabobs of the local council who have daubed the oak and ash trees with death numbers and who slyly wait for winter to denude the summer trees of leaves, so that when the woods look tawdry and shabby and down at heel, they can with impunity condemn them to death.

Alas! What shall buoy Peter up in the face of civic barbarity, in the face of impotence sexually and mentally. What shall buoy me up, Peddah asks himself again? The laughing memory of one old man belittling another. "See that old hoor across the road facing the century. He says he was a cowboy in Wyoming. The only horse that fellah ever seen was in a Schweppes' Racing Calendar." What if the harness maker dies for his red form is a seat of adventure and into his adventurous house moved the representatives of all the nations of the earth? Ped and Ned—we comfort him by telling him of places where the horse still is king.

What shall comfort me, Peter queries again. The cult of severed head. The three would hardly approve. Already the chill of winter is in the air and the blackberries have been raped by the pookas. The dahlias, those blown blowsy bitches of the garden, will linger for a few weeks yet to comfort brides like Mediterranean women poised before the menopause, slavering for one fond fling with whatever of nature's lubricity still ripe remained to assist them along the road to mental tranquility.

But as for the rest? Are all the outwardly meek citizens of Hero Town inwardly as turbulent as I am? The maids on their backs in locked bedrooms dreaming away, crashing through the roof. Oh yes! I hail thee. Life is like a cup of tea. It's how you make it. And again my house is small, no mansion for a millionaire. But there is room for me, aye, there is room for friends. That's all I care. Prrumph! Prrrrh! In imitation of wind of the lower bowel. Coward town, dirty, shabby, scabby. Snotty, scuffy, bloody lice-ridden town. So there!

Forgive me my love, my love, my love.

What was the outcome of the story of the giggly jiggly woman in the exciting emotive darkness of the castle banqueting hall? All the ingredients of wantonness were then present. Night, candlelight, claret. An atmosphere that yelled "Let's Go!" and again "Do not allow the emotionally significant moment to pass by unnoted only to be recognised and appreciated in dismal retrospect." Erotic! Electric! Here, no! Semi darkness. A bubble of giddy laughter . . . oh dear tired Jesus, the walls of our mortal halls began to move inwards to leave little space. Lost notions. O dear, dear America, hungry for human relationships, banter and quarrel, the constant need for reassurance that one is never isolated or alone. The ripe woman in the dark? How should Peter have left her? Dear lovely USA, my heart goes out to you this day. Lost notions.

Tick-tock, tick-tock. The young women drift past Peddah and one, one alone, could solve his difficulties and turning that key in the lock release him from the prison of Vulgar Fractions, Percentages, and musty History. And scarcely a day passes but young men from all corners of the globe with knowledge in their eyes pass him by, eyes that are secretly amused at his total abstinence badge, at his speak-Irish badge, at the pelican indicating that he has given blood intravenously scores of times to people, men and women possibly he shall never meet, faceless blood brothers.

Peter, strolling through the streets on route to the Diamond for his mid-morning stroll assured and consoled himself that the beauty of the inconsequential has yet to be appreciated and the insignificant and deprived have their uses also. They are humanisers. Yes, every pedestrian movement when novel of every individual is of surpassing interest. Is not the aim of every artist "to arrest motion, which is life, by artificial means".

Pedagogue: "You are mistaken, misdirected," the voice of the Piano Tuner snaps while the comrades nod in approval. "You have followed a prank-twisted finger-post. All your zeal and endeavour and diligence are in vain. On the brink of forty and still you waste your substance, your energy profitlessly." "Bring your ideas closer to home, to what you call Hero Town," chanted the Egg Tester, "though why you should call a gaggle of dispirited indolent shaggers and shagged heroes and heroines eludes me. Convey me down the street and indicate the heroic qualities of the place."

Fall into step with me so, this meek and mild autumn Saturday. Don't turn back or Margo will give me a job. Sweep around the back door. Are we free? Are we free?"

Poor United States, hungry for human relationships; hungry for a mid-morning stroll around the buzzing, greeting, gossiping, gaggle of streets. For a few moments the bright shopfronts that were newly painted for the approaching Race Meeting occupied Peter's attention, though the horse races themselves were probably the most insignificent part of the week's proceedings for many inhabitants. The hammering goes on. Platforms, lights, buntings, paint jobs, men up poles, a veritable fairyland. Harvest gold time. Put your best foot forward, the horse is king. Fun time, now and when the rates are paid. Ah but the man who makes the fences at the Races is equally troubled. So many horses fell at a city track in the heavy going that the jockeys grumbled. How was the injured Redmond boy in hospital? And the couple who sold their holding outside the town, a wren's nest, now cribbed and confined as urban dwellers, pass their time parading the town in style at night.

*

Races or otherwise, alive or dead, it mattered not to Cantwell who stalked the town streets, he was off again. There was no escape now, we're in for it. This time he kept it up for a week in every street and pub of the town. Questions, questions. No relief! Who actually cut out Daniel O'Connell's heart in Genoa, I mean he said, who cut out the actual heart with a slater's tool? Who slit, who scooped, who removed from under the ribcage the Liberator's ticker? He drove us up the walls. When Cantwell gets a pet subject into his skull he chews mercilessly at it non stop like a starving huskie at a leather strap until at last after a week he wears it thin and frees us all. He followed his victim of the day out of the pub to the street corner and into his (once her) own home where the dilated eyes of the sufferer's wife, as often as not upturned to God's abode, shone like twin suns in the comparative darkness of the kitchen. Trapped!

Was it a local surgeon cut out the heart or a butcher's apprentice? As Cantwell continued to spout, expound and air the subject the stuffy room in Genoa where the Liberator lay dead became almost materalised before our eyes. People at the foot of the stairs were speaking muted Italian and using muted gestures. The proprietor of the hotel in which the blustering Kerryman, now a deflated pig's bladder "thrun" on the four-poster didn't know the hell whether to be jolly or peevish that such celebrity should conk it under his roof. Cantwell wondered what time of year it was when Dan died, because if it was on a hot day the Liberator would stink almighty fast.

About this time a new personality, a woman for a change, suggested herself to Peter's erratic imagination. This was Switchboard Dolly.

In the switchboard of Cantwell's erratic imagination the Dolly was furiously plugging in conversation from all points of the compass and feeding them on to a multiple loudspeaker within the office of Managing Director. Into what did Dan's son put the heart? Was the heart big or small? A Tupperware receptacle would be the ideal thing to put it in if it dripped as indeed it must have . . . Was the body shunted back pronto to the Glasnevin or did the son go first to Rome with the bloody pacemaker?

Did he hand the parcel to the Pope, saying, "Your Holiness, my Da said you were to have his heart"? Cantwell also had some sadistic and barbaric queries centrifugal and to the kernel of the main enquiry. Could a man's heart be stuffed with breadcrumbs and herbs, pot roasted and eaten? How about that? Croí Dhónaill—à la carte—Dan's heart. Strange to say, Cantwell had no time at all for the soul case or body. He said he didn't give a shit if it was thrown into the tide; it was the heart that fascinated him. Peter concluded that it was a pig's saffron heart placed in a saline solution in the chemist's window which kept beating for three days that gave Cantwell the lead to this bone. Whatever it was, Hero Town went wild on the strength of it—until Switchboard Dolly collapsed exhausted on her stool and for a long period publican's wives looking over the perforated screen of their inner snugs were wont to cry out as in labour, "Jesus, Cantwell's coming again!"

Switchboard Dolly was snoring and no messages were reaching the boardroom.

Dispirited shagged heroes and heroines?

Cop yourself on—animated, alive and heroic!

OCTOBER

Autumn is walking in the woods. The foliage in Hanrahans', the finest farmers in the barony, grows wan. Margo gathers torytops, conkers and pine tufts, a few chestnuts, a spray of oak leaves tinged with the scorch of the fall, and arranges them in a shallow glass vessel. The arrangement is the autumn world in microcosm.

Heart or no heart the curtain of harvest-time spree, orgy, salt, sport, "greann agus aoibhneas" had to be hung down on the inhabitants of Hero Town. The ire of God falls on all hamlets and burghs that lack a festival and by cripes Peter was informed that their town wasn't to be an exception. The town spun around him: loudspeakers shrilled as they wrapped singing voices in cocoons of electronic steel wool. Walls of death raised an admonishing finger at walls of life, drinking women by their abandonment in bawdy song showed dimensions to their femininity that Peter the Pioneer never guessed and later in the night sent him out of the hotel lounge gasping.

Peter loitered on: his head swimming. Vertigo—hold off you merciless bastard! The speakers now played "The Thunder and Lightning Polka" something dulcet for the head. A jockey his horse hitting the dolly was lifted clean and clear into the air and thrown on his back. In the race stand lavatory a child picked up a piss wet tote ticket before the stewards announced an enquiry, and shaking the drops off it placed it in a plastic bag for later examination as to whether its owner had thrown down a winning ticket. The Rose of Tralee and the flower of Sweet Strabane were raped publicly on mattresses affixed to luggage racks on Ford Cortinas that whizzed through the crowded streets. In fast flowing flood water under the arches of the Race bridge tinker children stood thigh deep calling up, "Throw me down somethin'," pushing and shoving when the pennies from heaven rained into the shallows below. A community should possess a certain shameless minority to balance the scales, so uninhibited young women had the uncontrollable urge to vent the cask of tension which meant of course going reckless for a week and holy for the remnant of the year. Damnation! The horses are now about to leave the parade ring.

"How did you enjoy the Races, Minnie?"

"I got a belt of the nerves a couple o' months ago—tell you the truth—and I can't bear to face the people."

"You're not old, Minnie?"

"What use is that when I'm the way I am?"

"You should have seen old Jack Delaney on the stage in the Diamond last night dancing his heart out with a young lassie of nineteen. Would he be touching the sixty mark?"

"What are you saying, man, that dribblin' eedjit is facing eighty, the one age to my oldest brother, Mick."

"You should take a leaf out of his book—go out and meet the people. "I hope to Jesus I die dancing'—that's his cry!"

"That he might indeed—and soon—not wishing him harm before his time. Himself and his little cap in a jerk on the side of his skull, and his bloodshot eyes with one eye pointing to China. You can have the bastard. Himself and his bullock's notions!"

"All the same, Minnie, he has guts for an old cock: if he met a young gamey hen he'd let down the wing."

"Aye, with the wrenboys tonight, she'll lose a few feathers and if Jack Delaney is around she'll be threaded."

"You never lost it, Minnie. Good luck."

"Good luck my arse."

The horses are under starters orders. Peter Mulrooney contemplates the curtain falling in the growing year with an increasing sense of dark dismay. It is as if a fungus is growing steadily in the mind and in his emotions. I tell ye what races means for me. You'll laugh. It's the yalla piss running in the red tide in the lavatory at the back of the stand. It's the Tote man's rubber stamp pounding the tote ticket while he sets the dibs in the payout tray—it's going to the rails at the start to hear the jockeys cry, "Not ready yet, Sir." And the thunder under their humped bodies, a noise they never escape. It's the drum of all night tambourines, it's gulls' feathers on the dry fields, it's the effect of grass on young women. If only a senseless sensible woman would take me into a wood and talk urgent heated sense into my stupid head undoing me perhaps and telling me to hush when my scruples began to break into broken phrases, phrases begun, left off, recovered from a corded throat, and abandoned. Why am I this way? Is it that I am colour blind as regards the signals of women? Do they laugh at me behind my back? Do they demolish me in the quick intimacy of a woman's touch or with a sharp phrase that scorns my sorry manhood? The last of the visitors for the festival who meshed with the inhabitants of Hero Town prepare to disband and disintegrate into that cohesive mass known as the crowd. Now that the Races are over, here comes winter with a bay. We have been cavorting now since Patrick's Day, in God's name now let us hibernate to a normal routine.

Hero Town is happy. It is counting its money after the ructions. It is cat fat and purring. In an hour of national crisis Hero Town by its smashing of all records for betting and booze has cause for celebration. Economic crisis? Don't be silly, look at what was spent last week in Hero Town during the Races. What with elections and re-elections we'll soon create in this little island a true Utopia. Hurrah for us, we done it brother! Believe! Peter partakes of the publican's euphoria and sense of brotherhood as he walks the streets congratulating the tavern keepers on the serried ranks of empty ale barrels outside their premises.

Had they all gone mad, heavy with drink? Were all the puking Christians, critics, characters, all vicious, as a unit? Peter asked himself in astonishment as he walked the quiet dark streets. Poor heroic. A town and hinterland recovering from a feed of booze.

The pavements are a rink with the frying grease of chips and the slithery emissions from crubeens.

"Peddah."

"Yourself, Janey."

"I had this dream about you last night. A real sensual dream; you, you . . . you put the heart cross-ways in me."

"Me? How?"

"Come closer. I was after a bath, mother naked and well powdered and whatever tempted me I lay down on top of the bedclothes and not having a stitch on me."

"Sssh, let this matron pass. Lovely day, Molly."

"The door was locked but there you were, Pedagogue. Boy! You're no joke when you go into action. I screamed but you clasped your hand this way across my mouth and then . . . Peddah, I was slain by the silver sword of love.

"Oh, if I only had the teaspach of twenty back again. I'll never become reconciled. And I thought that the tide of my lovely lust would never ebb. Look at them passing me by and all they see in an old wan with dab eyes ablaze. Ah, if I were back, I'd flatter and praise, and extol men's graces. And what way would I be, Peter, only lonely after my youth."

Walk on, Peddah, this conversation could turn dangerous if overheard.

Does excitement vanish at close quarters? Still, life here is good. The streets tomorrow night will grow quiet and the Diamond shall appear as if it never experienced hullabaloo. Oh Lord, how butter melts. Slain by the Silver Sword of Love. Alas! The last blades of the gladioli in the bulbous vases. "Hey, Peter, will that nephew of yours play again after his long suspension? He should know better." *(Will they never give over those jibing tormentors!)*

There is the nub of it: the ever recurrents whose ideal place in the scheme of Peter—existence has yet to be determined and appreciated. One repeats the open sesame of life in the hope that the great rock of sentience will swing on its odd but accurate axis and reveal the full extent and immense richness of the treasure house within. Didn't the famed Kahlil Gibran and Mary Hackett in their correspondence come close to making the stone move? But such is the limitless variety of slogan, talisman, password, rubbing as in the tale of Aladdin— this lamp, the raising of staff as in the case of Moses, that one despairs of ever chancing upon it. How could one hope to chance upon the release word? "Rumpel stiffskin?" One could spend a whole walking lifetime trying to find the password to absolute happiness even ecstasy and still remain unrewarded. So what can Peter do? Repeat words or phrases that evoke and tantalise yet reveal little of the physical appointments of one's imaginative habitation. The Silver Sword of Love, The Hanrahans of Golden Hill, a sensual dream. Repeat! Repeat!

*

"Let them talk their heads off about power, Peter, but we the Unions have it and in no small amount." Behold the Cottoners' son. Home to his birthplace. Forty. Mousey hair. A deep voice, and glasses.

"I'm on the *Herald Tribune* now. A flat—a love nest in Manhattan. Four full rooms, paying a packet for it. Lumps on my thick skull from your belting the tables and spelling into me. It helped—brother, it helped. Jesus, we Irish have the New York newspapers sewn up. The reporters are fronts for us. Power! 'Twas O'Connor of Annascaul started it and Quill—what about the wasp that stung all New York—when he said, "Walk" by Christ they walked. And now our own Mickey from Cloone, as head of the stevedores union in Manilla, sure there isn't a lousy greasing lascar from Port Said to Adelaide but thinks he's Jesus Christ born again. P-o-w-e-r—power! A ball of feckin' fire! I came home for the Races and to see the Ma. You still don't drink, Peter? No! Too many young people drinking in Ireland now with the good life, shekels and women. Did you hear that I'm the next father of the chapel, the youngest ever? The silence before those presses begin to roar. Power, Peter, power!

"I'm off now to walk around Parkanaurd to hear the acorns cracking under my shoe soles and to collect the stockpile of puddings, black and white, and the meatpies. That's right, tie the mouth of the glassy bag well. It would never do to have it burst in the plane. Christ, we'll have a great feed when we get back. You won't buy them in Times Square."

You've wasted your life hereabouts, Pedagogue! You'd be president of the Patriotic and Benevolent in no time if you were in New York, and that's only for starters.

Sensual dreams. Meatpies. The silver sword of love!

Manhatten, the tall walls, Mary Hackett and the Syrian mystic. No intercourse—they made a pact. A love nest in Manhattan.

"The Ma is like a two-year-old. You're sizing me up now, Peter, I'm not a fool but I'm sizing you up too. Before I forget it, did any young couple skip to get married in the excitement of the Races? A few always do. You could do worse yourself Peter."

*

The wheel, the wheel, the wheel, round and round, as Hero Town exemplifies in microcosm the successive stages in the history of mankind. Man the hunter, man the nomad, there he goes in the person of young Dalton, with the pure-bred terriers protruding over the top of a box on the rear carrier of his bicycle and a pair of dead grazier rabbits slung across the handlebars. As for Archer from the Gap testing a spade on the pavement outside Harrington's hardware shop, he's man the tiller who had to stay put and see his seed ripen to harvest. Man the village dweller—that's Costelloe, stooped and limping, with his cans distributing loose milk to the houses of people with old manners, people with ess-hooks high on their door jambs on which the handles of slender gallons may be hung; the milch cows moving through the traffic, vouch for the abandonment of nomadic life and the settled life that followed. Technology—signs of this are everywhere. The giant trucks, the great creamery puffing on the skyline by the river's edge, water the beginning and end of the world. How technology roars, steams, stinks. Man crouches a little afraid. Excitement over for the season time now to cannibalise. All part of a psychological evolution.

But wait. Peter experiences beloved release on finding a piebald chestnut split and twinned with sides as flat as a wall. The chestnuts touching his fingertips solaces him to the innermost parts of his existence. *Dear piebald skewbald, partly albino chestnut, allow my fingertips to address you when I am bewildered by conversations and imprisoned by confidences from neighbours who treat me as a wastepaper basket or scapegoat for their sins.*

The horses are turning into the straight.

Power. Power. Power.

Kahlil Gabriel in all chastity viewing the new body of Mary Hackett. The silver sword of love.

Sunday afternoon. Peace.

*

"Stand in here, David. What hurry are you in?"

"Yes, Boss."

Into the hallway of the embossed wallpaper, the polished brass jardinière, the maidenhair fern, the red lean face well cut as that of a thin Indian in profile, the accurate black suit.

"I suppose, David, that you indulged a great deal this past week? Hmmm, No need to reply but before I give my donation you must run a discreet errand for me. Remind me too that I have a better pair of shoes inside for you. That nephew of mine, we aren't on the best of terms, you understand. He's after the widower's worldly goods and having his first son christened just now. I trust you, David. Saunter down at your bogadam and with discretion find out what the infant boy has been named. The christening is fixed for 3 p.m. If it is called Philip after me we shall relent in the matter of a certain payment. If not . . . well. That's another story. Off with you now. I'll see you right when you come back."

Time passes.

"Well, David, what is the name?"

"Kenneth."

"Kenneth! Shit for Kenneth—that's an ainm cúl le dúchas."

"I told 'em that. I said to that nephew of yours—what did ye call the kid? And when he told me Kenneth I said, 'Ye shit on the course!' Didn't I do right, Boss?"

"Dead right, David. You didn't say I sent you?"

"Think I'm a fool?"

"Job well done. Take the stairs. There's a bottle of Jameson and a cooked chicken waiting to be demolished in the room above. Kenneth my arse!"

"Boss?"

"What?"

"She got it out of a book."

"The bitch. I'll leave what I have to a fecking cat's home. Kenneth. Out of a book. The thundering shallow-minded bitch!"

"He laughs best who laughs last, isn't that right, Boss?"

"They call you the urban bum, David, but to me you're a philosopher."

"That's right, Boss. That's what I am, a philosopher. I'll pour your glass."

"Kenneth! How are you! Pure spite. They made their bed. See if I care."

The streets of Hero Town are quiet now. Darkness sets in fast, but do not be deceived: they are girding their loins, drawing their breath, watching their time, catching up on lost sleep. The nine publicans are back off the booze they went on after the tourist summer culminating in the Festival; any day now they'll be back to normal monotony. They must be understood. Hospitality, forbearance, and patience are required when dealing with excited, loquacious even pugnacious returned exiles (many of whom are subject to enormous pressures of climatic stress not to itemise amatory arabesques of a highly intimate and personal nature). So is it to be wondered at if the attitude of these now loud-shouting publicans has, ever since Pentecost, been "The very minute this shaggin' season is over, I'll go on one royal razzle-dazzle and the devil choke the begrudgers." Hero Town comprehends; the instant the publicans are raised from their hectic crouches in what the UDC toploftically terms rear-roads. Cleaned, cosseted and chicked they emerge man after manful man with the key of heaven devoutly locked in each pious axilla to step daintily down the Sunday pavement greeting every one with rectitude, on their road to last Mass. The matter is expunged from the record. In this particular instance the whole matter may be compared to a pool of still water which has known violence and turbulence and which has now reverted to the calmness and serenity of the traditional millpond, with the last ripple echoing in the words of the Parish Clerk spouting in the Diamond.

"The lovely tabernacle to be dipped in that butter-yellow shite. Across my dead body!"

Upstreet in the saddlers, a template for dog collars and leads is cut for an order to be collected by a greyhound owner on the coming Horse Fair Day. By name the stitching of the collars goes ahead. The clamp is losing its grip as the clock on the wall keeping God's time ticks on.

Peter is obsessed by questions that arise. Dare he throw up all this and begin afresh in some quiet Canadian town? Or even Garrachico at the foot of snow-capped Teide? Should there not be a sabbatical year? Is not his life here in this miserable huddle a banal existence of quiet desperation? How shall he master courage, to resolve this woman dilemma of his which one part of his brain tells him is unique to himself, and still another part assures him is the common lot of mankind. As in a trance he examines for the ten thousandth time the pattern of the tiles on the classroom floor. His exterior is placid yet inside his entrails are being poked at by the point of the Silver Sword, as he relives at second hand the details of a seminal dream. All the time wondering if there is a young woman in the mythical family of the Hanrahans of Golden Hill while he caresses the surface of the piebald and the flatsided chestnuts in the pocket of his showerproof coat.

*

Whnnn! Whnnn! The horses scatter in the street of horses, as the great lorries try to push their way slowly through the thronged thoroughfare. Whnnn! Pat the saddler stands on the edge of the pungent pavement under the ironmonger's public clock while three farmers, all cold faced in concentration, hang on his words as if they were the Gospel of the Lord. All four men are watching a big bay half-bred for which the owner is asking £1,000. Eyes on horse.

"A bit fine in bone. For his size," the saddler says, and again the underbreath whisper comes: "For his size." "Polished up in a hunt with the right rider on his back he'd look well."

"He'd look well," came the echo of the sycophants. Every syllable of this conversation will be repeated in hundreds of houses throughout the countryside. "I seen him. He was standing outside the ironmonger's! A bit fine in bone, his exact words." Then the hearers in the visiting houses improvise on the subject—"The working horse is a thing of the past. 'Twas all narra heads in the town." Peddah rejoices at the minor ecstasy of the harnessmaker. For this day he is King. He has had the wit to transfer his allegiance to the half-thoroughbred at the right time. This new interest solaces his sense of sorrow at the decline of the horse in the urban district. All rally round sensing his loneliness and pride conjoined at being the last saddler and expert in the town.

"What are you talking about, man? The last of the horses? Didn't the galloping horses bring half a million quid into this town last week? And here we have a thriving horse fair. If you tossed up a penny in this street today it would land flat on a horse's back." The pale-faced aristocratic harness maker continued to look at the animal. "I remember a time when there were six hundred and fifty horses in the urban area of this here town, and sure aren't we down to four working horses and a couple of toy ponies. How can you say that the horse is not defeated!" They counter by saying, "Pat, listen. We have colour televisions. Every time we switch on there's a horse on the screen. A cowboy's horse. A racing horse. A show jumping horse. Day and night our screens are filled with horses."

"Aye, and your screen is full of Red Indians and Vikings and early Egyptians too, and what are they but museum pieces." So they fall silent and they know he is overjoyed by the triumph of his sorrow. And in their minds they search for hoof prints on the grass and try to recall the anvil's song.

How can all these disparate tessarae of words with the images they invoke fall into a coherent pattern?

The festive part of the year now draws to a close. Night falls and Lily the Lonely comes to her discreet door near the corner with folded arms waiting for the few crumbs of words that Peter offers her. Five minutes idle conversation no matter how cold the night, and her day has some significance. Invariably she refers to a distant scandal which horrified the town involving a creamery manager and his concubine. Creamery managers, she ventures with a giggle, are full of teaspach. It must be the cream, Peter says, and escapes in the resultant faded wanton giggle. The names of the creamery Swedes hang in the air. Monson. Larson. Neilson. How many descendents of these same Swedes still lingered on in the hinterland of Hero Town? Lily is solaced. The door closes behind her. Whnnn! Whnnn! The nests of horse apples are lyre shattered on the road but still the aroma hangs ammoniacally pungent on the night air.

*

Again and again, though the month of the dead had not yet arrived, Peter in his walks past the cemetery was drawn towards a small grave that fascinated and exercised some mesmeric power over him, that of a young tinker girl killed in a car accident, its white headstone recording the details. There among the plastic flowers that carpeted the grave lay the headless señorita doll with minute hands set wide apart in a gesture of eagerness and life. The capacious red and black, flounced dancer's skirt upturned quivered in the breeze. More than anything else he had ever seen this higgledy-piggledy scene impressed Peter. It was beautifully Pagan. So now the headless señorita joined Peter's litany of the current noon and snuggled in beside Kenneth, a child who in one important matter of nomenclature had been forced to turn his back on tradition.

What has all this to do with me, Peter kept asking himself. Why am I annotating all this matter superficially, events, thoughts and observations, the ebb and flow of life as I know it? Is it that all these matters of small town life impinge on the reality of Peter bombarding the atom that constitutes true entity? Does this systole and diastole, this play and interplay, this pendulum swing, what I chose to call disarray of movement, shape me, and forge me on the anvil of Hero Town? Thus Peter for this Saturday in in-between October saw himself atom bombarded by such missiles. Some of these recondite missiles such as the remarks at funerals while the mourners sought the sun patches in the chapel yard a little to the right of the new deadhouse doorway where subsequent to the protoquery comment "she went quick in the latter end", the real geography lesson began. Didn't a son of hers get killed in Labrador?

Peter now screams. Me! Me! How does all this effect me? And the answer comes pat out of the void. Remarks such as these will be passed from lip to lip in this very chapel yard and your soul case will be gone and your eyebrows that meet will be turned up to the unpainted boards of the inside of the coffin bed. And how you came out in photographs won't bother you. Then the History cum Geography lesson in the absolute vernacular will be taught here in this blackboard chapel yard with your four bones and your stinking orifices as items in the object lesson. And remember, Schoolmaster, into that shagging box you will go without even the remotest knowledge of what carnal knowledge of a woman means. Sure, sure, you could recite "Byzantium" throwing your caibín into the air for joy and hilarity . But boy, the musky yeasty stealing ritual, the mesmerism, the pounding upwards, the gaol breaking crash out of self, the sense of being washed up after shipwreck on the aromatic sand of an island in the sun—that was as intelligible to you as the hieroglyphics on a tomb of a young Rameses.

Boys oh boys is the Pedagogue a mutt!

It was about this time too that Peter concluded and became slightly obsessed as a result of bitter experience, that his bowels had an identity, a conjoined organ all their own, as distinct from his own highly subjective identity as a person. They sulked when forced to drink strange water, became shy and withdrawn on experiencing strange environments and were subject to all kinds of bouts of manic depression. They were neurotic, often psychotic, and needed constant emissaries of comfort and stimulation in the form of bran, saline drinks, goose soup (which as every rustic knows is loose soup), sulphur water, fruit juice and homemade bread to keep them in any kind of acceptable humour. Their lord and master never ceased to be amazed at their capriciousness at times even whilst walking on the grimy edge of a grimy railway station, the bowels signalled benevolently that they were ready able, and willing to evacuate to their surprised but discommodent owner, Peddah. With no option but to obey and seek asylum in a strong green-doored, red-tiled station lavatory where after Peter had inserted the offering of a penny coin and withdrawn the finger-grooved catch, trousers-trapped he crouched backwards over the naked porcelain to release a salubrious and satisfying stool, having already raised the stout mahogany seat as a minimum precaution deluded to him by hygiene. The bowels chortled, or so it seemed, at such a prodigal emission of diurnal wee and a stool, twin signals of health in any man. But the bowels, they could wear collars and ties, striped dark lounge suits, black conservative shoes and a bowler hat. The resourceful bowels that were in a certain fashion as impish as civil servants.

Out in the open fresh air again, relieved, Peter Mulrooney marched along until he came to the beginning of finality in the urban enclave. Finality, the ultimate, after this no more to it, the last shoemaker, the last faltering ass on its roadway to the creamery, the final cooper and nailer and weaver, all figures in a boyhood haze of para-recollection, the final naturally balled cow, the final hurling ball. This realisation of finality egged the neurotic schoolmaster to begin his magnum opus, the setting down in words placed in such an order as would again imaginatively evoke the scenes, the dramatis personae, the properties, the action offstage and on, so that a century from thence a reader would be able to understand the five great divisions of the oracular drama: the exposition, the complication, the climax, the resolution and the catastrophe or conclusion. Peter could not for the life of him visualise a catastrophe occurring to himself; in secluded inner candour he was capable of conceding that he didn't wish to visualise this catastrophe but the others he could indeed come to terms with. There would be a woman in the climax, his fingertips moving delectably down the firm shivering small of her back, but then again there was always a climax with a woman in it, for a man that is, and perhaps he was acting the goose in trying to fake it.

Meanwhile, the benevolent late autumn in sunlight gilded and gelded all things. Not all indeed: for the red flags were everywhere in the countryside lanes calling the artificial bulls out of the cars to bull real cows. And proper order too!

Be assured of this. Everyone except me shall die, this my delusion. I am never come to congruence with the idea that I shall die, unless of course I wish it so. And yet world pollution shows its face here in Hero Town. Sewage untreated pouring into an otherwise clean river. Urine, detergent and bobbing faeces. Does the Council give a damn? It does not. It was all there, Peter thought, and I am not. And yet I am part and parcel of them all, as indeed they are part of me.

Raise your hat, dearly beloved bowel. Place the black square on your head, O awesome Cervical Smear. Slice me, castrate me, O Silver Sword of Love and period to my agony and seeming impotence. O piebald chestnut, turn into a tinker's shaggy pony and carry me off on your smelly matted back. Dear Immaculatus Uterus, give me a new birth. O Sensual Dream, ravish me and initiate me into the fullness of manhood, and do you the friendly Hanrahans of Golden Hill, plough me in the hope and promise of a full harvest, even as you plough your south facing hill flanks of manly loam.

Tessarae Disparate. The prosaic succeeded one another. The biopsy, all the fecking, jacking inhabitants of Hero Town were aware of the imminence of the biopsy, and the instant the doctor phoned the result to Peter, brother of Margo, the whole of Hero Town placed rejoicement on one pave of the scales of contemplation and disappointment on the other and allowed them to swing until they were demonstrably in equipoise, and then placing a pensive forefinger on the edge of the hurrah-pan, they three-quarter heartedly phoned the news to each other. In the wires underground the message thrummed. So Margo the Master or Her Ladyship in the middle of the street, or the Widdah Mull or whatever you call her hasn't the Boyo after all. The Boyo being cancer.

*

In the Diamond the clock on the church steeple banged as the figure of Dick McGonagle approached Peter. The two mad eyes deep in his socketed skull, eyebrows meeting and mating under a tweed cap, stopped him, and said:

"It's King Lear I am now. With two mad daughters. And a third in a convent who is in a stranger caper. Goneril, Regan and Cordelia. And what's more, listen, I've a niece in the state of Missouri who's a drum-majorette at football matches. She leaps up with her fork spread. I have a picture of her winning a baton twirling competition. I never laid an eye on her but I'll leave her every goddam penny I own to spite the other pair o' bitches. Divide my kingdom—do you think I'm mad?"

"I do," Peter said quietly and Dick after scrutinising the Pedagogue snorted for a second, put out his hand and said, "Shake hands, brother!" Peter did so while Dick still chuckling marched away.

A Baton Twirler, Peter mused. Is she fit to be included in the menstrual roster of the usual with Piebald Chestnut?

Doubtful, he said, and threw the image aside. Yet there she lurked in an eyecorner of his imagination twirling at midnight two batons, one in each hand, the batons having torches affixed to their extremities. Could I not mate the Baton Twirler with Kenneth Cúl le Dúchas? You can't mate yourself, came the shouted interruption of the heckler on the edge of the imaginative dark. The days passed. The whitethorn hedges were bare of leaf but were blood red with the plentitude of the haw harvest.

The coursing season had opened. The whippet walkers were abroad.

"See that brindled bitch, Peter? She had a shit you could put out in O'Connell's window. With the boxes of chocolate and the Belleek vases. With luck this year, Clounanna. She's a good thing for the Trial Stakes."

Dick, crazy Dick again, this time a hundred yards further down the street.

"Schoolmaster! You still know me? King Lear?"

Two still madder eyes.

"I've made up me mind I'm going to die where I was born. Money makes the mare go round and I'll have it done. I was born in Friary Lane eighty-four years ago in a back room in Mick the Yank's. Under scraws and thatch. The cabin still stands. I fought me way up to a house in the Diamond with steps up to it and a baby grand in the parlour. I have it fixed with the Yank. The bed is aired. The minute I feel death leaving Limerick for me I'll stagger into that crabbit room where I was born and I'll strip to the pelt. Who's to stop me? I'll creep under the crazy quilt and by Jesus, my Lord, I'll go out of this life as I came into it, from between my Ma's wide thighs. Bollocks naked. You'll see, Peter, no word of a lie. You'll see. That'll put the noses of the bitches hereabouts out of joint. I have the Yank well tutored and salaried to stand guard over my dying bed with a slasher. Yahoo. A slasher—and that's as true as Christ is my mortal judge. Shake hands, brother!"

Again Peter shook hands.

Hero Town? You refuse to admit?

I refuse.

The Baton Trooper? The marble cake?

Inanimate.

King Lear?

Without doubt.

The torches tossed high making a tracer light. A plentitude of haws. The sign of a hard winter.

"Sure she hasn't the Boyo at all," whispered Minnie. "They were on the phone while ago. Don't let on I told you, she'd want to tell you herself."

Minnie from the hill had shadowed him on the street and plonked herself in Peter's path with a yelp. "I'm in rip-roaring, tearing form." Minnie, a marvelous sort but always giving out the pay in the coinage of talking shop, leans against the wall and makes her spectacle glasses into twin moons.

"What way is your aunt, Minnie?"

"Gone in the noodle. Still she will hould together for a while more but after that—curtains."

"You should be good to her, Min."

"Good to her! I'm more than good to her."

"You remember the time you were in bed with the last baby months ago?"

"I have cause to remember it. I went the back of my nail of skeeting it."

"Well, she told me a secret."

"What secret had she, Peter?"

"When you were in your sickbed, Minnie, she went down into the church of a quiet evening with no one in the house of God, and climbed over the altar rails, straight up the steps of the altar, and with the tip of her wet finger she printed MINNIE on the golden tabernacle door!"

"She never told me that!"

"Gospel truth, Minnie, no word of a lie. That's as she told me."

"She never let on a syllable of it to me. Was that the same morning that I felt strong enough to leave my bed and go down to the church only to walk in on the Mass of the Angels?"

That Mass for the child who had been pandied against a wall, red lolly in hand, by the bumper of a runaway motorcar, defective brakes, silent down creeping, a scream and the child dies with an easy squelch. When the body is taken so lightly away the red lollipop melts on the inner pavement by the side of the shop doorway. The child's classmates, class mites, are lined up outside the dead house. The two irregular files fingertipped into linear manifestation by their teacher. At half past eleven Patricia, a child of eleven, enters Heaven, and to the list of assorted menstrual familiars that had been absent from the imagination of the blackhead pore-squeezing Peddah for days, as if they had vanished into a fog of their own making, was now added Mass of the Angels—with loud approval. As for the interloper nurse from south Chicago, strenuous objection and disapproval, she has no right to be among us. Objection upheld! Dismissed.

Peter dared not tell anyone about the pain across his heart. He feared angina. Perhaps it was only muscular. Now angina on top of cystitis and Meniere's. If he told anyone in town he could be certain that the other had the exact pain a week before, only it was a little above or below the place indicated by Peter. *What the feckin' hell did the begrudging bastards want stealing my highly personalised and unique ache. Was anything sacred in an intimate huddle like Hero Town? If pain-sharers, why not wife-sharers like the hospitable Eskimos? I hope my friend the harness maker lives out the winter. I hope I live it out myself.*

*

The sea is never far away from the heart of Hero Town and in this end of autumn day the wind is icy, but in the shade of the cliffs where the north wind is cut off, a suntrap is formed. From the cliff top Peter sees the wide mouth of the estuary, and the ranked pinnacles of the black Towers, rocks that have survived erosion. There he transiently experiences his terror as a child of this cliff top cracking slowly off and swinging downward like a grotesque trapdoor into the sea. Again, Peter stands silently screaming on the patch of grass. Time concertined.

The frost-polished wonderful waves gathered, listed, lofted mathematically inwards and broke beneath the cliff walk. The cold airs stung the face. It would kill the dahlias; it would deface the beautiful surface of the piebald chestnut. South-west of the calm wide estuary in a straight line lay Valparaiso.

It would soon be winter and the fight against cystitis and bronchitis and vertigo would be in full swing. He wouldn't like to grow old and have a malodorous fork to his breeches. No, by God. Bowler hat and Cervical Smear, spilled tessarae of imagery, why have you left the forefront of my consciousness? The wide capacious light material skirt of the señorita doll on the grave of the tinker child had stepped down over the dolly hips. The torso was almost bare. One laughing prurient child looking up at another prurient boy. Incipient lust over the body of a child. The sidelong leer upwards. The Hanrahans of Golden Hill.

The wheel of the year was turning. The assorted nuts sold at 10p per quarter. The shopkeeper's wife put a lot more monkey nuts than hazel or walnuts into the bag. Out on the ice cold but dry street boys had candles lighting in turnip skulls. "Booh!" From a distance it looked African and voodoo-ish. It was the year when turnips were as dear as honeydew melons, and spuds as shaggin' bananas, when big farmers were drawing fat creamery cheques and Government doles.

Turning his overcoat collar up around his ears, he recalled the local advice: "Lag your pipes, for the heat is gone from the sun."

NOVEMBER

Ta—Ra—Ra—Boom—De—Aye!

Here comes the ectoplasmic dead! Booo!

This is their month of course, the alleged gibberers. But as the country people remark with a wink behind the priest's back, we know where we are but we don't know where we're going. The month of the dead is a dangerous time for the inhabitants of Hero Town. The reaction to summer has set in; there are no diversions—there are no visitors, no hikers, no US kinsfolk, there is suddenly seen the need to gnaw at each others' vitals. Booo!

In the sky, intimidators, thunder clouds, gather up rear and threaten to browbeat the heavens above the streets of Hero Town. The crows perform their mock terrified antics in the sky. Peddah is filled with remorse born of an opportunity missed. Remorse!

"Oh yes, we shall make love. Stroke me and I shall respond. Denied, I shall scream."

The voice enticing Peter was a distant echo, indicating that she was truly woman, yet she flounced away and slammed the kitchen door. The terror in the heart—the terror of refusal. Boo! Terrified, Peter walked on as thunder roars in a leaden, livid sky.

But hold softly, we observe, all are observed. The function of the brain and the nervous system is to protect us from being overwhelmed by our ability to recall all that has ever happened to us. The brain is a sieve or screen, which eliminates the irrelevant and allows through to consciousness all that is useful to us as individuals. In Peter's case there's a bloody big hole in the net and every thing swims through. In the local paper there is an advertisement for the sale of three thousand headless mackerel. *Has a mackerel a soul? Presumably they are smoked. Hurrah for the headless mackerel!*

Peter drifts through this incipient cold death time seeking solace, release, even diversion welcoming the intrusion, the wild eyes, uncontrolled gestures and mouth-cornered foam of Darkie who confronted Peter out in the cold air of the Diamond. Darkie, intelligent, high with excitement, is troubled.

"Pardon your presence, Peter, can I curse? Amn't I shagged to death by a double negative and ignorance of punctuation?" The red gold flame of the plane trees has been brushed together in a heap outside the doctor's door. Rain. Spluttering. The wet, cold, whinging wind enclosing the shins, thighs, genitals, warns that it will refrigerate the bladder and turn the urine yellow. Darkie in Cowardly Custard Town.

"Give your attention, Sir. Pay me heed! Isn't it a pure cobweb to have me asking you for attention? For years now as you know well, I'm drawing money for VD—Valvular Disease of the heart, not the other thing. So I got this proclamation from Queen Granuaile to present myself at the Clinic a Tuesday last and place myself before a doctor to see if I'm fit to work. Up with me. Monty the Janitor beckoned me, when my turn came, to walk into a room where there was a clean nurse writing behind a desk. I don't know the geography of the Clinic very well so I kept looking at a white door wondering when I'd be told to go into the doctor. This nurse I took for one of the Gleeson girls from the Crosses so I whispers to her, is it the drunkard from Mitchelstown or the Total Abstainer from Glin is on duty inside? If it's the drunkard I'm frigged for he'll put me working. 'Strip off', says the nurse without looking up. 'Is it out of your mind you are girl,' I says. 'Strip off', says she raising her voice. 'I'm the doctor.' 'The curse of Christ on you, Monty,' I said, 'that never warned me.' I bared bollocks naked and I shivering. She put the tackle on my chest. I gave a convincing kind of a gurgle and I answering her. 'Is that brandy I smell?' she asked.

"'A spoonful for courage,' I said.

"'I'll cut it short, Peter. I'm outside the door and home to my bothán and I still mystified. Two days later the letter came. 'I certify that he is not incapable of working!' 'Hurray, Ma,' says I, 'I'm past the post.' Back down to my own doctor. Down for my cert. 'You're shit out of luck,' he says. 'It's a double negative.' I'd write my life story only I don't understand punctuation."

Ha, ha said the wind to Peter. I'll scald your bloody bladder. Peter drifted home through Cowardly Custard Town—hurt.

*

Glug, glug, glug. Gurgle, gurgle!! O Fons Bandusiae, will it never stop spitting rain? The river roars by under the spindle shins of the race bridge. Is that the Chaser knocking at a fanlight, a born trier, the same man? Peter wishes he had his neck. A fine looking lad. Athletic, barely thirty, but let him talk to a woman for two minutes and he eagerly beaverly overwhelms her. He gets down to bedrock, to rock bed right away. No finesse. No sense of protocol. No terror. The women all respond. But who under God is Peter to judge? Should not their two natures be fused, mixed, shuffled like playing cards or the ingredients of a barmbrack, baked and halved—then the overhunter and the underhunter would average out in proper proportions. There he is, hunting in sight, tapping out the coded knock for the lady visitor at the Castle Guesthouse. Tally Ho!

Noontime Saturday. It was raining heavily again, the down delving rain shot lit with sunlight when it hit the roadway had transformed the black road surface to a lawn that sprouted erratically in fleeting clusters of silver grass. A trick of configuration had ensured this, Peter told himself as he walked downtown on the quest of a living day in the tied-to-one another houses of dark Hero Town, that once had seventy-eight pubs for three thousand residents. Imperial intrigue in action, keep the Paddies blotto and faction fighting, all good cannon food when they sober up and memorise their regimental number in Chatham Barracks. Since the great truck was stopped and impounded by the Head Water Keeper with boxes upon boxes of Undersized Oysters, a new character was recruited to see Peter the Pedagogue to the year's end.

Fáilte, O Undersized Oyster!

The new girl at Madden's looks . . . feminine. Very feminine. Peter is not sure what feminine means, but thinks that she is just that. The Undersized Oysters certainly had a colourful story to tell their prosaic stick-in-the-mud mates when they got home after the buggy ride and the legitimate hijack. The problem is that Peter realises that women like men have desires but in a situation of reality he simply cannot imagine their translating these desires into deed. A mystery.

As the mind of women is said to oscillate between boudoir and altar, like every man Peter's oscillates between thoughts of blasphemy, lust and pious obscenity to thoughts of sanctity and bright white chastity. At the most sublime moments of the colourful, wonderful, ceremony of Ordination of a curly polled local in the thronged expectant church the voice of the mother of the candidate is recalled.

"The night before John was ordained he asked me to speak to him alone in his room. I sat on the bed. He put his head on my lap and cried bitterly, his head battering between my thighs. Few words passed between us. "The woman,' I said in a low voice whispering in his ear. He sobbed in a final convulsion. He sat up and dried his eyes. "Yes,' he said, seemingly satisfied that I had recognised the source of his trouble and his grief. He smiled and was an extrovert."

In the church the wonderful spectacle went on, the chanting

of the choir, nostril titillating smell of incense, red and gold, colours reminiscent of John Duffy's Circus and before Christ no disrespect is meant or innuendo. The sunlight of the winter day strikes crazy-wise and the colours of the assembled prelates and clergy danced against the limestone grey in the crowded church.

The woman at Peter's elbow in the church, the beautiful girl with no wedding ring on her finger, when I went to shake hands with her, she trembled visibly. She did not understand. Was she too in the boudoir?

Peter is perplexed, yet later he breaks into laughter when he considers the verdict of a gabby old parishioner on the truly ennobling ceremonies. The old woman emerging in the wet crush of people turns back to the now lighted Gothic doorway saying, "Wan thing anyway, they needn't be a bit ashamed of the carry out." Peter, pondering this statement over, realised that this was the highest praise she could give. In effect she was praising to the full while propitiating evil spirits who lurked everywhere unseen on the alert, to wreak the havoc as a result of rapid overpraise. The child, or young priest, overpraised should by the protocol of dead religions be gently spat upon, in the old days, or at second remove in their moment of overpraise the acrid tobacco spit is cast on the flag of the hearthstone, the old bootsole drawn across it as if to say such beauty should not be greeted with unqualified praise. Hush! Demons are in the wings. Or perhaps it is the legacy of God's judgement ever since the fall of Lucifer.

Outside the rain had ceased and the bright sky from the south-west hastened to rush up the sky. With the trees now in rod, Peter glanced at the hill on the far side of the river and thought how the goldfinch would show up against the winter landscape.

*

The clock in its clock case ticks out Peter's life as he sits and watches the scene in Hero Town. From a rooftop a jackdaw swoops to the asphalt of mid-road and delicately and hurriedly places its beak under the almost flattened but almost completely clean pleated circle of a drenched paper bun case.

He smiled when the new chemist girl at Madden's passed him by. Would her body ever emerge from the white coat even if she were to burn all her clothing and don new clothes, as the old people say, from the skin out? After the vacuum left by her passing had gone he sniffled the wind that beat upon his face. He couldn't smell the woman in her, it was all overlaid with the thousand smells of the chemist shop.

A world of thoughts from Peter as he closes the door and arm pregnant goes to the scullery with an offering of vegetable marrow and a cluster of celery the whole harvest festival in miniature in his outstretched hands. "These are for Margo," the kindly neighbour had whispered, but the flecked marrow causes havoc, as it bounces and thuds to the polished tiles of the hall. "Awkward," Margo shouts, and dropping his load Peter thumps back out into the street in a hasty retreat telling himself, you can't win! Beaten to the ropes he returns later for lunch. Margo was generous. She acted as if nothing had happened. Woman is at her best when she acts as if nothing has happened. Her return to workaday world of routine, her calm acceptance and recovery after she has been man-ruffled is admirable. It is as if she accepts her role of being the sort of creature against whose body, mind and spirit it is wholesome and healing for man to be mad against.

Dark, dear dark dread, dreary, dismal, depressing month of the uncountable hosts of the dead. Their ambitions, their urgent desires, their cries, their virtues—puff, a lump of sweet shit all. Booh-ghost and booh to all other familiars of a semi crazy schoolmaster. Our Lady of Perpetual Extension, look down with favour on the recumbent form of thy obedient servant, Peter Mulrooney. NT in Hero Town, south-west Ireland. Voluntary Health number 100085 629 18. Amen. P.S. And aborted scribbler.

Knock. Knock. "Will you buy holly? The finest of red knobs, Sir?" "No, son. Too early."

*

Later in the week Peddah awoke to find the sky high, wide, blue and flawless and a winter sun breaking through with all the bravery of a summer's warm smile at the unexpected and as a consequence exhilarating change of battle fortune. The whole effect on him was that of an explosion. Margo too found the unusual day exhilarating. Our bodies or our metabolism must be on trial, Peter explained to himself, when he found she was arranging small variegated holly mixed with rosemary, its awkward lovely ungainly attractive sprigs evoking a sense of winsomeness. Interesting, but no more interesting than Restless Wife en route to encounter God.

As the traffic swished past, she gently manoeuvred Peter into standing with his back to a sun-warmed painted wall, for such walls can really exist even in the bland month of Booh-Ghost, to observe the life flow of her most beautiful town. "Do you ever raise your eyes, Peter, to watch the skies this time of the year? You should. And the sunsets, a pure delirium of delight." Restless Wife, her face is turned to the sky, as she began a delectable treble layered conversation with Peddah.

Watch out, she smells continence from you, Peter, and she's out to crack that continence in you and having cracked she'll run off leaving you with an emotional problem to tell other hecklers about. She tried all her tricks; she introduced words calculated to inflame the passion, bed, spread, fed, ejection, reflection, erection, trick, wick, click, and still he refused to see. "Your big empty bed, Peter, what a waste of talent! Aren't you ashamed? Admit it now." Restless Wife who knows he won't repeat what she tells him but will certainly if he is unguarded repeat what he tells her if in any way whatsoever it can be considered salacious or risqué. Restless Wife laughed lasciviously and walked off to encounter God in his silent but incense aromatic church. But perhaps words satisfy the restless ache she endures, and deeds not at all. Walking home to his tea Peter thought what it would be like to tell one's sins to a woman priest. Would a youngish newly ordained woman priest prove embarrassed on hearing from a man tales of rich concupiscence? Ah but when women get a set on a young priest, May God help him!

"Hey, Peter, watch yourself, chatting to that one. Gossip travels and she has a husband even if he is tormented. I'm only for your good, that's why I'm telling you."

The cordaline tree dark green was grumpy against the winter sky in the neat trimmed lawn while the witch's cap of Halloween with the book of spells dispirited lay soggy on the pavement. Near by the winter cherry tree in the Diamond, her garment blossoms spread about her feet, stood stark naked against the northern sky tempting the sunlight of spring that is yet in the remote future.

Oh well, fall back on the familiars, touch them lovingly, allow the sense of touch to become a protocol of obscure reference. Good old Undersized Oyster. Good old Headless Mackerel.

In the schoolroom Peter now became aware of a coiled spring of intensity within him, a powerhouse of intensity, when the word images and rhythm and cadence could be almost seen penetrating and fertilising and fructifying the minds of the children. It was a process akin to heterosexual coupling he dared to tell himself. What had terrified him before he realised could be translated into terms of penetrative power. Could Castle Cutjacks be included in the monthly list of totem words and phrases? Cry havoc! The Undersized Oysters would yet grow to maturity if returned to their beds. Only the thoroughbred shivers.

The day smells with sunshine. Downstreet close by the delicatessen the JCB snorts and bucks and farts like the offstage stallion in the house of Alba. The stallion roaring for mares designed to counterpoise the man roaring for the unnaturally cooped up woman in the house of the Spanish nobleman. The ground too in its own mute way cries out since the beginning of time to be broken. The digging head of the JCB like the head of a prehistoric monster dwarfed the donkey tied to a rusted black railing in the shadow of the Bank. A gleam of November sunshine is reflected in the chrome of the old motor parked with its rear against the kerb. Framed in the rear window is a small plastic skull which of its conformation can do little else but grin with a black mantilla flowing from the poll of the skull. Power begins to flow in him as again he strides home.

The new girl at Madden's is heading for the Post Office. Does he get a distinct vibratory feedback there? Her clicking heels echoing in the tappety-tap of a tinker's spring cart driven swiftly upstreet. Tappety-tap, into my life, out of my life. Peter grew in self-confidence and considered the ebb and flow of desire and sublimation at the other end of the keyboard in the convent outside the town. For Peter without his beliefs and the celebratory church ceremonies of the year, those accompanying birth, mating, death, the fabric of his life in Hero Town was reduced to ashes. The liberals with their promises of life free from flaw or sanction or poverty or injustice—he would wait and see before he chose. Given time they would evolve feast days and rituals of their own and sanctions and jealousy, poverty and injustices.

He'd stick by what he had . . . *but wait, the card in a shop window gave notice of a lecture on the life of the mystic Padre Pio in a singing pub by a singing river. The final line caught Pedagogue's attention—"Relics present to bless the assembly!" Relics, and the man not even a Blessed. But Hero Town did not mind such niceties of papal protocol. Skull and mantilla present to frighten the shit out of the assembly. Tappety-tap. All tied together. Salubrious, bran-begotten stools are to be saluted. The equals of women in the house of Bernardo Alba.*

While these sad, mad, glad and bad events were in train the trees peeping over the roofs of the townhouses mimicked and imitated the colours of the final fashioned winter garments in the mock mullioned white windows of Widow Holmes' Boutique which stood two doors from the urine saturated archway that led by a lane to the market. A splendid show outstanding against the backdrop of the ageing castle.

"Will you want holly?" the voice intruded.

"I will want."

"Well you won't want now as all mine is gone!"

*

Did all this make a single scrap of difference to Hero Town, to an intimate community with their yellow chrysanthemums, to the corner houses behind which the shared backyards were like rabbit warrens? It was all a game like Ludo or Snakes and Ladders.

The way forward was to find women when they were already emotionally aroused and to cash in on it. What did the widow woman mean by saying, "You should speak to Violet. She's tense and nervous." The lock on the front door clicked indicating that the widow had left them alone in the house. Peter found himself wholly inadequate to meet the situation and the whole dismal failure became appallingly Gothic.

The winter came, and mild. No strangers in the town. People said, "This mild weather will kill the winter." A wise listener replied, "If you kill the winter you kill time, and time is how precious life is measured."

*

"Hey, John, you're the very man I wanted to meet. I'm sorry to say that I was laid up when I heard of Francey's death. I'm sorry," Peter-he went on, this conversation was held beside a wet church at a bridge in the moorland hills, "that I wasn't present in person to pay my respects at the funeral. You and he were the best bodhran players in this barony. They found it hard to separate the pair of you at the Drumming Final in Oldcastle. By the way—did you drum over his grave?"

"No."

"Why not?"

"I didn't like the priest's eye. I thought that if I produced the tambourine at the graveside he'd rear up on me. And maybe bullrag me off the altar the following Sunday."

"Still and all—you should have drummed over your brother's grave. Yourself and himself were the last great drummers of our time. Ó Riada gave it up to ye."

"It troubled me, I can tell you, Sir. Listen . . . I have the bodhran above at Connolly's pub. If you hang on there a few minutes I'll run up and get it and then I'll hop over the stile and drum over his grave."

"But . . . But . . ."

Hang on there now one minute—no buts, Peter . . . I'll be right back."

Led with my jaw. This'll be in town before me. Is the Schoolmaster going off his nut? Up there is Slieva Nossil in a dripping churchyard and himself and the Drummer floggin' the goats skin. Over a grave. No one but the two of them. What harm but the local Peepee is a touchy boyo.

"I wasn't long, Peter. I gave the skin a small heat to the fire to tighten it up. Watch the flagstone at the other side of the stile—'tis damn slippery. That's it."

The grave. Unfolded plastic flowers. Grass struggling through clay, drip, drip. Make the best of it. Take off your cap, Drummer. Hang it on the cross. Stand here by the grave. Face the east. The knuckles only. Don't work the rim. The naked skin is your man. Imagine there are 500 mourners around you. Now. Make it deep. Ornament first. Then deep, deep! Burrum, burrum. Deep. Skittle across the face of the skin. Knuckles bare. Barrumtitty, bumtitty bum. Good bloody man.

Close the eyes, Pedagogue. Are the people at the doors of the cottages? *I think so.* In the pub doorway? *Yes—yes!* Burrumditty dum. Dum, dum, dum—*Go on, Drummer, let 'em have it, send the rev-er-ber-ations far and wide.*

In a dripping churchyacd. Up in the hills in dark November.

Voodooland. Crazy Billygoat for sure. The Master. No! Yes—yes—yes!

That I may be dead it was Peter Mulrooney!

*

Time passed—time galloped for Peter on the ten streets of Hero Town. The ten in time had become sixteen. Pining for the aristocracy they called the new clusters of buildings estates, the roads drives, and the bothareens avenues. There he waited among the people, his eye most remotely hoping that he would come face to face with the new chemist assistant at Madden's who seemed to spend the day running from one chemist to another in the town so as to fill prescriptions of drugs they did not keep in stock.

"You're doing the rounds, Peter. Shove in here off the street and witness my application to be exempt from Rates. Didn't I tell you, friend, that my eldest son married a common whore? I don't believe half of what she calls my grandchildren are any blood relations of mine at all. Amn't I out of my mind with that upstart!"

Stories. Queries. Questions. Is there no end to it, the Pedagogue asks himself? Have I nothing to show for my time? This is a query that stabs home. Peter is lost in thought as the loud voice of the grimy Mucking Man, who halts his tractor with its full load of steaming manure in the bottleneck that siphons off the main traffic, booms at Peter. He opens the cab door.

"Hey, you seen me coming up last night from behind the castle?"

"I did."

"I had my torch with me, the powerful beam with the red blinker on top."

"Corr-ect."

"Well, she calved. A bull calf. A white head. Twenty past five this morning. Already sold for seventy pounds."

"Well done, Joe."

Peep, peep. Hoot, hoot.

"What the hell hooting have those blasted cars? Let them go to hell. Can't a man salute his neighbour? The calf . . . you won't take offence if I name him N.T. Will you, Peter? 'Twas the young tinker fellah suggested it. He thinks it's dynamite."

"Have I any choice?"

"None." The reply was drowned in the engine's roar as the tractor shunted upstreet and passed the cemetery, where in the nearby field the whine of the newly purchased chainsaw was audible. The double first cousin of the vice chairman of the Town Commissioners had purchased the saw and arranged on the q.t. that he was sold the five oak trees that were standing at the demesne corner which the Council had taken over, moryah, as if to widen a dangerous corner.

The chainsaw slavered for the municipal timber, and it was likely that the fine trees would be disposed of as suggested unanimously and quietly.

Dear small town, miserly bitching intriguing small town Ireland at the ghost time of year. When the sky presses down on the barometric eardrums of the inhabitants you can be the lousiest, meanest, shabbiest most unpleasant minded hoarder of camel crap, rat crap, muesli crap, thrush crap that ever existed. Peter made up his mind not to have familiars unless they forced themselves upon him and already a quotation from the mouth of Oliver Cromwell intruded. "I beseech thee by the bowels of Christ to think that thou mayst sometimes be mistaken" kept offering the Bowels of Christ as a final familiar. If Holy Heart in Rome, then why not bowels—it was Satan whispering. No mistaking his soft, succulent, sibilant, saccharine suggestion.

Dear Sister Norina. You are engaged in trying to house tinkers, and you are encountering opposition from those already housed by the Corporation. Well. Society's fear of the outcast outweighs the outcast's fear of society. And now they threaten you . . .

Wouldn't doubt you, Hero Town, you never miss a trick. It's visceral.

New games for children appeared in the windows of the shops. Retrace, Ulcers and Blackmail, developments of the Monopoly and Snap syndromes. The chainsaw whined in the woods.

This time of year the pulse of life beats faintly.

Soon, soon Christ will come and blow his clarion over the dreaming earth, over rotten bitching Hero Town with snorting JCB and haunting skulls, over destructive saws and grasping paws as the dropped calf is sold the moment it hits the hay.

The pulse of life beating low, low and slow, slow, slow.

DECEMBER

The spirit of Christ is suddenly in the streets of Hero Town. The tinker kids with up and down snots stand guard above their small bundles of holly.

"How much have you made, Martin?"

"Three pound."

A boy of eight, not bad for a morning's work.

Christ in the cold streets of Hero Town. Warning everyone with His presence. The greetings of cold Booh-Ghost are over.

Colder still outside the window-frosted room of the great house in the Comeragh Mountains where the invited guest, Peter, is dining in style. The talk is of history and the far out branch of their family who had ventured to the south-west close to Hero Town. Across the candlelit table the goodlooking girl hitches the emerald green stole over her bare shoulders. Dare he out-gaze her over the fish and the cut glass? Illiterate in the literature of love. She is a book he is unable to read. Wanting a woman to make the first, second and third move and by her so doing, he is repelled.

Dare he tell the De Burgo gathering what the barefooted mountainey girl who came up along the winding avenue said to her ladyship in 1835? "Well," her ladyship said laughingly when the girl had come close to the main door. "Nothing for you today."

"Be that as it may, your ladyship, but I have something for you. A fine romp of a grandson sired by your blue-eyed son Tom." And with that she lays the child on the steps of the great house. Peter chances telling it, and for a moment the listeners suck in their breath, and then explode in laughter. Human-feckin-ised! Well done, Peter!

Next morning when the red-faced rustic pushes the frozen car down the winding avenue, the engine at last pulls into jerking life down into the streets of Graiguenamanagh where the Hero Town exile, a bookmaker friend, heads for the butcher's shop.

Am I illiterate or daft or just crazy this sleety miserable gusty December day, asks Peter frozen in his raincoat, standing guard over a cow's head dripping blood on the edge of the wide pavement in this south Leinster town?

"I get all the fall of the shop for my greyhounds. I buy honey by the stone weight. Yes, it flavours the meat—that's my secret. Sing dumb. Keep an eye on that," and with a thud a second cardboard box of stinking offal is dumped on the ground. The cow's head with a skelp of Fresian cowhide still in place on its elongated nostril squelches at Peter's feet.

I hope to God none of the elegant Burgos spot me here on the pavement. Squelch! A second head oozes and drips at Peter's shoes. Guardian, he stands on guard. Are the people in the shop staring? Is there no limit to the permutations and combinations of the adorable incompatible in the context of this brother of Hero Town?

One of the Burkes, the chick of the clan, speaks up, and says before proffering the note of thanks, "There is certainly room in our extended family for Tom's baby and much else. Cheers!" Martha Rothwell, standing on the glebe porch, baby in arms, is welcomed. Events unknown in the context of the closed circuit of the university, but outside its walls in small intimate communities anecdotes, conundrums, legends, yarns, parables, observations are always in close communion with the reality of life, for ever conscious that imitation is the first sign of decay in a community. *The blood of damsons sparkles in the cut glass of the benevolent candle flame, and O boy, the green stole on the olive shoulders above the black dress.*

Mystery! And as sleep falls against the gurgling of the old pipes in the castle a voice echoes—"Face your fears, man. Life is the evidence of tactical errors but it is also the courage to make them for how can one ascertain whether the exercise of tactics is erroneous or not unless one employs it? The employment of tactics lacking the omniscience of God indicates that there is a grey area where there may be error, there may also be success."

All are recalled here, under the stand of fine beeches with blood around his shoes. And now to home again we come. The long and fiery strife of battle over to regurgitate the delectable morsel of reality of Madden's Chemist and the white-faced friend the harness maker, glancing out at the devilishly sleety street, his pointed wax end hitting the needle's eye as if by instinct. Damson juice is a portent of bright arterial blood but courage, Pedagogue, dulcissima rerum. Madden's Maid! Euthymol and Hibissen's Hair Cream stand still as of yore.

*

"Bloody cold today, Peter. You'd be hard set to find midges." Come to think of it he found cows heads not to mention lights and livers and a marvellous conglomeration of guts and adherences.

In Hero Town hell, Dunsinane, the shop fronts are being downtorn for plastic illuminated elongated rectangles with the proprietor's name and ads for cigarettes. Sorry substitutes for a treasured generation of painters and craftsmen. Oh Jesus! The old chestnut tree that gave ecstasy to our generation—down—as the politicians scheme. The up and shagging coming, cocking their lúidíns, a birdie at the fourteenth, lady shagging Bracknell. The intoxicating limelight. The inebriating licker of publicity.

"Nothing wrong with your guide book, Peter, we all liked it. But let me tell you something else. That poor hoor John Crotty, the publican, is sweating blood and going off his skull. I wouldn't be surprised if he K-r-r-c-k-cut his gad. Sshh! He got it into his napper that the Guards have a set on him, the most honest man that ever lived. Raided twice and his licence endorsed. He happened to say that he thought political publicans were open till dawn. He's got so bad that the sight of a silver button can drive him batty. Do Guards get sets like that? Is the present set up, the bother in the North, giving them the heeby-jeebies? Police are police. Individually they're marvellous, they have wives and children to support. But if they gang up in a small community and are directed by whisperers. . . . It's a different story.

"Hey, Peter, are you making any stir towards getting a woman for yourself? Take my advice, go somewhere foreign and chum up with a middle-aged widow; put yourself in her books and put your cards on the table. Say you're a bit of an eejit where women are concerned, you're sexually illiterate. . . . . was sick perhaps while the subject was being taught at the school of life. A widow, a Spanish señora, in case of later litigation she'll find it hard to give evidence without an interpreter who'll be sympathetic to a foolah like yourself. I see you as a comic genius, as true as Christ I wouldn't wrong you."

Peter's attention wanders inwardly and is again captured by the green, green stole on bare shoulders. Will he ever get that green stole out of his napper? Point his imagination in any direction and off it races. There you have it, this bitter end of the year day with the back gate gone bow-ways and skew-ways in the wind of night and the ambulance hooting and moaning and twirling its poison blue roof beacon as it hastens to the rescue of a man and his three children who crashed into the railway bridge. Damson children swimming in a Salome bowl of blood.

Then again she'd want to be an understanding sort of woman, the kind you could go mad against, or even "with". No emotional hold afterwards. Never mind the morals. The against reminds one of a haystack against which you can throw yourself till you are exhausted.

And I keep imagining in my heart disintigrate, disintigrate, I'll masturbate! I'll masturbate!

Is that mad brown dog in the broken asphalt roadway still chasing the cars? Soon they'll have silicone chips in the monstrance in place of the host. What use is this or that? "Ballymacon turf filled with water caught the frost, and nothing after." Still it is aromatic enough. Go in harness maker, dear friend, or pneumonia will deprive us of happier interludes in a lovely summer yet to come.

It isn't the same way any two people go mad; madness—as individualistic as a painting or a signature or a frenzied fit at orgasm.

In the yard the three disconsolate sparrows perch in the naked rods of the lilac, their beaks to the last of light oozing from the cold, clammy afternoon west.

Die, year, die. Die as Christ is born. Now, old Carpenter Joseph, place your straw sack on the ass's back for the child has flattened in Mary's womb. Off you go. See the ripe Mary vouches for urban greenery.

*

Give 'em something for Christmas, Peter. You can't pass the collectors of the local football club without leaving something in the biscuit box. Within, the church is holy day warm on the festival of the Conception in the womb of the Blessed Virgin. Did he give the football collection enough? Too much? Madden's maid kneels by the pillar. She's plain. But her every gesture is so feminine it spells attraction. The short-sighted priest drones on; "Mary, bright spot on the dark screen of human history, intuitive foe of all evil." The word conceived keeps recurring in the liturgy. It is Peter's imagination that the female nubiles in the church mentally accommodate their bodies at the sound of the word and are pierced and penetrated by the Holy Ghost.

Aha—what's that he said off the altar? So Jim Taaffe's uncle, Old Warm-the-Po, is dead out by the shore. Uncle of the well-known TD, that whips shit. Every post a winning post. And he not from this parish either. Funeral will leave the bonesucker's hospital. Easy now, ribald Pedagogue. The Bon Secours were wonderful to you in the recent past. *Mea maxima culpa—it was extracted from me by the fact that a TD advertises, canvases and controls his supporters by demonstrations such as funerals; it shows his standing in the community. A poor funeral and he's out on his ear next election.*

Let me tell you something, Schoolmaster. Next thing before you know it you'll get a clatter of the old nerves. Then you'll be Mr Hug-the-House like the nervy bank porter questioned about a missing postal packet when he was twenty, who never ventured outdoors again for years.

Well, well, the stole, Lady Bracknell, Cow's heads, all familiar faithful servants of the schoolmaster about to seek his grotesque fortune at the end of the world of his grotesque mind.

*

In the cobbler's the lasts are serried in front of the worn counter. "Go on now, Peter, give her advice, she's going to get married. Education? Sweet you, holy divine God! Me, me mate? I was long enough a slave to that bench out there. In my time, Peter, there were schoolmasters not plastic bastards." The cobbler in his morning kitchen, bald, voluble, blasphemous, garrulous in front of an electric fire, with "The Times of Ireland" on his chest issues orders to Peter. His gentle adoring son admiring his father's Rabelaisian vocabulary looks around in admiration as every rock of profanity falls from the cliff top of his tongue echoes resoundingly in the chasm of the hearer's attention.

"Aren't you a man, Peter? Can't you speak up from the male side of the fence?"

"Minnie girl, you're venturing into territory that's never trod. I'll echo what an old man said when advising a girl like you. From the woman's point of view she must always fix up arguments as when she quarrels with her man she's quarrelling with her own flesh. And she should by the way shyly lead her man to be a full man, to enjoy every inch of her, to use her freely without let or hindrance, and vice versa in a different idiom. And for God's sake, feed the brute, and by way of small ceremony—a bunch of flowers, an oval plate, and a bit of religion to add spice to life."

"Oh Peter, it was far from oval plates I was reared."

"I know. But we must climb up, generation after generation, and I am only a signpost telling how many miles it is to a Babylon where I've never been. Good luck, Minnie. Don't be gabby."

"I won't. I'll try my best, Peter."

So it goes.

Down by the laneway, under the shadow of the castle bulk Peter strolls. Friend castle, you have looked down on friend river for over six hundred and fifty years. Friend river, are you there, are you still alive in the fading light of evening? You are a link with all the former inhabitants of Hero Town. You are a friend, river, transient, anonymous and inscrutable . . . Oh well, if that's how you feel about it I'll leave you there in the first frosts of the afternoon dusk!

Jesus, who's sane here? Look, there's a facsimile of the Book of Kells in the window, thirty quids worth, for sale on top of bananas, grapes and monkey nuts. Mad town. Dumb river. And yet the community lives ahead. Down in the mouth, Peter rambles on by the river path. Cop the colour of the sewage spout. Oh Lord God—saffron piss and soap suds! And the UDC blames the tinkers for the fever outbreak some years ago. Watch your step, the pathway is like a rink.

The open air oxygenates the blood. Madness is a decided asset. People will forgive anything. "If you jam a widow against a hen house—they say—sure he's not responsible at all. Now and again he gets a clatter of old nerves."

"Was your Aunt Julia batty?"

"Crazier than a coot. That's where I get it from, from Aunt Julia. Me? I love insanity—it's like freewheeling through space. If I get prosecuted for indecent exposure or whipping a few quid, the Guards'll say, "Not the full shilling. He gives no trouble. He's a borderline case. Let him off with a caution.' "

"I never looked at it that way," Peter replied.

The pinnacles of the mid Diamond church burnish with pale morning sunshine. Christ-time gallops with Joseph who is now on his road to Bethlehem. Isn't the Junior Chamber astute now to get the Santa Claus business going? Business is right. Two drunken Santa Clauses at Corrigan's Hall separated by a Garda. Any minute now the inadequate carol singers will begin to perambulate. To chant the fecking helm. Will angina stab eventually, Peter wonders. Does the God who made beseeching demand to be besought? How can clean, clean women bear to clean up from under dirty old men? There's a mystery for sure. Novice nurses unrevolted. Kahlil—how did you view Christmas?

From his frustration, and be it conceded his joy, at finding recurrent uniqueness in a small module of people clustered on a few heroic streets, Peter sends out what he hopes are telepathic mental radio signals that will twin and twine with other humans, with other citizens, elsewhere in the world. Literature is sharing with the entire world now and in time to come.

*

Peter still on the river path longed to crouch under the whirling hair-rippling of a helicopter blade and be glass-borne high, high over the foothills so that he could see Hero Town in the perspective of the countryside where it lay crouched beside its silver paper river, with the Diamond ever faintly showing. Then his gaze could ramble over the hills and brown boglanded plains with the authentic mountains far to the south to the great pimple of the single historic hill north of the town to the eventual tardy Shannon spreading like a sea and as the books on Geology say, leaving in his consciousness important trace elements. The beauty of disparity of difference, of incongruity of variety, of the order of disorder, of the loveliness of the unexpected fascinated Peter. Once again he was a child clapping his hands and demanding a surprise from a parental God, or his haphazard creation.

"Sing and shout for joy for in your midst is the Holy One of Israel." The river underneath the castle thrust into the eye of the bridge as a stallion into a mare. Peter watched the water for a while, it was getting dark, and that invested the service with suitable mystery. He lusted to tell the approaching old soldier still erect and tall at ninety the story of the fishery meeting but it could wait.

"What thoughts have you, Fred? Tell out the truth now."

"I'm thinking of a little Asian girl I slept with in Madras. That's God's truth, Peter, without a word of a lie. Nineteen, and I like a stallion that was in first year of standing. Look at me now, I am stumbling along between the immensities of birth and death."

"You put me thinking, Fred."

"Too much thinking is bad, Peter. Good luck to you. Wait. Did anyone wish you a Happy Christmas yet?"

"No, Fred."

"Then let me be the first one, friend."

Christmas came galloping onwards. The doughty pedagogue began to feel the first madness of the approaching festival. "Sing and shout for joy all ye familiars who gather about me," Peter prayed silently. Were I to recite your names lovingly—my dear familiars of this month in Devout Town—and if I add the intention, Pray for Us, would I be guilty of blasphemy.

Each end of each street was glazed with an indigo blue spare pave of sky. The inhabitants of the town were the warp and the woof was composed of country people. Patients discharged themselves from hospitals prematurely—this because the madness of Christmas with its concomitant strong drink had seeped through the cracks in the ward windows. The red berried holly with the dark green glossy leaves glistened.

Christmas was galloping . . . Tatta Tatta . . . Tattatatata. "Excuse me, Peter—you're the very man." "What way are you?" "Tired and prepared to pull into the headland. This is what I want you to do. Since the missus died John Danaher the fiddler at the corner have been very good to me. They talk to me and cheer me up! I'm giving them a bottle of Red Breast whiskey for Christmas. Write out this card for me and sign my name to it. "To John and Mrs Danaher, in keen appreciation . . . take it easy . . . of their kindness to me during . . . I'll find myself: don't fuss me. . . . during the past year'."

"Gobble Gobble"—the voice of the turkey was scarce in the land. The smell of aftershave had replaced the odour of sanctifying grace. The new lady chemist, Peter could see her through the great window, was hearing the confession of an old countrywoman, faces up close together beside the glass cases.

Christ comes galloping in. He is equipped to interpret the apparent mystery of Lady Bracknell and the other familiars. "Bless me, Father, for I have sinned. Six months. I spilled my seed." O Jesus of the Stable, O Madonna of the Chair. Sing and shout for joy. The greetings called across the street. Mary visiting Elizabeth in a little town in the hill country. The child leaped (the priest said lepped) in her womb. A little town—Peter found the term evocative. Good. A child imitated a hen saying, "Boca-Boca-Awock." Peter tested it to see if it could be promoted familiar but decided against it on intuition.

Outside the church Mary the Barrister stood with another woman under umbrellas making a collection for research into the origin, prevention and treatment of cancer. Dressed in regal purple and with a hat of cream and yellow, she allowed her intimidating eyes to enfilade the churchgoers in the oncoming mist like a machine-gun swivelling through a curtain of rain. Mary never gave a penny to any charity in her whole life. She had her own methods of administrating charity she told collectors for various worthy and unworthy causes who stood insubordinate on her metal door doormat. Mary was a liar. She never gave in charity. Today was different. She was mortally afraid of carcinoma in its many manifestations. So today she intimidated.

"Boca-Boca-Awock." Had he done right in rejecting Boca-Boca-Awock, Peter asked himself. Let it remain in the limbo of his

consciousness as a valuable trace element. Do women despise men around them who avoid the logical climax? The gobble gobble of a white turkey striking the walls of the town without warning bore an affinity to the sudden squeal of brakes on a heavy vehicle. No wasps now. They lived in warm crevices and wall crannies.

*

Hero Town gathers speed as it races to the final down-torn calendar leaf. The tearing, racing along the line of perforations.

Still a cutjack, eh Peter? Does schoolteaching emasculate the teacher? What I mean to say: does the essential juice which is the basis of jissom ebb away as a consequence as a tithe—paid in the imaginative effort of classroom communication. Still snatching the brilliant green shawl off the woman's shoulders—eh Peter— in your little town in the hill country?

The fog on the hill seeps and clouds the ground in Hero Town. Like Queen Victoria at Balmoral, Mary the Barrister as distinct from Mary of Hero Town Nazareth again stands guard at the church gate. Boca-Boca-Awock still like the ghost of Roger Casement is beating at the door. The days grow vertiginous.

Where women are concerned Peter was convinced that Christmas was a form of insanity. Margo, his sister, was fit for the straitjacket. "Did you send e'er a card to Minnie?"

"Will you for God's sake take your old books off the chair? I can't do out the room while you're in it." She became a hen blackbird nest building, a calving cow leaving for a clean stall, a doe beaver dam building, and a hen salmon butting the gravel of the riverbed. Christ the Saviour is born—the birthing of Christ again re-echoed in labour pangs vicariously experienced in their oh so different bodies. Clean out of their minds. Queries, instructions, admonitions.

Peter tried laughing—but it failed. Margo bustled; bodily motion is a natural consequence of emotion. Bustle too, and confusion in the shed across the back lane as Feathers, the turkey man, plucked for the fowl merchants at Christmas. The poinsettia-tinged heads hang downwards; lifeless after the electric rod laced their necks. When eviscerated the edible parts rescued, the offal awful stench rose. Blood oozed. The great revolving drum rolled—plucked clean. The church bell had become automated. People grumbled saying they couldn't hear it. The parish clerk said they could shag off. He had given fifty years swinging off a rope and he was finished. Finished with hardship. Anima bloody mundi. *A form of insanity but a lovely lunacy just the same. If Christmas didn't exist we'd be forced to invent it. Buggar the begrudgers. Double buggar those who substitute King Winter for the little Lord Jesus asleep on the hay. With my final breath I'll wager their names.*

The candles are lit now and the beloved townlands speak up in holy flame. Hero Town Bethlehem. Even now in every house, in every lane, in every canvas tinker tent, the poetry of Christ is lapping, making Hero Town a womb.

Dear Mary of the stinking stable, help me come to terms with this woman business. Do not let me die without the experience of coupling. Lawfully as protocol so demands.

Galloping onwards. The country people have bent the feast of the birth of Christ to their own metaphors and idioms as carol singers continue to crucify essentially decent songs. Still the spiritual insanity invades Peter's consciousness. The cold wind from the north-east whistles down the perished streets.

Ever onwards Christmas Eve gallops, gallops, is suddenly here. Hero Town begins to think in terms of wine. Of charity. Of love. It's down on the door with us. And the personality of each person blazes up. Monica the Good who offers her guests wine recalls the childhood words spoken by the butcher at his block. "If right was right you'd be my daughter." Happy Christmas, and many happy returns. An old admirer brings Margo a crucifix made of horseshoe nails with the figure of Christ a tortured copper. So Christ is born and dies on the same night in one bright kitchen.

The rain falls hell hard on Hero Town. Then suddenly the benign in league with Christ's approach the streets became cheerfully bone dry. The country folk poured in and in all towns everywhere wire baskets were being filled in the microcosmic mart of the supermarket. Purses were raised near faces to hide the open contents. A child in a pram looked out at the Alladin's Cave of comestibles and exotic goodies. His eyes were the eyes of a grandfather Peter knew as a child and who died, the people say, of starvation. By Christ the British kept us down, Peter concluded. The faces in the crowds were burnished with the winter sunlight that brought out the frilled glory of the painted cluttered shops. Peter saw it as an Eastern bazaar. At the corner of Canopy Street two old friends approached—the Womaniser and the Bright.

"This is it," Peter-he said greeting them. "The beautiful afternoon before the Nativity. And though your morals and your music I find miles apart I extend across the barrier rather cautiously the hand of temporary friendship, in other words I demand a truce on this celebrated night of nights."

"Oh Jesus," said the Womaniser, clapping his hands to his ears, "the basterin schoolmaster is drunk." On the polished mahogany table at home friendlier words on paper from an English gaol reached Peter and a sentence moved him.

"Mentor, I attach to you only the stigma of my love, the ill advised contact of a rotten cored fruit upon the tree of life."

The painted houses responded to the limelight of the spent day and a Happy Christmas also to you, John, from Hero Town.

It was a polished Christmas of frost. At midnight Mass the choir of the schoolgirls was woefully but beautifully inadequate. In Mary's body the waters of birth had broken, charity was benevolent lava creeping down from the crater of Christ to engulf everyone in the town. Peddah took his seat well before the time Mass was due to begin beside a pillar and radiator.

"Let me inside you, Peter," Miss Denver said. "You know I

must have a pillar and I must have the heat." For Miss Denver since her childhood, a black pillar had taken the place of a man—she had confessed this to Peter some years before and had forgotten that she had done so. A pillar of black marble strength and the tepid radiator of her faded womanhood. The newly automated bell in the spire timbred head over heels joyously. Peter recalled seeing outside in the Square a frozen octopus of ass's piss brilliant on the asphalt between him and the Turkish crescent moon. He felt good; he had dared to speak to the lady chemist at Madden's as he deliberately contrived to bump into her at the corner. It sounded rehearsed but later he came to the conclusion that her recognition of the rehearsal would serve in her mind as compliment. From the altar the priest also complimented the congregation. The only drunk present at Mass slept silently behind the pillar at the door. The lava poured down. A little town in the hill country. Nazareth. Mary of the Labour Pains was now Mary of the Afterbirth. Christ the Saviour was born. The whole of the year that was drawing to a close passed in review before the Pedagogue's eyes as he sat in the pew in the warm church.

My familiars, Peter schoolmaster of Hero Town, I who am about to die after a fruitless existence, salute you. The drums are already beating out their tattoo—not real drums of course but local tambourines beating out a blood rhythm in the narrow spaces that constitute the towns streets as their accomplished strummers with black and red faces collect money for the ultimate booze up and down in honour of Major Wren. Barrum, durum, durum. Have the bloody bums under my window any other tune except Roddy McCorley? The chemist's assistant was now before a log fire in Westport, far away. Drums and bums were out. And yet he would have stuck his finger in your eye if you suggested ending the custom of the Wren Boys with their giobals, gauds and daubs. Oh pillar that for a dessicated virgin approximated to a man. How now brown cow, Peter. What softly reiterated mantra from Hindu Buddhism or Judean Christianity will tranquillise the tortured dangerously disturbed mind?

The music comes powerful and dies at the mouth of a pub. Green stole, shoulders fit to be stroked by fingertips. Fingertips with eyes that recall in the dark of winter's night the touch of the bare small of a woman's back experienced in an early morning context in an island in the long ago. How much more educated, how much wiser she was than the poor ignorant young schoolmaster of Hero Town. On what shall he thread the beads of his yearly narration? On the street, Peter heard the old musician; his dancer's heels hitting the ground as he stumbled valiantly home on the late evening of St Stephen's Day.

In the kitchen Margo had left a smear of lipstick on the edge of the liqueur glass. Ave Maria, Tia Maria. The stones of Stonehenge shall pass away ere my love for you shall fade. He was tempted to go upstairs and locking his bedroom door allow himself free rein. M-S Anonymous. As valid as the Gay Rights people. He still hoped he was a lock yet to be opened by a women's key. A reversal of traditional roles he told himself. Peter now recalled when, as an infant in the country school, he was given into the custody and curse of the surely nubile girls of the sixth class. Echoes of delight to be pressed to just burgeoned breasts. The new tumult of sensation against a novel warmth and security. To be enfolded with cries of "Me!"

"Me!"

On the dining room table a cineraria flowered deep purple, as the inch of ice thickened in the polythene pail outside the back door. Downtown, the windows of the toyshops were in disarray. It was a point of honour that those toys unsold should be poker-knocked in the darkness late on Christmas Eve so that the slur of poor business should not be flung at the house.

"They tore 'em out of the window, girl."

Hero Town has mercantile pride. After the shops open the bastards in the Town Council will fell more trees. That their metaphorical arms may rot from the metaphorical elbows out. "You parcel of drunken whores, will you come out of the pubs and finish the deliveries of coal." The Christmas was now reduced to a few frost-rimmed thin crouches of holly bearing a meagre burden of berries lying on the cold floor of a tinker's flat cart.

*

Later Peter ventured out to the beach where horses raced the tide. The weather broke to sleeting snow as he stood under the rim of an anchored umbrella and watched the mad horses career dangerously through the people, their hooves salting the air with an almost solid spray.

Bock-Bock-Awock! Mary Twee dropped a bitter word. "Peter Boy, make a New Years resolution, take a drop of hot whiskey going to bed. Irish firewater—it might make you brave. The women are sniggering at you, leanbh bawn."

Burrum, burrum.

"If you were a cock with one leg on my father's farm he'd put a clutch of eggs under you so you wouldn't be idle. Are you going to the McNamara woman's funeral, Peter?"

"Yes."

"We'll be seen so."

A Christmas month to hang on the walls.

*

Light the tired candle to greet the year's end. Let us go out in minor reference. Take a last look at the sparrows mathematically spaced on the rods of the lilac bush and the nut brown faded heads of the hydrangea blooms—heads of ageing prostitutes. Sniff the rosemary, stiff arthritic and aromatic. Fly, carpet, fly. Oh winter of remorseless rain. I pray to God that out of this environment, I may win through from the room of full awareness to that room of ecstasy, not to dwell therein for the rest of my days for that would cause the imaginative river to break through its levee, but to experience the adventures of that room in its fullness and to live thereafter in the nutriment of its memory.

Dear familiars, you spawn and are spawned. For Peter-me relief depends not on any theory of therapy but on the personal magnetism, the essence of the therapist. Peter-I who have always believed in the aristocracy of ability now stand witness o'er a bewildering episode of change, where the passengers on the bus of education fight to control the steering wheel and the final destination. Classless Hero Town now possesses a new freedom to climb the ladder of life with all the expected risks. In the tribal system too, one had faith in one's chieftains yet now political Johnny-Jump-Ups, men without standards or vision, are in posts of authority and power. They seek an epitaph, a good man to do a turn. Will the integrity of the individual and the vivid personality of the therapist be shackled by the mediocrity of the committee where status preoccupation grows like the invasive ivy? Only time will tell.

Peter now muffled in topcoat in the afternoon gloom gazes at the black and astonishing gold of a gutted and smoked mackerel in the fishmonger's window. Are individuality, spontaneity and flexibility to be things of the past? A stitch in leather and a nail in a horses hoof are real; so is the sunlight through stained glass.

Night falls, the final night of the year. Electric candles now, like false teeth too perfect. The time—ridiculing memory of the fading postcard family album reign—remains Happy New Year. May the home-ridden Christ reign in the year that is upon us—this is Peter's prayer. People in far out places who hear only the curlew's cry can become sages too.

"Shit, is that schoolmaster still walking round and round the Diamond talking to himself? I have a reel in my head watching him."

Why stand I here like a ghost, a shadow, a mast? Anonymous at best to be numbered among you.

"That bloody candle of yours will blacken the ceiling," Margo warns. Even the familiars tire one now. Hilarity breeds community cohesion. It was ice blue cold in the outer spacious air of the Diamond with the clear sky drape that extended to infinity. Shall the sweating hikers ever come again bringing us rumours of other lands and peoples?

The thought depressed Peter. He was aware of the transient nature of his existence. To snatch the delight of the day he was unable.

Who, what had maimed him?

It spits sleet. Margo is chastened by the immense prospect of another year. In the dissection of anxiety will anxiety disintegrate. Snow would fall before morning rendering benign and anonymous and endowing with the specious warmth the houses, streets, roadways and lawns of Hero Town. The tambourines would soon be appearing abroad. Their blood beat would prove tributary to his heartbeat. He awaited them with fear commingled with joyous anticipation.

Burrum, burrum, burrum!

At last they come. The bodhran for him was an elemental familiar, its thumping would track him quietly through all his days. Burrum! Beat louder still, bastard and beloved instrument. Louder, raise the knuckles to bleed and bring blood to boil. Louder until trembling Peter Mulrooney begins at last to earn a need of defiance and bravery.

Midnight strikes from the steeple. The schoolmaster stands at his door on the narrow street, his ears probe the air for the blood-stirring sounding beaten goatskin.

"Shut the door, you'll perish the house," Margo scolds from the landing, polishing to the veins of niceties in preparation for the farmers' social on New Year's Night. Hope springs eternal in the female heart. Peter gives a last look up and down the street— nothing—no one—no sound. He retreats into the hallway, closes the door and mounts the stairwell to bed.